Also by Robert Reuland

Hollowpoint

SEMIAUTOMATIC

ROBERT REULAND

SEMIAUTOMATIC

a novel

🏠 Random House • New York

All rights reserved under International and Pan-American Copyright Conventions.
Published in the United States by Random House, an imprint of The Random
House Publishing Group, a division of Random House, Inc., New York, and si-
multaneously in Canada by Random House of Canada Limited, Toronto.

RANDOM HOUSE and colophon are registered trademarks of Random House, Inc.

Library of Congress Cataloging-in-Publication Data
Reuland, Robert.
Semiautomatic : a novel / Robert Reuland.
p. cm.
ISBN 0-375-50502-4
1. Brooklyn (New York, N.Y.)—Fiction. 2. Public prosecutors—Fiction. 3. Trials
(Murder)—Fiction. I. Title.

PS3568.E778B57 2004
813'.6—dc21   2003046806

Random House website address: www.atrandom.com

Printed in the United States of America on acid-free paper

123456789

First Edition

Book design by Mercedes Everett

For my parents,
Robert and Mary Reuland

A defendant may not be convicted of any offense upon the testimony of an accomplice unsupported by corroborative evidence tending to connect the defendant with the commission of such offense.

—Section 60.22, Chapter 11-A,
"Consolidated Laws of New York," *Criminal Procedure Law*

You down with a partner on that, and the cops work him? You're fucked.

—overheard in the tenth-floor men's room,
New York Supreme Court, Brooklyn

SEMIAUTOMATIC

CHAPTER 1

Here is **Phil Bloch** standing in my office doorway. He does not sit after panting up the five stories from his own office. He stands heavily breathing and does not sit in the sorry solitary armchair that bleeds beige crumbs of foam through a gash in its orange vinyl onto the gray-green linoleum before the metal desk where I sit watching him shift anxiously from one foot to the other. I put down my sandwich.

Silence behind him in the desolate noontime hallway. He shifts from foot to foot. For ten minutes, ten awkward minutes of throat clearing and Knicks bullshit and great yawning silences I do not fill—ten minutes that follow his unexpected, unwanted appearance here—ten minutes more than we have spent face-to-face since all the jazz that got me sent upstairs in the first place—I sit watching him as my brisket-and-gravy sandwich grows cold. The brown gravy congeals on the waxed paper into an oil slick, and a rainbow glints dully on it, and I watch him and wonder why now? Why, after more than a year, and with the elevator broken, did Bloch come to see me? He wants something. To apologize, maybe. Something.

Outside the Municipal Building, on the other side of my ninth-floor window, the snow falls, giving Bloch another topic, another excuse to avoid saying what he came here to say. "Look at it come down!" et cetera. I shift in my chair; I do not want to hear his opinion on the snow. Walking through it this morning, the first snowfall since the Brooklyn sky closed gray in November, I fell reluctantly under its spell. I put my hands in my pockets and it came down. Just yesterday pale denuded Christmas trees alongside the road in my neighborhood were the only relief from the hard brown and gray of everything else.

So I ask him what's on his mind, and from the sound of my own voice I know that I am impatient, that the novelty of Phil Bloch in my doorway has worn off in those ten minutes. When I speak, Bloch faces me, turning his gaze away from the window as if he had forgotten I was here, forgotten he was here, and he is startled and does not say anything at all. He blinks once or twice. I ask him again for his own good, thinking that if I do not keep on him, he may lose his nerve and wander off, spinning away like a comet on an elliptical trajectory, not to return for another year or two.

Yet Bloch still wavers, tongue-tied. At least now he comes fully into my office. He stands with the vinyl armchair between us. For safety, I suppose—as if I might decide at any moment to come around it and punch his face in for him, as a thank-you for putting me here. He reaches forward and takes a snow globe from my desk. He holds it in his mittlike left hand, and still he says nothing. He shakes it, and fluorescent snow falls on pink palm fronds against an azure sky, the lurid hue of a Miami nightmare. A souvenir not of Florida but of another life, flotsam from a memory of a wife, a child, a family trip. Another desktop memento, along with the school portrait of Opal, age five, near some drawings she made when she was alive.

"It snow in Florida?" Bloch finally asks with blank curiosity.

"What?"

"You got this with the snow on the palm trees in there," he says. "I don't think you get snow down there. In Miami, I don't think."

"Phil."

"It's not—right—"

"Phil," I start again. And Bloch, mistaking my tone for something more benign, at long last sits in the upholstered armchair, which gives off a plaintive breath beneath him. Sitting there with the snow globe in his hand, he makes a sweeping motion, as if to dispel the poisonous miasma he imagines in the air between us. Truth is, I have not spent a lot of time missing him, much less sticking pointed pins into a voodoo Phil. I have hardly thought about him at all since that day two Septembers ago when I sat in his office, trying hard not to laugh as he assumed a fatherly demeanor with me, or tried to, and went on about how he was doing me a favor if I would just think about it, goddammit. I knew it was not his idea, but I let him pretend; I let him tell me what I needed. "What you need," Bloch told me then, "is to—just think about it, goddammit!—is to get some air. *Just air yourself out!*" He was my doctor, writing me a prescription to this place: the Appeals Bureau. *Appeals!* This ninth-floor backwater bureau where you never see a jury, never see a defendant, never see a judge. Where no one shouts, no one sweats. Where the men wear glasses and women long skirts, their nyloned thighs hissing as they pace the quiet library stacks. Here you can shut your door and hunch over your computer and type and smoke 'em if you got 'em and leave at five on the nose without seeing anybody all day. Or, more important, without letting a killer go free. Which is how you got here. For air.

I have not thought about Bloch since then, except in those comic moments when he saw me in a hallway or a nearby street and would have sold his immortal soul to disappear. Mostly what I have seen of Phil these past eighteen months has been his pantomime eye-widening at fifty yards, his double takes, his flinging of himself bodily into women's shoe stores, or broom closets, or offices of people he does not even know—so afraid he was that I might walk over and say boo. At those moments Bloch seemed more afraid of a routine hallway encounter than he ever had of losing his office to me.

Before I decamped here, safely out of Bloch's way in Appeals, that nightmare image must have featured regularly in his Cranford, New Jersey, bedroom: Andrew Giobberti returning to reclaim his once and future office in the Homicide Bureau, carrying a cardboard box containing law books, a stapler, coffee-stained papers, a snow globe, photographs, drawings, and a pencil holder made from a soup can and construction paper. Bloch's abiding fear—that I would stencil my unpronounceable name on his frosted-glass door and would again be his boss and not he mine, like it was before everything changed—was nothing next to the terror of a simple morning hullo.

So I understand what it means for Bloch to have come up here. That is why I remain patient. That is how I know he wants something, and that it was not his idea to walk up five flights to see me. And yet Phil Bloch, his face white with discomfort, his skin dewy from the steam radiator knocking away in the corner, is so evidently pained when he tells me, "I'm not going to apologize," that I take it as an apology anyway.

But I cannot resist asking, "Apologize for what, Phil?"

"You know . . . that," he says, again sweeping his hand to indicate my office, Appeals, and what landed me here. "This."

"I thought I needed to air out," I say, sounding more sarcastic than I intend.

"Look. You didn't hear this from me," Bloch says, taking a backward glance at the silent hallway, a line of closed doors with all the dormitory appeal of a Manhattan apartment building. As he turns, an even roll of white fat appears over his collar. He shrugs, then without standing scoots his chair closer to me. In the process more beige crumbs of foam silently fall.

"Luther was pushing to can you then and there," he says in a throaty whisper.

"What?" I ask, although I can hear him fine.

He frowns, shifts his weight, and stands in a sudden jerk. He walks to the doorway and bends into the hall. I see his khaki behind, wide and flat, the material creased into the deep, patterned furrows of a mountain range seen from high altitude. He shuts the door.

"Luther wanted to fire you," he says in his natural register and sits again. "After that business with the, um—the mother—"

"Nicole Carbon."

"—who, ah, killed her own kid."

"After I let her go, you mean."

"Yeah," Bloch says after a moment passes, during which he does not take his eyes off me. "After—after, you know. What happened."

"After what happened?" I repeat, quoting him with mild incredulity. He does not say anything else. Nicole Carbon means something different to him. For him, she is something to be for-

gotten or ignored. If he ever understood, he never let on. For him, for all of them, Nicole Carbon was a brief embarrassment, a page-three headline quickly forgotten. For me, though, Nicole Carbon is not so much the reason I was sent upstairs as the reason I have stayed.

"I let her go, Phil."

"Well," he says, ignoring me now as well as Nicole Carbon. "He wanted you gone anyway. Luther did."

"He should have fired me."

"But I said, you know, 'Let him—' "

"Air out?" I say, frowning seriously at Bloch. I frown so that I do not grin stupidly as I say it. He nods. He doesn't get me and instead mirrors my expression. We are both sitting here frowning at each other and nodding in agreement with ourselves.

"Yeah," he says. "Get some air is what I said you needed."

I nod some more, understanding. Whatever else he came here to say, Bloch wanted me to know he put in the good word with the D.A. after everything went to hell. Saved my job, maybe, or so he lets himself think. Like flowers after the fight, that is what he carried up five flights to lay across my desk. Who knows what he said to Fister? Not much, if I know Bloch, and certainly nothing that would have affected how Fister handled me after I gave Nicole Carbon a pass. Fister and I have our own history, but clearly Bloch nourishes the belief that I still have a job because of him. I am abruptly glad I did not smile when he told me. I will let him keep that.

"You want to know what Fister said?" he asks. "What he said about you, I mean?"

"No."

"All right." Bloch frowns abjectly. His loose face, like a child's, betrays every emotion. He had, on the spur of that fine moment, very nearly told me something we both would have regretted—

something the D.A. let drop within Bloch's earshot, an offhand compliment that meant more to Bloch than it would have meant to me. I shut Bloch up because he would have regretted telling me the second after he did, and I would have regretted his regret. Besides, I do not care what Fister thinks of me. I know, and I know what it is worth. I am a coin in his pocket, tarnished, one of many. He will spend me when he needs to. "Well—he likes you," Bloch says.

I am laughing, I realize. Not hysterically, yet I cannot stop.

"What?" Bloch says, looking hurt, thinking I am laughing at him. "What?"

I am imagining that scene: Mark Luther—the D.A.'s number one boy—pacing the worn carpet in Fister's office, holding his rolled *Brooklyn Daily News* like a field marshal's baton beneath the arm of his double-breasted suit. Fister, meanwhile, would have been staring out the window at the display of Brooklyn brick and pavement, surreptitiously sticking a thumb into the rich lode of his nostril when he thought no one was looking. And I imagine Bloch sitting silently in a corner armchair all the while, working himself up to offer his piece of unsought advice: that all Giobberti needed was some air. Whether he did say those words is neither here nor there, so I am not laughing at him. I am laughing at their world, a world so small that its problems can be rolled into Luther's newspaper like fish guts and thrown away.

This is new. Lately, as if in exchange for everything I lost, I have been given in compensation—*what?* Perspective, I suppose. There's a word. Not the happy horseshit of God opening a window when he closes a door. Not the blind man's acuity of hearing. Not the numbness that spread like an anesthetic balm over the pain of Opal's death. This—whatever this is—is new; this sensation of sitting high above the swirling universe of people with their concerns, their unexcused absences, their bad-hair days, their lost keys, their parking tickets, their what-to-have-for-dinner, their runny noses, their unplanned pregnancies, their what-do-I-want-to-be-when-I-grow-up, their entire fucking *lives* from the cradle to the grave. All of it! All of it, when seen from my ethereal perch, from my ninth-floor window, is—for want of a better word—*funny*. When your universe is pulled from beneath your feet, those few remnants left dangling, almost entirely without support or context, seem ridiculous. Like a hanged man dancing in the air, it is at once repellent and inexplicably comic.

"What?" Bloch asks in a different voice, and with that he puts the globe back on my desk. I stop laughing and look at it. Inside, it has stopped snowing.

"Fister couldn't fire me," I say as a matter of fact, and before Bloch can answer, I tell him, "Fister couldn't fire me, and Luther knew it. He told the papers we didn't know—we didn't know Carbon was the shooter until it came out in the grand jury." Bloch nods and waits. "To cover his own ass, Fister had to cover mine."

Bloch shrugs and smiles in the open, guileless way that makes him hard to dislike. He is not one of them, I know. He is not a politician. "Guess Whitey likes you."

"Yeah, you said," I tell him and sigh loudly. "That's why you're here, right, Phil? Fister wants us to play nice? No hard feelings and all?"

"Something like that."

"Whatever the reason," I say, "it's not your idea."

"Christ, you're a prickly pear," he says. "Here I am telling you you're out of the doghouse and—"

"Doghouse?" I say. "That's where I am?"

"The fucking *Appeals Bureau,* Gio? Come on." He stands and hitches up his pants. He stands there with his priapic thumbs hooked into his waistband and scowls at me. "That's what the D.A.

said—I'm gonna tell you anyway, goddammit. That you being up here is like a thoroughbred pulling a, pulling a—what?"

"Donkey cart?" I volunteer, frowning at him. He sees through me this time but is too disconcerted to be angry.

"No," Block says, flushing a damasked crimson. "The hell with it. A goddamn plow or something—you know what I'm trying to say. Now you're making me feel stupid."

"I told you not to tell me, Phil."

"Just stop making this hard," Bloch says. "You gonna come back or what?"

"Come back? To Homicide?" I say, not hiding my surprise. Then I begin to laugh again. I laugh and shake my head. An instinctive, biological no, for never—quite literally *never*—did it occur to me to want to go back, or that I might be asked. The thought of me back in the old bureau, my old bureau; of me in those hallways and metal cubicles, of me on trial again, standing before a judge and jury. After so long! The idea is weird and wonderful; a stranger image for the mind to get around than Giobberti here in Appeals, Giobberti behind his door, Giobberti among the professors with their whistling nylons. *Me here!* After having seen what I have seen, after having done what I have done. Me thumbing through law books, black letters on a clean white page, leaving smudges of dirt and blood and gore, accumulated on my fingertips and under my nails from twelve years out there before I came inside.

Bloch furrows his brow. He does not understand why Whitey Fister wants me back downstairs any better than I do, and he must believe I am laughing at him again. "So. What is it?" he asks. Solemn, almost curt.

"No, thanks."

"Funny guy."

"No, Phil. I'm good here," I say, and he sets his eyes on me resignedly, certain I am jerking him off. With nothing tangible to reprove me with, however, he just stands there and breathes through his nose. All I hear is Bloch breathing, and I am no longer laughing so much.

"Listen, Gio. You want to stay up here, fine. No skin off my ass, you know." Here Bloch pauses for effect. In the quiet I hear my fingernails drum absently, arrhythmically, on my metal desktop. "This comes from Fister," he tells me, and when I say nothing to that, either, he tries again: "I'm asking you to come back, but I'm not asking you. You read me?"

Then he also asks if I heard him. (I did.) "Keep talking," I say.

"You hearda Haskin Pool, right?"

"No."

"Baloney."

"No."

"Come on. You hearda him. Kid that bumped the guy in the bodega. Out on Sutter Avenue last year."

"That sure as hell narrows it down."

"Wiseass, this is the one that got all the press on it," he says. "Don't you read the papers?"

"Tell me about it," I say, although now I realize who he is talking about. I have a Dr. Brown's on my desk, the balance of my forlorn lunch, and I sip that through a straw and put my feet up while Bloch starts talking about the kid Haskin Pool. A short story, because Brooklyn killers do not have long stories. Brooklyn killers do not deserve long stories. Brooklyn killers have no imagination. Brooklyn killers are the dumbest killers in the world. They are unimaginative, stupid, petulant, unlucky, and—unlike the lilies of the field—generally unwatched over by God. Haskin Pool is no different. One fine morning he walks into a bodega in East New

York and pulls a gun on the owner. Right there you know Pool's not the sharpest tool in the shed. (You never stick a bodega in the morning; there is nothing in the register.) Why the owner decided to reach for his own pistol is beyond me. I guess twenty bucks meant more to him than it does to me, but then I don't work for a living. Maybe he was tired of getting stuck. Maybe that's why he pulled out, or maybe that's what you do when you got a burner in your face. The dick starts to speak. Once a twelve-year-old kid pulled a box cutter on me in an empty subway car. I ignored him, and when the train pulled into the station, I walked away. He followed with his little knife and was shaking all over, but I threw him to the tracks. He was cursing me from the trench and crying, and when I got outside and stopped walking, I was shaking, too, because I knew it could have ended different.

"So?" I ask Bloch when he is done talking, although I know what comes next. Even so, I want to hear him say it.

"Fister wants you on Pool."

I nod and notice my carotid artery pulsing in my neck, and my throat is dry as I consider what this means. I nod because I saw this the instant he started to tell me about Pool, and I nod because it explains everything—why Bloch is here, why he pounded up five flights, why he is studying me now with an expression I could not describe. Yet his answer fertilizes other questions that immediately begin to germinate into buds of doubt. *What's wrong with it?* for instance, and also the question that Bloch is asking himself: *Why Giobberti?* And I suppose the answer to the second question is because Fister said so; and the answer to the first you sometimes do not know until too late. There are other questions, too, other questions without a ready answer, and because of those questions, I tell him no.

Bloch is too tired to fight with me. Nor does he need to. I have no choice, and we both know it. "Yeah, well. You think about it,

Gio. For two minutes, maybe. You got jury selection tomorrow."
He shrugs when I give no answer, and almost apologetically, he
tells me, "Just talk to Ashfield, okay?"

"Who?"

"Laurel Ashfield. She indicted him." When I say nothing, he
offers, "Her first homicide in the bureau. I guess Fister figured
you might want to show her how it's done. I guess."

"I don't take second-seaters," I say, but already it seems like a
concession.

"You can think about that, too." It is his turn to smile. He
smiles at me and comes closer. He stands over my desk with his
big face, and he stops smiling and says, "Take it, Gio. Get the hell
out of here. Get back in the goddamn game."

I stand abruptly, tasting anger or something like it, and I am
surprised to hear myself say, "I never asked for your advice, and I
don't want it. Tell Fister to go to hell."

Bloch gives a wave of his hand to show me I am not talking
sense. *Cry me a river,* he seems to say, *and it won't make no difference. You're up.* He starts to say something else, then he changes
his mind. "God Almighty, what are you eating? What is that,
brown gravy on there?"

We both look at my brisket sandwich and at the gravy, which
has spread out over the waxed paper. I roll it into an uneven ball,
drop it in the trash can; it drums hollow and metallic, a fitting
punctuation mark. Not an exclamation mark, just a fat period.
Bloch shrugs and walks over to the door. There he hesitates, and I
think he might tell me something he left out.

CHAPTER 2

Behind a partition wall, painted beige and topped with frosted glass, a woman speaks. Her telephone voice is precise, solemn; I form an opinion about her although I cannot hear a word she is saying, although I have never met her. I check my watch and wait in the hallway. Almost five o'clock, here in this familiar space, this narrow corridor of painted metal and linoleum that runs the length of the Homicide Bureau.

Two ADAs pass by me talking, hands in motion. They see me. One of them regards me longer than necessary, and after he passes, he glances back. I know the look. Like he knows something interesting about me, and he probably does. Me, I know nothing about nobody. I do not even recognize anyone, or this place. Like the gymnasium at the high school reunion: it was yours, but now it is theirs. I check my watch again. I still hear Laurel Ashfield talking, so for kicks I walk down the hallway to my old cubicle. A sentimental journey. Some joke. Someone sits there working, his sleeves rolled up. Behind him, huge snowflakes beat soundlessly like moths against the window glass, backlit by nighttime Brooklyn, the winter sun already set. I do not know him. "Hey," he says, smiling in a way I never could. He is a friendly white boy with the pale carbohydrate look of a Limp Bizkit fan and the shaved head that goes with it. He is also, as far as I can tell, about twelve years old. He tells me his name; he already knows mine and stands to shake my hand. His is callused and dry. He makes polite conversation, but I can tell something is on his mind. Meanwhile, I listen for whether Laurel Ashfield is still on the phone. When I ask the guy what he's got cooking, he thinks I actually want to know and tells me all about it in too much detail. He is new in Homicide and is working an open investigation Bloch threw him to cut his teeth on. Sounds like a dead-end caper, but the kid doesn't get it. He thinks it is a real case. He thinks he can do something with it, and you can tell he's been eating and breathing it for months. He is talking to me without pausing for air, calling all the players by their first names and their street names, as if I know them. After four minutes, I am lost. Then he asks me what I think.

"Well, it is what it is," I say and swing back around into the hallway. I am feeling antsy, but not from the kid. Being back here puts me on edge. The look, the feel, the flavor of the air, the antiseptic color of the light, the notices taped to every wall, the sound of everything. Being back, I get that familiar feeling—forgotten but remembered with a concrete immediacy—of riding on the axle of the wheel, of watching the outside world spin around me, of being in the center of it and knowing that whatever happens out there in the violent world at night will end up here in the morning. There is a heartbeat here, so different from the placid upstairs where I sat all this afternoon staring dully at a wall or out the window, picking up the phone, putting it down, trying to decide what to do. After three and a half hours, all I accomplished was to walk downstairs. I came to find Laurel Ashfield. Bloch did not give me everything; he is holding something back, either because he does not want me to know what's wrong with Haskin Pool or because he does not know himself. Ashfield will know. Whether she will tell me is another question, but there is always something to tell. Even nothing wrong is something wrong. Nothing wrong makes a jury more nervous than something wrong. You give them a case with no flies on it, with nothing for them to think about, and they start inventing something wrong for you. They go back to their room and smoke cigarettes and start asking one another questions that start with *Well, maybe*—

"Hey. Giobberti," the kid says as I turn away from him. I turn back and see that he has started to rise from his seat, prepared to follow me down the hallway if necessary. I have forgotten how junior ADAs are like abandoned cats, wrapping their hairy little tails around your ankle if you feed them the milk of attention. This one will soon learn if he has not already that homicide prosecution is a lonely trade and no one is ever as interested in your case as you; you dream about it at night; you make opening statements to yourself while you floss your teeth in the bathroom mirror. No one cares like you care except the dead guy's family, and sometimes not even them. Sometimes you call them on the telephone and they tell you to fuck off. Sometimes you are just another reminder.

He sits and asks me if I am coming back down to the bureau.

"Who said?" I ask.

"Just what I heard is all. Anyway. You better catch her before she splits."

"Catch who?"

He points. "Ashfield. Laurel Ashfield."

Yeah. Ashfield, Laurel Ashfield. Shaken, not stirred. The spy who hates me. No doubt why Fister kept her on, knowing I hate second-seaters worse than ketchup, was to keep an eye on me. He will let me out of the doghouse, but he's not ready to let me run around and pee on his threadbare carpet. He knew she had to say yes if she wanted to keep a hand on this, her own case. That is not how it is supposed to work. Fister knows better. And I know better than to poach someone else's trial—that alone should be reason enough to say no. But even so, I feel myself ignoring Laurel Ashfield with a shameful selfish vigor. I find myself thinking of Haskin Pool less as hers and more as mine. I am willing to shrug and let it happen, as if it is all beyond my control. What I am feeling is nothing as pointless as nostalgia, nothing as useless as sentiment, but being back here, what I know is that I have been too far from the campfire for too long. What I want is not a reason to say no. What I want is an excuse to say yes.

"Ashfield?" I repeat, playing dumb with the kid for some reason.

"Heard you were gonna try Laurel's case for her," he says. *Laurel's case,* but I nod, which could mean anything. He takes it as a yes and keeps talking. The kid enjoys talking, so now he is talking about Haskin Pool, and meanwhile I am thinking about the marvelous velocity of office chatter—my nose barely out of my warm warren, and already I am a topic again. Jesus. When he stops talking, I realize he has asked me a question. He is waiting for my answer.

"What?"

"No, don't get me wrong," he says, lowering his voice and seeming defensive all of a sudden. "I'm just saying."

"Saying what?"

"You know. Why Luther fucking—you know—lost his shit and all."

"When?"

"Last week," he says and relaxes, his smile reviving and turning distinctly naughty. "In Bloch's office. I mean, we all heard it. Figured that's why they brought you in. Right? She fucked something up, maybe."

"Listen," I start to say with a wave before I walk away, but then I change my mind and just walk away.

Back down the hallway I walk, hands in pockets, looking inside other cubicles, some occupied, some not. A couple of uniformed cops sleep audibly in one, their mouths agape, their feet up, their hats on their laps, their heads lolled against the uncomfortable partition walls. In another a detective is giving his version to an ADA in a worn-out voice. They each seem sick of the other and sit with their ties undone and seem to welcome the fleeting distraction of me walking by. Closer to the door, paralegals and secretaries wait in small perfumed packs of red fingernails and accented English. They sound like birds to me. They wait by the door for the time clock to hit five. In their hands are purses and time cards. Across from them, outside Laurel Ashfield's cubicle, I pause and listen. Nothing. I listen some more and hear only the voices of the women by the door and the heavy clang of the time clock as each inserts her card, and I hear the trail of their voices as they walk to the elevators. In the enveloping quiet that follows, I hear a woman in a faraway interview room. A long slow wail, then nothing more.

I step inside Laurel Ashfield's cubicle. Empty, so I take a seat and wait. On a metal chair in front of her metal desk in this cubicle office, the same dimensions as a king-size bed, I sit. I run my eyes quickly over her neat desk. There is nothing on her abbreviated walls except a map of Brooklyn pulled from the phone book and taped up. Everything gives the impression that she just arrived, or that she will soon be leaving. Then I notice that her desk lamp is off. I notice an empty hanger on a nail pounded into a seam in the wall.

"The hell," I say, and I stand up. I walk to one end of the hallway and then to the other end, where, from Bloch's office, I hear the incongruous sound of violins swelling behind his shut door. I feel oddly abandoned.

I walk back to Laurel Ashfield's cubicle, passing the kid standing outside his cubicle with a sheaf of papers in his hands. He wants to talk some more, but I am not in the mood. I brush by him in the narrow hallway and feel him watching my back, but I do not care if he thinks I am as crazy as they all say. *Goddammit,* I am thinking. *Goddammit goddammit goddammit.* And when I get to her cubicle, she is not there, of course, but I sit in her cubicle, at her desk, and absently pick up her telephone. It smells like a girl. "Goddammit," I say aloud at last and drop the receiver into the cradle, but it goes awry and pendulums from the side of her desk until it starts making an angry dissonant tone. I hang it up. "Goddammit," I say, my rancor spent. I know this should not matter so much. I have done this before. I have done this a hundred times. I have picked a hundred juries, but this time—

I am picking a jury tomorrow, and this time I am scared. That is all.

I snap out of it, smiling to myself, and begin to open her desk drawers, seeking the Haskin Pool file. I open three different drawers, all stocked with bulging blood-red case files, all neatly arranged. In the third drawer, in its proper alphabetical place, I find the Pool file. I place it on her tidy desktop and open it. Then I take everything out. A dozen manila folders, legal-sized, thick with papers. I spread them haphazardly over her desktop. Something about her office makes me do this. Within handy reach is a dispenser of hand sanitizer, bought at Duane Reade, to be used after handshaking witnesses, or cops, or after touching a suspect doorknob or subway-station handrail. A pen set, affixed to which is a brass plaque: MOOT COURT CHAMPION. Paper clips in translucent cubes, arranged by size. Spare change in enamel dishes, arranged by denomination. Pens, still in their boxes, arranged by color.

Among the folders I locate one labeled PRESS in her fluid handwriting, and I spill its contents atop everything else. Newspaper clippings subside slowly into the disarray. There are too many of them, too many for just another bodega job on Sutter Avenue. I have tried the same case twenty times, each time to an empty courtroom. I thumb through the clips, cut neatly into rectangles. One from the *Times,* as tiny as a mailing label, tells only that Habib al-Hamadi was killed inside *an East New York grocery store during an apparent robbery attempt.*

"No shit," I think out loud. "He wasn't killed in an apparent Snapple purchase."

Beneath that is another, from the *Brooklyn Daily News.* A full tabloid page. Page three, in fact, featuring a grainy photograph of the bodega itself, in a neighborhood that could only be east Brooklyn. There are too many adjectives, and the newsprint gets all over your fingers, but at least you know the reporter knows something. He calls the D'Vine Mini-Market what it is—a bodega, not a goddamn grocery store. Then I notice the byline. Roger Cully.

Cully, his gangly form, his froth of red hair, now comes into focus in my head. When I was around, Cully covered Brooklyn homicide like a moldy tarp, so I knew the guy pretty well. He was often a disheveled presence in the courtroom corner when I went on trial. Of all the men and women you should forget when they no longer matter, of all the judges and lawyers and court officers and police officers and detectives and men and women who sell coffee from little carts in front of the courthouse, of all that ugly miscellany, some you remember. I remember Cully.

I read a few more clips. All Cully's. He milked the story for a couple of days, but after the hard news ran dry, he kept on it. No arrest for two weeks, so for two weeks Cully talked about that shady block of Sutter Avenue, which was easy enough to write about. Sutter Avenue in East New York. (Jesus Christ.) He wrote about the bodega, too, and how many times Habib al-Hamadi got robbed up. And he wrote about the young mothers and old women who shopped there, and the kids who went there after school. He wrote about Hamadi, about how he came here from Yemen and how he liked baseball and chocolate-chip ice cream and all that happy horseshit. Everyone called him Gomez, Cully wrote without explaining why. Probably because in that vicinity you were either black or Spanish, and Habib al-Hamadi was not black. Everyone liked him. Everyone misses him. And there is a picture: mostly bald with a caterpillar mustache, an arm around someone. A brother. A son. By now I am cursing Cully for making me care. Goddamn him for getting to me with another bodega-owning sonofabitch who couldn't simply hand over the money. Another dumb bastard who got himself killed for no good reason. *Don't they get it?* No one ever dies for a good reason in Brooklyn, but dying for your cash register is worse than a bad reason. Goddamn Cully, and goddamn Gomez, too.

All of a sudden I smile, because through the halo of adjectives and ink, I see Cully's game. I see where he was going. No surprise; he was going after Fister. Cully hoped to immolate Gomez's dead corpse and let the flames lick Fister's tidy house. For a reason I have never fully understood, Cully detests Fister with unaffected vigor. He would spit Fister's name onto the sawdust floor where he bought me drinks inside one of those Irish joints in south Brooklyn where you cannot see anybody, on purpose. He would bring me there on occasion to fish for an unattributed quote that I never gave him, or rarely, or we would drink and not talk about the shared world we watched from different angles. When we did talk about it, though, the conversation inevitably would turn to Fister, and Cully's face would change. He had covered Fister for twenty years, and the hatred was something deep in his blood. He never offered an explanation, but I suspected that it was a thing between two men or their fathers or their father's fathers and I would never know. But then again, maybe it could be explained by nothing more profound than Fister's little foursquare in Forest Hills. Cully could not abide that Fister lived in Queens. "You know the fuck ain't even from around here," he would say and knock back his liquor, his Adam's apple moving. Hatred, I suppose, is even less explicable than love.

I thumb through the clips with a new understanding and re-call that a year ago Fister was up for reelection. All the unsolved homicides in Brooklyn last fall, all the men shot dead in bodegas on Sutter Avenue: Cully only needed to pick one and let no one forget it until November. I smile again because I know that Fister asked for it, too. He had been in subway posters featuring himself, airbrushed. "WHITEY" FISTER MEANS SAFER STREETS! he declaimed, and repeated himself in Spanish. There he was, setting himself up for another landslide against a token Republican nobody when along came Cully, waving Gomez's bloody shirt.

Fister got his arrest, though. For two weeks Cully had his run, and then Fister shut him up with Pool's mug shot, poster-sized, at a Borough Hall news conference. Here is the clip—from the *Post,* since Cully left it alone. A black-and-white newspaper photo-graph. Laurel Ashfield next to Mark Luther who is next to Fister who stands in front of a flag and behind a microphone. What a trio they are! Queerer together than she and I will seem tomorrow at the prosecution table. There is Fister, his preternaturally white hair plastered to his skull with Brylcreem, his little black eyes un-readable behind black frames. There is Luther, snarky with a car-nation in his lapel. And there is Laurel Ashfield, a prim and pretty cipher in the background. The three of them at the first news con-ference called in the three-hundred-year history of Kings County for a dead bodega owner. But Fister hit Cully's knuckleball out of the park, so why the hell not run the bases? If not for Cully, who would have cared? Ashfield, perhaps, and you can sense that from her mien of dazed apprehension. Even in the halftone photo-graph, you can see that she is terrifically uncomfortable with the public display and with them, the men sticking their fingers into her pie. Luther and Fister. And now there is me. Now she gets to watch me try it.

I begin to return the clippings to their manila folder when I see—paper-clipped to the folder—a Mass card. An ordinary Mass card, Victorian pastel, plasticized, featuring a saint I recognize from his myriad appearances at services for Brooklyn murder vic-tims. I myself made many such appearances, standing in the back of the funeral parlor until I could slip my business card into the hand of a family member with a promise that the office would do everything it could, et cetera. I would stand in the back and take angry stares from uncles and cousins wondering who the hell the white boy was. I got a nice shiner once from a father who thought I was chasing an ambulance; he did not understand that my job was to put the kid who killed his kid in jail. I collected many Mass cards in my day, and I slipped them all in the file, so I know this beatific face well—better than some other faces from that time. An ostensible Catholic, I always felt I ought to know who this par-ticular saint was. Perhaps if I knew the saint, I would understand why it is invariably he who is featured on Mass cards for young men killed by guns. Some wiseass in the bureau once cracked that the saint's fingers, arranged in a solemn benediction over his heart, resemble a semiautomatic pistol. As good an explanation as any—he is the patron saint of street violence.

Smiling for a third time, now at this peculiar nostalgia, I square the clippings between my fingers, but they are tissue-flimsy and slide to my lap and from there to the floor and—

Why would a bodega owner named Habib al-Hamadi have a Mass card at all?

I unfasten the card from the folder, turn it over, and there, beneath the italicized prayer, beneath the winged dove, is a name, but not Hamadi's. *Lashawn Sims,* I read. *Who is—?* But I give it no more thought than that. I put it on my growing list of things to think about later. I rub my eye sockets. I need a Coke. If I am going to get through this file tonight, I need something. I stand and step gingerly around the press clippings on the floor. Halfway to the vending machine, I find I have no pocket change, so I return to Laurel Ashfield's office and root underneath the disorder I have brought to her desktop. I uncover her dishes of organized coins and scoop a handful. An errant quarter rolls across scattered folders, and I hear it fall to the floor as I walk to the machine. When I return a minute later, Coke in hand, she is standing there.

CHAPTER 3

I see Laurel Ashfield in profile, in a long black coat that comes down nearly to her shoes and is oddly elegant against the backdrop of her beige cubicle and empty walls and the disarray I have made of everything. She is staring at the floor. The only movement for a moment is the silently swirling snow visible in the thin light cast from a solitary street lamp. She sees me, but I do not seem to register entirely. We seem like bystanders at the aftermath of something. She turns her attention again to the floor and then— keeping her knees virginally locked and holding her coat so that it does not brush against the dirty-dull linoleum—lowers herself in a single lissome movement and, with careful fingers, picks up one clipping, then another.

"Here, let me," I say, and then I am on the floor, too, kneeling next to her as she balances on the balls of her feet, her white-stockinged kneecaps peeping inquisitively through her coat. Close to her, I look at her in side glances that she does not return. Her coppery hair is plaited back, and she is brown-eyed and brown, but lighter here under the hanging fluorescents than you would suppose from the newspaper photograph. She smells like her telephone.

She stands, and so do I. She is tall, taller than me, maybe, in her shiny black heels that glint in obstinate counterpoise to the linoleum and to my own shoes of a black gone gray from walking on salted sidewalks and through half-frozen puddles. She knows who I am or can guess, but I tell her anyway and give her my hand as a peace offering. She takes it, and I realize as she does that it is cold and wet from the Coke, sooty from the floor. Still, she takes it without wincing and says with subdued, perfunctory politeness, "Pleased to meet you."

We stand there, neither of us knowing quite how to start. When at last she says something innocuous regarding, of all things, my pants, I recognize that it was my responsibility to speak first. What she tells me about my pants I do not altogether hear, but I see that my knees are dusted gray from the chalky film applied to the floor weekly with dirty mops from dirty buckets. I bend and slap at them, and Laurel apologizes for some reason, as if it were her fault. She sits at her desk and begins searching through a drawer, presumably for whatever she forgot, whatever she came back for. She came back for that, not for the pleasure of seeing me. Her coat is still on, and she is a stranger here. She does not belong here, not here in Brooklyn, not here in Homicide, not here burglarizing her own desk. I sit now across from her in a metal chair, shoehorned between a metal wall and a pea-green filing cabinet covered over with peeling stickers and graffiti, and she says nothing.

Thirty seconds pass. A quarter after five now. Early. Too damn early, in fact, for her to have left the building. I nearly say that to her as a joke but not entirely; something in her expression tells me to go slow with her. Something about Laurel Ashfield says that while it may be early for me, it is far, far too late for her. So I say nothing, more interested in how long she can avoid dealing with me than I am in being polite or breaking the ice or apologizing to her for the file, for the clippings, for being in her cubicle, for taking her case.

At last I yield to my own curiosity and say, simply, nothing more than her first name.

"Yes," she immediately says, and her gaze startles me with its caged fierceness, with its pointed opposition to the bland sound of her voice. She is deceptively delicate, a tendriled wasp flying in slow motion before a screen door. Her face, over the smoothness of her bones, is all lit up with some emotion. She is flushed pink beneath the cover of her skin. Whatever she is thinking, whatever she would like to say, she keeps from me, for certainly she is alive with thought. Compacted within that single word, by force of her self-government, are her hurt and her defiance and her anger all sugarcoated by a deference to me that I have not earned. She says none of what she wants to say only because of *who I am;* of who she thinks I am. For I am, to her, *from them.* I am one of theirs, one of their darlings, one of Fister's beauties, and I think she might append a scornful *Mr. Giobberti* to the end of her *yes,* and that would be a slap. That would be the backhand to the forehand of the look she is giving me. Her politeness has teeth that bite; whatever she gives me now, along with her case, she gives because she has to.

Still, the impression I had of her moments ago, formed entirely in her absence, is different. She is hurt and beautiful, and that makes a difference. Men are that way.

"Laurel," I say a second time, but whatever I wanted to say is gone. She seems to expect something, but nothing comes to my mind to fill the gap except idle talk. "So, what's wrong with the case?"

"I don't understand." Her voice is flat.

"Always something, right?" I ask. *A good way to start with her*, I think, although it has been so long since I played at this. Years since I sat around in cubicles with people who do this job, years since I sat around with my feet up and my tie undone, throwing crumpled paper basketballs at wastebaskets and bullshitting about what goes wrong. She is not ready to be that way with me.

"What are you saying?" she says, as if I meant it as an accusation.

"No. I'm just saying," I say, still smiling because this scene is so comical. We don't get each other. We are talking about different things. Her chin comes up a little, and I expect her to say what I am thinking—*Don't bore me with your war stories, with your glory days, with the way you were, because I don't care.* Have I become one of those office ghosts who linger ignored in doorways and hallways and throw out advice like old men throw out seed to pigeons, for something to do? I wonder if I know anything anymore, or if what I knew went with me upstairs and stayed there like a locked steamer trunk of polyester ties and pointed collars, never again to see the light of day without reeking of mold or seeming unbearably quaint. And for the hundredth time today I wonder if I can do this. Even under the pretext of saying I have no choice, I wonder if I can stand in front of a jury with my attic ideas and do it like I used to. I wonder if they will be able to tell.

But exactly when she appears poised to tell me what I expected to hear her say at the outset—that this is her case, that she worked it for months while I was upstairs thumbing through my law books, typing on my computer—her expression falls and she lets go.

Watching her, I wish she would say it. *This is my case!* she should tell me. *This is my case, now fuck off!* I wish she would, so I can tell her what I want to say, too. That I am from Fister but I am not his boy. That I am on the case, but this was not my idea. I want her to know that, although it would make no difference, really. Aren't I just being a lawyer? Contriving a hair to split to make myself feel better? Aren't I, after all, Fister's willing accomplice? If it were a crime to steal Laurel's trial, I could be charged with the larceny. I went along. I went along because I want it. This is what I expect her to say. That I am a thief, and there would be enough truth there to shut me up. I would have to sit in her metal chair and take it. I am ready for that, but I am not ready for this—her meek obeisance to the inevitable. And I have not prepared myself to hear her say, "Please don't make fun of me."

She is feeling inside her desk drawer as she says it, then abruptly she withdraws her hand. She examines her fingertip, where a ruby dewdrop forms against the nail. *Unlike her,* I think— to misstep, to bleed. *A feature of her makeup worth remembering,* I tell myself. I would offer her a clean handkerchief, if I had one. As it is, all I can do is tell her I am sorry. "Sorry," I tell her, and her expression changes. She softens as women do when you are that way with them, but she does not understand what I am saying; she thinks I am talking about her finger, but if that is what I meant when I said it, I recognize now that I was talking about something else.

She shows me her finger, which is not bleeding any longer, as if that settles that. "No," I say. I have had enough indirection with her, enough of her anodyne tongue-biting for my benefit, for the benefit of *Mr. Giobberti.* I want to shine a light on this thing so I can do what I need to do—to make her my accomplice, perhaps, as

Fister made me his. I do not have to take her case. We could try Pool together, she and I. Together we could stick her manicured finger in Fister's eyeball.

But first I would need to make her understand, and I do not know how. We cannot even say hello, so how can I tell her I am not taking Pool when I am? I cannot confess to her that I did not ask for this trial, or that half of me still wants to walk away clean because I do not know if I can do it. Certainly she asked someone about me. Certainly she was told. When they took away her case, when they told her it was mine, the first word from her mouth— even before *no*—was *who*.

Who?

You know.

Giobberti?

Up in Appeals, you know. Giobberti.

No.

Come on. Giobberti.

Giobberti?

Fine fucking trial lawyer, if you ask me. Used to be, anyway, right? What happened? What happened is he lost it. Just, just fucking lost it, I don't know. Cracked up, is what I heard. Yeah, let a defendant out. Jesus, that was a while ago. Yeah, he used to be chief of the bureau; he used to be something around here. Could do some shit on trial I never seen, then—you know. You know what happened, don't you?

No.

You never heard this? Saddest fucking story. Lost his little girl. Traffic accident. Yeah, a fucking tragedy, that was. Wife walked out and everything afterwards because—

Why?

Blamed him, I guess. His fault? Dunno. I suppose so. Came back after and wasn't no good. That's when they made Bloch chief.

Oh.

Yeah, wasn't no good after. Let that defendant out, like I told you already. The one who killed her own kid. Shot her own kid—said it was a mistake, but where have you heard that before, right? Anyway, that got him sent upstairs. Anyway. That's what happened—

That is what happened.

And yet, despite everything I lost, I believed I remained a man who tried men who killed men. I thought I could never be mistaken as anything other—as one of them, for instance. As one of Fister's upstairs boys, which is how Laurel is looking at me now. I never thought I would be her *Mr. Giobberti,* just as I never thought that outside, out in the wide world, they would see me in my suit and think, *Ah, here is a man who sells insurance, who represents old women who fall down in supermarkets.* I saw myself as I was, even after I went to Appeals, even after no one thought of me at all and I became a name typed on a legal brief filed away in some wooden cabinet. I saw myself as a homicide prosecutor.

I remember myself as I was. As much as I gave the job, it gave back. I loved it. Every fucking inch of it. I loved standing up. I loved picking a jury, winnowing out the twelve solid citizens who could do business. I loved making an opening statement, telling my jurors how I would tear away the thin veneer of civilization that separated them from the man over there. I loved the judges who slept during testimony. I loved the defense lawyers who worked what they had and knew the score. I loved the witnesses who hated my guts. The cops who never showed up when I needed them but, when they eventually did, would sometimes bring a cup of coffee as an apology. The families of the dead boys. The mothers and sisters and aunts who came to court dressed as if for church and looked to me with unreasonable hope and apologized oftentimes and told me that despite whatever else their dead sons or brothers or nephews had done with their short lives, they had some good in them, they did not deserve to go out of the picture that way. While I never gave them an answer that would make them whole, I could give them a verdict. No matter what that was, it always helped.

And I loved the verdict.

I loved the interminable, agonizing wait, pacing the courtroom after the note comes from the jury room. You get the note, and the torpor of the empty court shifts, and people start to filter in, and the court officers stir to life, and you stand up and start pacing. Then the defendant is escorted in and he does not know why; he does not know it is the verdict until his lawyer tells him, and then maybe he puts his head down on the table and starts waiting, too. Everyone is waiting, and you are still pacing off your seven lucky footsteps in the well, seven this way, seven the other, and looking at the floor while you say Hail Marys and pray a vaguely blasphemous prayer for *guilty,* to which you would always add, *if he did it,* although you always knew he did. Then the single elongated minute when the foreman stands, and your table is close to the jury box, so when the foreman stands he is right there and you can see the sheet of paper that he is holding with the verdict written on it. Time grows heavy and slow.

And afterwards, if the defendant hugs his lawyer and goes home, you thank the jury anyway. You thank them all but privately hope they fall down the stairs walking out. You hate them all for the dumb sonofabitches that they are. And you sit in your wooden seat in the empty courtroom and tell yourself what you always tell yourself when bad men return to the world—

He'll be back.

As if that makes any difference.

What made a difference then—the only thing that made any difference—was knowing that you did everything you could.

Everything you could? Not like now. Now—Christ. Now I do

as little as possible. Shuttered away from the fray in Appeals, sliding over the surface of events, insulated from the muck I once wal-
lowed in to my knees. Now there is only legal error, the dry fodder
of appellate work. No longer do I bother with stark human falli-
bility, particularly my own. I no longer trust myself, and more
than anything, a prosecutor needs to trust himself. Gun-shy, I
have become something vaguely detestable: a small man. That I
have the best possible excuse for shrinking into a flat and irrelevant life does not matter. I am still enough of what I was to remain
intolerant of excuses. And while I never overtly indulged in self-
pity or offered it to myself as a reason for leaving everything outside my locked door, it festers in the damp unlit recesses of my
mind, infecting everything.

A homicide prosecutor! The expression on Laurel's face rips
aside my happy self-deception and I see myself as I am underneath, as I have become. I see myself as she sees me, and while she
does not know me and her perception of me is wrong for the right
reasons, she hits close enough to the anesthetized nerve to send a
painful jolt coursing along my backbone.

So I will take her case.

I will try Haskin Pool. I will try Pool not because they said to.
Not to get back here. Not to give Fister an opportunity to extend
his ring for me to kiss. I will try Haskin Pool even though something is wrong with the case that no one has told me. I will try it
even though Laurel Ashfield will despise me for it. I will try Haskin
Pool because I have no choice. Haskin Pool is all I have left. And
I will try him the right way or else I will have not even that. I want
myself back. A better version of myself.

"Laurel."

"Yes."

"This. This wasn't my idea, okay?"

"What idea?" she asks me.

"This. Taking your case. Everything."

"I don't understand," she says.

"I never asked for this. I want you to know."

"What do you mean?"

"This was Fister's idea," I tell her. "He's trying— I don't know what he's trying to do, but they came to me. Do you understand? I was—"

"What's he trying to do?"

"Fister? Do me a favor, I guess. I don't really know."

"How's he doing you a favor?" she asks.

"By—by giving me your case. Giving me Pool."

"Giving you Pool?" she says.

"I told him no, if that makes any difference to you." I regret this bald lie at once. My *no* was not for her sake but for my own, and I have already recanted it, in any event. Here I am, after all.

"But. But you talked to him," she says, not caring one way or the other. "Fister—yes?"

"No. Bloch came. Why?"

"Bloch knows?"

"Of course," I say.

"I mean, he talked to you. Bloch talked to you about the case?"

I nod.

"And . . . ," she says and waits, but not for me. She is carefully choosing each word as if struggling to make this topic bland enough for her tongue to shape. "And you—you agreed to try it. You agreed to take the case. Didn't you?"

"I don't think he asked."

Now a pained smile. We share at least that: we know what it is like to be asked a question without an answer being expected or required. "Goddamn office, right?" I say, but she will not let me play them-against-us. Her smile was for herself alone, and as it dissipates in the thin air of her cubicle, I feel an inexplicable disappointment at being left outside. "Listen," I say. "My say-so still has some weight around here. If I make a stink about it, I mean."

"I don't—"

"We can try it together, is what I'm saying."

"Giobberti, you don't understand."

"Or I could second you—"

"You don't understand," she repeats, her voice revealing a quiet, breathless astonishment. "I don't want it." She shakes her head as if in disbelief. When I say nothing, she elaborates: "I told them to take me off."

And I suppose this is it. At long last, this is the polite fuck-you that I was waiting for. She would rather walk out the door on general principle than take the second seat to me on her own trial. *Fuck you*, she is telling me in the only language she speaks.

"That," I say mildly, "that's just stupid, Laurel."

A short, pained laugh. "Well—" She stands, and then she walks out.

CHAPTER 4

Alone again with Laurel Ashfield's pen set and her hand sanitizer and her file, its guts spilled everywhere, I hear the purposeful clip of her black shoes fade, and then I hear the bureau door close behind her. I am alone with her things and the lingering brush of her perfume, sweet as jam.

Thirty minutes pass in which I do nothing, really. I sit at her desk and feel as much a stranger here as she seemed, rummaging for her forgotten house keys or whatever. I think about her, not the case. I played it badly. She caught me off guard and I came off like a dope. I should have done something different, said something different, and I replay our four minutes together for some clue to help me. I need to do better with her. I need to do better with people in general, if I am going to be around them again, if I am going to talk to them and get them to testify for me and ask them to convict that man sitting over there, ladies and gentlemen. Convict him and send him to jail! I was once clever with people that way, but so what? I was many things once. Once is nothing. Once is an accident of fate. Once is winning the lottery. You must earn it every goddamn day.

I sit in her chair. The folders and papers are spread over her desktop. I reach past her pen set and shoot hand sanitizer into my palm. I rub it over my hands, slap it on my face like after-shave. Wake up, Giobberti! Now everything smells like rubbing alcohol.

Ah well, let it pass. Let her have her sulk. She will be back. She said what she wanted to say, as pointedly as propriety allows, and when she has ridden the subway back to the Upper East Side or wherever she sleeps—certainly not Brooklyn, or at least not my Brooklyn—she will realize that she wants this, and she will be back. That is how Fister gets us. What he forces down our throats is what we want to eat.

All around me the daytime sounds of the bureau yield gradually to the nighttime trill of the five or so of us left here. When this was my life, when this was what I did, now was when I would get down to business: when the shouts and curses and cries had died away, when the cabinet drawers had quit slamming, and the file carts had quit wheeling, and the telephones and the fax machines and the copy machines and the fire alarms had stopped doing their incessant thing. Now the corners are silent and dark where paralegals spread rumor and innuendo by daytime, and the hallways are empty of sweatshirted red-faced cops pushing handcuffed prisoners in and out of interrogation rooms and bringing with them the stink of jail, the odor of men incarcerated in their own bodies. The reception intercom is silent, and the fluorescent tubes fade to black on schedule, and all business concentrates itself under the few desk lamps throwing private pools of light.

I pull the beaded cord on Laurel Ashfield's desk lamp and study the empty file again, a thick accordion affair edge-worn from months of being carried to court and back again and ripped a little on the flap but repaired nicely with white tape as you might bandage a child's scraped knee. PEOPLE OF THE STATE OF NEW YORK AGAINST, the caption reads in preprinted capitals, and beneath that, in neat cursive handwriting, "POOL, Haskin." Under the caption is a list of every court date since Pool's arraignment. He was arraigned, and then the case was put over for him to get a lawyer. And then it was adjourned again because he could not afford a lawyer. And then again so that the court could assign him a lawyer. And again so everyone could see where things stood. Again for defense motions. Again because the defense served its motion papers late. Again for the People's answer to the defense's motions. Again for the People's cross-motion. Again for the court's decision on all pending motions. Again because the court said so. Again for the People to complete discovery. Again because the defense lawyer was on trial in Queens. Again for court conference. Again for conference. Again for conference. Again because it was Christmas, and then again to last Monday, when the case was marked ready and passed until tomorrow for jury selection. The life of a death case, pretrial.

Next to every appearance are her initials. She stood up on every date. She went to court and stood up on it because this is her case.

What is not written on the file is what happened between last week and today. That she mostly told me, and I can guess the rest. She did not write down, for instance, how she came back from court Monday in the cold and did not feel her feet walking. She did not see the people on the sidewalks and in the hallways that led to this desk. She was thinking only about the thousand things that needed to be done between then and now. There were cops to schedule, witnesses to subpoena, evidence to be brought from the police department's Property Room, witness lists to prepare, an opening statement to write, photograph exhibits to enlarge, diagrams to be mounted—Christ! And with the thought of all there is to do, if she has not done it already, my stomach starts to roil with a familiar, almost nostalgic sickness. The same sickness she must have felt, the same dreadful elation that begins when you get sent out on trial. You teeter then, at the top of an icy hill, seated on your worn accordion file, all alone except for the boot that sends you going down the long, uncertain plummet to the base. Or headlong into a tree.

She wrote none of that, nor initialed it, but I know how she felt because I have felt it every time, and every time it is the same. A hundred trials that end a hundred ways but each begins the same. After the first one I stopped excusing myself to walk then run to the can and vomit before the jury walked in, but the sensation remained the same until my last trial. Two years ago.

Nor did she write how they came to her and took it away, all of it that made it hers alone. I can picture her at this desk, irked to be called by the staticky intercom to Bloch's office, wondering what the hell he wanted, and did he not know she had other things to be doing? Nonetheless she would have hurried over the linoleum in those shoes of hers, with that fine posture of hers, until she came to his door and knocked three times in rapid succession. And when she opened the door, she would have known from his expression that it was not good, whatever he wanted, for Bloch is no poker player. Luther was there. There was an ugly scene, the kid down the hall said. Maybe Luther offered her the same tolerant smile Bloch gave me when I said no—the smile you give to a child pounding his foot by the car door, saying, "I won't I won't I won't!" Luther would have told her the way it was going to be. When at last she spoke, she told them to go to hell. God bless her.

Yet it worked—whatever petty extortion they used to get her back in line, it worked.

Thinking about her with them shames me into activity. I sit up and shrug off my jacket, letting it drape over the back of her chair. Then I start as I always do: I examine the fucker. I push the manila folders around until I find Pool's mug shot. Ugly. Ugly, thank God. I look at his sheet, too, a tissuey streamer of paper printed in dot matrix. Haskin Pool—alias "HAKIN POOL" alias "HASKIN SPOOL" alias "POOL HASKIN" alias "THOMAS ANDERSON"—is twenty-six years old. He is five feet seven. He weighs 145 pounds. He has brown eyes. SKIN COLOR: BROWN. HAIR COLOR: BROWN. HAIR LENGTH: NORMAL. TEETH: NORMAL. FACIAL HAIR: NONE. TATTOOS: NONE. SCARS: NONE. But none of this tells you anything about him; except for the color of his skin, the man described on the rap sheet could be the kid down the hall.

Pool has a Social Security number and a welfare number. He has lived at five different addresses known to the National Crime Information Center, all of them in Brownsville and East New York. His proliferation of pseudonyms has less to do with active deceit (except for Thomas Anderson) than with the booking officers' fat-fingered typing. He has been arrested eleven times, mostly uninteresting collars. Stolen bikes. Fare beats. Narcotics, assaults, larceny, narcotics, narcotics, disorderly conduct. The usual diploma to hang on his wall. Here is something interesting: an arrest for murder when he was eighteen—but we dropped the charge to gun possession. Pool copped and served eight months on Rikers Island. Misdemeanor murder. I love Brooklyn.

Next I open a large envelope and shake out a thick packet of curling color photographs, 8½ x 11, that stick together and have to be peeled gingerly apart: crime-scene photographs taken by a detective with perfect objectivity, getting right up close while a partner turned Gomez's head obligingly toward the camera with a gore-stained blue rubber glove, the sort my mother would wear to wash dishes. On one side of Gomez's head I see a fingertip-sized entrance wound; the other side, where his right temple would be, is mostly missing. There are others as well. Interior shots of the bodega. Rows of corn chips and breakfast cereal and well-ordered cans of Dinty Moore beef stew. You can tell that Habib al-Hamadi was a proud man by how neatly he arranged his stock. There is, in one shot taken behind the counter where he died, a perspective of loaves of Italian bread and rolls scattered haphazardly to the floor and spotted with sesame seeds and blood; Gomez would not have liked the mess at all. There is, in fact, blood all the fuck over the place, as if someone popped a bag of it as a joke: on the counter, on the cash register, behind the counter, on the mess behind the counter, where Gomez can be seen lying in a semicircle of his own blood the color of eggplant, his arms and legs loosely askew, bent into the angles of a swastika. His body is limp, utterly subject to gravity, pressed to the blood-soaked cardboard he had placed on the floor as a sort of carpet when he was alive. I've seen worse.

There are some long shots of that corner of Sutter and Williams, the D'Vine Mini-Market under an uninteresting sheet of sky and light rainfall. A fine September rain. Cool rain in the still-warm air. The rain darkens everything in the photographs and gives some variety to the usual gray of everything. On this block of East New York—as familiar to me as the contents of my sock drawer—everything is washed out, monotonous: the red and yellow of the meat signs in shop windows, the green of the garbage Dumpsters, the brown and pale red of the masonry in the procession of buildings that line this block of Brooklyn where no trees grow. The street washes up on the cement sidewalks that lap against the buildings, and, in all the right angles, paper accumulates: paper cups and newspapers and wrapping paper from sandwiches made in the corner bodega.

A murder scene. The men standing in front of the bodega are detectives. I know they are detectives because they are eating. But beyond that is something else. Something ineffable in the corner's grimy everydayness tells me. There are places where murder happens, like this one. And playgrounds. And littered sidewalks. And stairwells. And clothes-strewn bedrooms that smell like incense and fast food. Maybe in Manhattan or Cleveland, murder happens in some places you would never expect, but not here, not in Brooklyn. In Brooklyn, murders are pulled where you expect them. That is why murder seems less like murder when it happens in Brooklyn. That is why the *Times* gave Habib al-Hamadi a mailing label for an epitaph. That is why Cully would not have given him much more, except that he wanted to throw Fister a beating two months before Election Day. All I know is that the borough is, for me, awash in blood, and there are some blocks where I cannot shake the ghosts in certain doorways and vacant lots, on stoops and manhole covers. All around them, unaware, children play. Women push strollers and shop. Old men sit on benches where dead boys leer at them. From my car window I see them. Do the living not know, or do they forget? And if they have forgotten, how do they do it? I would like to know.

My beeper goes off, sending a nervous current through my gut. I swear colorfully, less startled than embarrassed in front of myself for jumping. I cant backward in Laurel's seat and unsnap the beeper from my waistband. Makes me feel ridiculous, like those Glock-wearing cops must feel working in the file room at 1 Police Plaza. As if.

I wonder who even knows my number. (I don't.) Ann, I see.

Of course, *Ann.* Called me upstairs, no doubt. And at home. But for once I was neither there nor there. For once I was not out the door at five, catching the F train home with the secretaries and insurance salesmen and lawyers who sue supermarkets where old women fall down. I should have called her earlier, for now it is nearly seven, and she will do the math. She will count the hours between now and when Bloch told me, examining the minutes like entrails for signs and portents; women are always looking to stick a thermometer in the ass of your need for them. Nonetheless, I should have called. If anything, Haskin Pool will mean more to her than to me.

"Medical Examiner," Dr. Ann Greenlun says wearily when she picks up. I say hullo, and in a different voice in a different register, she tells me to wait and I do. I hold the phone to my shoulder and half listen as she talks to someone else, and meanwhile the kid from before walks by, his shaved head moving atop the partition wall like a bobber jerked along by a nibbling sunfish. I start to push the folders and papers of the file into some sort of order, and then Ann says, as always, "Hello, Joe."

We talk for five minutes about nothing in particular, and that is all right. I only want to hear the sound of her voice. The truth is, she need not worry about me. She can put her thermometer away. I have learned that I can live with nothing, for I have had everything taken away; I can be solitary as a spider, but I want to be with her.

After the five minutes, I tell her, just like that. She does not understand at first, and I have to tell her again. Then she understands. She makes me tell her again what Bloch said. *What exactly he said,* she wants to know, and I tell her what I remember, but of course it is not enough to satisfy her. She is very excited, and it makes me feel I have given her a present I did not pay for. Or bought for someone else. And then she is quiet for a long moment, after which she asks what I am going to do.

"I'm—you know."

"You don't have to," Ann says. "I mean, you don't—do you?"

"No. I suppose not."

And I suppose I do not have to take it. I suppose despite Bloch's *asking but not asking,* all that would likely happen tomorrow if I refused is that I would go back upstairs to Appeals and shut my door. I would open my books and read them. I would type my briefs with two fingers and file them. I would not see a defendant, or a judge, or Laurel, and everything would continue much as it has these last fifteen months. Except for this: from tomorrow on, I would be my own jailer. No longer would I have them to blame, and that would make all the difference.

But hearing Ann's reticence over the telephone line, hearing her suggest the possibility of saying *no* and meaning *no* makes the word blossom into vivid reality; only a moment ago, *no* was a fantasy I contrived to give myself the illusion that I had a choice. *I have no choice,* I see now, but not because they have left me none. I have no choice because I will let myself say only *yes.* I have already said *yes,* although I cannot yet say it aloud.

I expected Ann to get that somehow. I expected her to know me well enough to understand I have no choice, yet hearing her reaction makes me wonder. With the phone pressing into the cartilage of my ear, I wonder who I am kidding. I can smell Laurel's perfume, and on her desktop there is her file, devastated by me, and the hundreds of pages of police reports and grand jury testimony I have not read, the evidence I have not seen, the names of witnesses I have not spoken to. I have not done this in two years, a lifetime, and the mess I made in two hours underscores my conceit: to think that I could roll out of bed into a murder trial!

But Ann lightly sighs. "Oh, Joe!"

I was wrong about her. She does understand. In her voice is distilled every hope she holds for us, and everything she fears. As she says her private name for me, her Anglo-Saxon construction of *Gio,* the relief of knowing that she understands everything makes me love her with an inarticulate childlike love. Nothing will be the same for us now. Even if I stay in bed tomorrow and pull the blankets over my head, the landscape will have changed overnight. She would pull aside the curtains and find the Kansas wheat fields replaced by a meaner topography. I have been living in the safety of doing nothing. I have taken shallow breaths of the thin air of the ninth floor, high above the Brooklyn streets where I belong, the streets where Opal died.

CHAPTER 5

Immediately awake from a dreamy flatness. A car alarm calls in the middle distance, but that is not why. I push myself up against the headboard. All I can see is a patch of diffuse light against the far wall. Another, yellow, moves ghostlike across the ceiling. Car lights and winter moonlight through the curtains—Laura Ashley curtains my wife left behind, along with the IKEA entertainment center and other remnants and bad ideas, when she split for Manhattan without me.

Next to me Ann stirs, turning languidly onto her side and releasing from beneath the blankets the heat from our bodies, the smell of sleep. I run my hand along the rise of her narrow hip and follow it upward, tracing the sudden dip in the architecture of her form as it falls away at her waist to the flat triangle of her lower back, which I can cover with a hand and do. Always surprising, how small women are up close. Beside her I seem to hulk. "What . . . ?" she says. Talking in her sleep. I do not say anything, although I want her to be awake with me. She has, after all, been with me in my exile since Nicole Carbon. Nicole Carbon was her case too, or more accurately the dead daughter was hers and the mother was mine. We divided them between us, and while it was too late for the girl, I could still do something about Nicole Carbon. When she went home, Ann came home with me and that was how it started.

I pretend to sleep, but I am still awake, still thinking about the case and tomorrow and Ann. The darkness has become syrupy and close. I am weighted down, pressed to the mattress by the weight of the black air. I slip silently from the blankets. Over the squeaking floorboards, every sound exaggerated by the cold silence, I walk down the hallway, habitually brushing my fingertips against Opal's unused bedroom door, as if it were a dish of holy water.

Quietly I shut myself inside the bathroom and breathe and blink under the abrupt white light of a bare bulb. On my feet I am less awake than I thought as I lay on my back a moment ago. I can hear nothing. My ears are full of cotton. My eyes are full of sleep. My legs are tied to bricks, and I stand upright and shut the medicine cabinet Ann left open, as ever, and there I am in the mirror with a shower-curtain backdrop. A parody of a school portrait, like the one of Opal caught in a posed smile against a maroon drapery hung on the gymnasium wall. I have three sheets of them in a drawer, wallet-sized, uncut, like newly minted money and equally unreal. I run water from the tap and put my mouth under it and rinse and squirt toothpaste on my tongue and rinse. Then I slap water on my face and neck, and when I straighten, the cold water runs down my chest and down my back. I dry my face and hang the towel around my neck. I study myself in the mirror and wonder why I am awake at two in the morning, but I know.

I look all right, considering. Good enough for a Brooklyn jury, anyway. Better than I deserve. Hair still there, still black. Eyes black. Black eyebrows. Black eyelashes. Skin a healthy pale from a Florentine ancestor. I raise my chin and let drain away what little animation this hour allows in my expression. Without blinking, I make myself into a hard customer, someone you would leave alone on the train. Then the look dissolves into a self-conscious smile.

From the bathroom I walk to the kitchen over the peeling linoleum to the refrigerator, which is Brady Bunch moderne, unlike everything else—the outsize enamel sink, the chrome-knob cabinets, the Chrysler-like stove complete with tail fins. I take a seltzer bottle from the refrigerator and shoot an effervescent stream into a juice glass and notice in my periphery the Haskin Pool file, out of place in the kitchen, as if dropped by a flying saucer into a display of birthday cards and Christmas cards on the countertop. There is the card in the shape of a cartoon Santa, signed with love from my twin spinster aunts who bankrupted themselves to put me through Columbia. There are others, cards from friends who still think of me as someone's husband, someone's father, someone else. The cards are from good people living stable lives in stable loving relationships with flocks of orderly children—good people who, out of goodness, invite me to the odd housewarming party, bridge party, cocktail party, Hanukkah party—whenever my wife, Amanda, is otherwise engaged, evidently, for she is never there. I suppose they are being kind, these old friends. More and more often I go. Ann makes me, leading me around therapeutically on a tether, making sure I do not wander off, asking me to introduce her to people whose names I do not entirely remember and herself drawing subtle stares, from men mostly but also from women: fertile women with tired eyes and square asses, women who do not understand why Ann does that to her hair or dresses like that.

Then there is the plain Gustav Klimt card from Amanda, neither a Christmas card nor a birthday card but, like everything with her since Opal died, neutral, self-sufficient. (On Halloween I learned that she was not seeing anyone—Ann asked someone in my wincing presence.) I wondered how much thought she put into deciding to sign it not *Love, Amanda* but simply *Amanda*. And I wondered why in hell she sent me a tie. A fine tie, though. I turned it over—Ermenegildo Zegna. Meant nothing to me, but now I remember turning over the Mass card and seeing another unfamiliar name: *Lashawn?* Something else to do tomorrow. Another reason not to sleep.

Yes, a fine tie, I will admit that. *Too nice for my Moe Ginsburg suits* was my second thought, and then I noticed underneath it a small watch. A woman's watch. I stood wondering what the hell. All at once I remembered giving it to Amanda on the occasion of something. I remembered that the watch had a story attached to it, but the story itself I did not recall. I held the tiny watch in my hand and wanted to remember, since she evidently remembered well enough to include a little note saying, *I thought you should have this, not me,* written on an ivory card imprinted with her initials— *AMB*—in deep blue copperplate. I noticed the *B,* and perhaps she wanted me to notice that, too. Anyway, I could not remember the story, and not remembering it made me realize that I had lost more than I thought I had before I opened her goddamn box.

Amanda's card—which Ann gave a cursory, proprietary once-over and set back down without comment—stands next to the Pool file, already beat to hell from one largely uneventful night with me: Laurel's cubicle to the F train to Windsor Terrace and a late dinner with Ann at the Japanese spot run by Koreans, next to

the Chinese spot run by different Koreans. I had the file, and neither of us mentioned it once, although it could not have been more
present if it were the dead body of a dwarf. Ann said nothing
about it until I set Haskin Pool on my kitchen counter. "Planning
on doing some work?" she asked me at last and pressed her lean
gunslinger's body against the doorframe and laughed a little at her
overture.

But as it happened, she was more work than I had planned for
a Monday night. Lately her thirty-four-year-old uterus ticks so
loudly in our ears that some nights it keeps us both awake for
hours. And last month her diaphragm sprang a convenient leak. I
thought she was more clever than that, but I checked in the morning and behold, it had! So there was another long conversation.
And a week after, another. She knows why I am not ready for fa-
therhood and all that, but there is a difference between *knowing
why* and *knowing*. She's a pathologist, what does she know about
death? She knows I am not ready because I told her I am not, but
what she does not know is whether I will ever be. When she asks—
never with words—I have no answer to give.

The sheets were cold when I pushed her back up against them
tonight, and I could not unfasten her bra. She had to stop everything while I lay there and do it herself. So after that, after we
started again, I was thinking too much. Thinking about the case
and Ann and her biological clock. I could not stop thinking. Nor
had I drunk enough to pretend I was drunk enough to enjoy doing
it. Afterwards, as we lay there in the dark, exhausted and discon-
tented, she had sense not to talk about anything—not about what
just happened, nor what did not, nor children, nor the future like-
lihood of, nor about us, nor the case, nor what if. We lay there
appreciating the cold air, and she smoked a single cigarette. All I
could see was the orange ember.

I open the refrigerator door and stare at the peanut butter. My toes are cold from the cold air rolling onto the linoleum, costing me money. I take out the milk carton. Open it. Smell it. Pour it down the drain, where it swirls momentarily, indiscernible against the white enamel. Some kitchen, I think—neither of us knows how to use it, so we do not. Instead we treat it like a knapsack. Thank God for Koreans. Since Amanda left, I have eaten away at her stock of canned food and frozen chicken, some of which still remains in frosty clumps at the rear of the freezer, no longer recognizable as chicken through the Ziploc bags. She was from the Midwest, where they have grocery stores, not bodegas, and the Hy-Vees and Krogers and A&Ps spread out for acres without murder and New York rents to keep them small. After we married, even after she had lived here for years, she would drive to New Jersey on Saturdays, to grocery stores with parking lots, and she would fill our crappy little Honda until it raised its nose like an inquisitive pig. I would carry paper bags up the wooden stairs to our walk-up, two in each arm, and Opal would go through them all looking for treats. Here I am still rationing out Amanda's canned tomatoes and industrial peanut butter like a snowbound man, knowing that the last can of navy beans will be the end of something— what, I do not know exactly, but something final. Then again, it may only mean I need to buy more navy beans.

Looking out the window for something else to do. Outside, the only sign of life is a neighbor's television making his window blue. A minute passes, then I sit at the table and open the file.

Crime-scene photographs spill onto the tabletop, reminding me that someone is dead and this is not homework. I sit reading for an hour, but it is no good. None of it stays with me for long— trying to remember what I read ten minutes earlier is like trying to remember a smell. Worse, nothing very interesting happens for the first two weeks of the investigation; I go blind reading about dead-end interrogations, witnesses who aren't, fruitless canvasses, pointless lab reports. There is nothing. No one sees anything, knows anything. The usual for that neighborhood, but there are no forensics, either, no fingerprints, and the ballistics do not trace to any gun on file. For two weeks all the PD had was an Arab in the ground and Fister up their ass because Cully was up his. (I read a dozen pink DD-5's headlined TELEPHONE CONF. ADA LUTHER, meaning Fister sicced Mark Luther on them almost daily.) I can only imagine who was more relieved when, after two weeks, this kid Darnell—Dellroy?—Dellroy Dunn walked into the precinct with his story. He saw the shoot, he said, or at least he saw Pool come inside and stick a gun up Gomez's nose. At that point Dunn, unseen in the back, on his knees arranging soup cans, tried not to move or breathe too much. When he heard the first shot, he did not know whose it was; he knew Gomez kept a little nine-millimeter under the counter, but when he heard the second shot, a full minute later, he knew things did not look good for his boss. Ten minutes after that, when he could no longer hear anything at all, Dellroy Dunn slipped out the back door and kept his mouth closed.

I think about his story and decide I like it. I like that he took two weeks to come forward. I like that he did not see how the murder went off. I want the jury to have some business to do. They can yell at one another all morning about why Dellroy lit out, about how Gomez died, but by lunchtime they will remember that Pool had a gun and that Gomez is dead. And they will come back with guilty.

But the case is all Dellroy Dunn—they have to believe the kid or I have nothing.

I am aware that I am thinking right, thinking about what I should be thinking about, not lying in bed with butterflies or eyeballing myself in the bathroom mirror. Yet just as suddenly I know—at three o'clock in the morning, six hours before I begin jury selection—what is wrong with my case.

I thumb in reverse through the sheaf of pink 5's, back through the diaphanous pages that curl maddeningly upon themselves. "Goddammit," I am saying, realizing I already saw it and went right by it an hour ago. There it is, headlined INTERVIEW—DUNN, DELLROY, a detective's DD-5 memorializing a conversation that took place the afternoon Gomez was killed:

> *On this date the undersigned detective interviewed above individual who did state in sum and substance that he works sometimes off the books in the D'Vine but was not at work today because he is sick.*

"Goddammit," I shout and hit the table with my closed hand. I pretend to be angry because I should be angry, but already I have decided that it does not matter. Before my fist hits the Formica, scattering crime-scene photographs, I decide that I like this, too. So the kid didn't want to play ball, so fucking what? This is Brooklyn, and if you get a witness who wants to cooperate, start asking yourself, *What's wrong with this guy?* Let Pool's lawyer ask the jury the TV question, *Is he lying now or was he lying then?* Let him. Dunn has no reason to lie now and every reason to lie then. The oldest reason there is in that neighborhood—*snitches get stitches.*

I laugh at myself. I am a freshman holding hands with an ugly girlfriend, kissing her openly in study hall. This is my first trial in two years, and I am a sucker for it, warts and all.

Ann comes padding out in my white shirt. She stands in the kitchen doorway with crossed ankles and crossed arms, hugging herself in the cold air. She yawns and blinks, am I okay? Half

asleep still, she cannot entirely open her green eyes, yet she asks if
I am okay in her doctor's intonation, the clinical tone that Amanda
always used when she asked the same question. When doctors ask,
I suppose, they actually want to know.

I nod yeah, then she comes over and sits atop me, long and
light. She presses her head under my chin, and her hair is going
everywhere—dirty blond dyed blond dyed Jell-O pink in places—
and she smells like cigarettes and her work. Cigarettes and form-
aldehyde. We sit like that for a while, and I run my hands over her
and she shivers from that or from the cold, but I do not feel cold.
I kiss her a little, and in a moment she wakes up and becomes serious about it, so I take off her shirt. She plants her feet squarely
on the linoleum floor, which gives her a fulcrum to press more emphatically against me. Her bare skin is a translucent white, nearly
blue, like milk in an enamel sink, and is constellated with red-
brown freckles and marked with creases from pillows and sheets
minted on her body in sleep. We kiss for a long time, like teen-
agers, but my leg is asleep, and it is all antiseptic in the blunt white
light, with Amanda's tomato cans looking out at us, with Opal's
drawings magneted to the refrigerator door, with Gomez bleeding
all over the kitchen table.

I stop, and I can tell she thinks it is the usual—that I am going to start opening drawers and medicine cabinets for the purple Trojan box (which I swear to Christ she is hiding, now that
she has already stuck a black-painted fingernail through her diaphragm) while she would patiently wait, knowing that I would
only be underscoring my unstated answer to her unasked question, and in the quiet interlude her clock would begin to hammer
in our ears like a kettle drum.

But that is not the reason. I do not stand up. I do not move at
all. She sits still and we both do nothing. Then she puts her small
fists on my chest and licks her full lips, chapped from kissing. We

sit like that, and I move her some, and when she changes her po-
sition, she sees what is on the table and I feel the line of muscle
and tendon inside her thigh go tense all at once. She turns fully
around on my leg, leans forward, and looks closely at the photographs. After two minutes, her head still down, she asks, "This is
Pool's work?"

"Um-hmm."

"Dirty goddamn scene," she says.

"Um-hmm."

"You have two wounds—the head and here," she tells me,
touching her own shoulder. "He was already down when he took
the head shot. Look. You can tell from the blood spatter."

"Coup de grâce," I say. "Wonder if he was dead already."

"I doubt it. But ask your M.E.," she says, turning and smiling
the way she does. "Who is it, anyway?"

"Meyers."

"He's good—a little cautious, maybe, but good. Don't ask him
for too many opinions. He'll get nervous."

"Not like you, I suppose."

"I *love* to give my opinions," she says, meaning it.

"You're not a scientist, baby, you're an actress."

"And what are you? All trial lawyers are actors. Mostly."

"I'm an appellate lawyer," I tell her.

She scowls, but not at what I just said. "If you're coming back
to this—if you're going back to Homicide, I mean—I wonder if I
should transfer out of Brooklyn."

"We'll see."

"To Manhattan, maybe," she says. "It wouldn't be good if we
had a trial together."

"We'll see."

"I mean, I wouldn't want to get asked 'Isn't it true, Doctor,
that you're fucking the D.A.?' "

"We'll see, Ann," I say, and she senses my gathering annoyance and leaves the topic alone. I am not ready to think about the trial that happens after this one, or the one after that.

"Do you have one of him?" she asks after a moment. "Pool?"

I nod and reach into the file.

"A face only a mother could love," she says when I show her Pool's mug shot.

"If his mother's Ray Charles."

She does not laugh, and I wonder if it is because of the word *mother*. *Mother* and *motherhood* and *children*—all are words and topics we come across together and ignore; in movies and in commercials, we pretend not to hear them.

She stares intently at Pool. Front and side, ugly as a Brooklyn street, pixilated in the color copy and leaving only a general impression, as if he were fashioned from three shades of clay. You could study this face for an hour and still not recognize him on the street. Ann is quiet, mostly naked, and I lean forward with her and see in profile her expressive mouth part slightly, a tiny line of saliva in the corner. She strains to see a killer, but the killer in the photograph is invisible. Pool is too ordinary, and that is not how we want them to be, believe them to be, need them to be for our own sanity. We want to believe them different from the rest of us, marked in some indelible way, like Cain, so we need only to squint our eyes and we will see. But it is not that way.

I run my hand over her bare back to change the subject, and she lets go of what she is thinking. Ann leans forward, flat on the kitchen table, and stretches her arms out. We do that for a while, then we walk to the bedroom and make up for before. At dawn she kisses me on the front stoop with her arms around my neck, and when she opens her eyes they are so full of faith that I nearly believe it myself. She does not let go, and I do not leave for the train.

CHAPTER 6

I, Andrew Francis Giobberti, am forty years old. I am sore and un-slept. Melted snow seeps into my unpolished shoes as I walk to court for the first time in more than a year. With me is a woman too well mannered ever to describe aloud how much she hates my guts. She walks two steps behind me, like a Japanese wife, but not out of respect. She has not said anything this morning except in answer to my questions, and even then she gives me only as much information as strictly called for. Despite everything, I am smooth-shaven, combed, wearing a decent dark gray suit, undeservedly loved by a woman, and completely at ease with myself and the world after a coffee-cart bialy and four Advils for breakfast.

Earlier I whistled a tuneless melody to myself as I pressed the wrong button on the elevator out of habit. I was on the ninth floor before I noticed, and someone in the hallway cast me a quizzical look as I stood in the car without getting off. I blew her—and Appeals—a goodbye kiss as the doors closed and I rode back downstairs to the fourth floor, to Homicide. There the receptionist quit talking on the phone to stare at me, slack-jawed, the expression on her spongy face indiscernible from fright. In the hallway, with people running and detectives lingering, I said hello to a couple of ADAs I did not recognize. A paralegal, one who has been here forever, actually stopped in the middle of the morning crush. Blew her a kiss, too! She reacted as if shot in the eye.

Now Laurel and I walk without talking in the clear winter sunlight. Yesterday's thin snowfall has been shoveled mostly into the gutter along Joralemon Street, where already it has turned gray or black or melted into pools in the shape of shoeprints and tire tracks. The sidewalks are scattered with smooth white pellets. As we walk over them, the small snap underfoot is all I hear.

In front of the courthouse I see white vapor billowing from manhole covers; a judge double-parking a rust-bucket Celica blowing blue smoke from the tailpipe; a sorry face in the window of a prisoner van; a shady character in a tricked-out Acura smoking a joint for breakfast with the seat way back. His feet are on the dashboard, and on his windshield a decal spells out his personal credo in six-inch capitals: MONEY BEFORE BITCHE's. With Laurel behind, I walk to the head of the line of men waiting for court. The men smoke and spit and kick their feet in the cold and fuck this and that. Some look scared. Some already have that prison stare: ready to get it on or get it over with. The line runs around Schermerhorn Street to the corner of Smith Street, where it turns and frays at the tail. There the Greek works his cart, like he has for as long as I remember. He sells coffee and bagels and buttered rolls. He says *thank you* to men who do not. The Greek has a sign of his own: WILL NOT HOLD KNIFES OR PHONES FOR COURT.

At the door I show my badge to a court officer, who does not bother to check me out. Inside, in a broad foyer of beige columns, men stand with their arms in the air beside metal detectors as the plastic sound of keys and pocket change thrown into Tupperware resonates dully. The men seem like they have done this every morning for the last thousand years, as if their fathers did it before them and their grandfathers before them, before the marble columns were painted beige to match the walls. All over this place is the sleepy calm of inevitability. And the waiting everywhere, inside, outside, in the elevators, on the hallway benches, in the courtrooms—waiting for the judge, waiting for the lawyers, waiting for the paper to be signed, waiting for the next date to come back so you can wait some more—all of it is part of the same thing. Everyone is waiting, already serving time.

We all wait for the elevator. Laurel casts wary glances at a lady eating Skittles and drinking orange juice, the gristle in her jawbone popping occasionally. The lady smells like her breakfast and powdered folds of fat. We wait five minutes, watching on a tarnished brass display the tortured progression of the two working elevator cars. Two out of six. Some of the numbers illuminate in pale green. Four. Five. Nothing. Seven. Nothing. Ten. One car hangs fire on the tenth floor, and the ten stays lit. Then the light goes out. Then the display goes out. Nearby an old man babbles unintelligibly; all around are misdemeanants and jurors, and you cannot tell them apart. No one is talking to anyone. No one cares that the elevators are fucked. Everyone waits. Everyone faces the same direction. Our eyes turn slightly to heaven and see no one, as on subway trains. After a minute, an elevator door opens. There is no bell, only a wan light that blinks then falters. The metal door—runic with tags scratched by keys and otherwise defaced with peeling stickers, and gum, and dried spit—opens. Then, just as abruptly, it shuts again.

I feel someone sidle up too close, and automatically I brace myself.

"Whoa, look out," the guy says. "Step aside, Homicide!"

"Luther," I say, turning and seeing Mark Luther's waxy face, on which he has fixed a practiced smile that efficiently dissolves my fine mood. He extends a hand for me to shake; his arm is at a perfect right angle to his body, as if he were a marionette and his hand were being yanked upward by an invisible thread. When I take it, he does a feint sideways as a sort of joke. "Look out, now!" he says. When he stops moving, I ask him what's new. He winks at Laurel, but she is behind me, so I do not catch her reaction. Meanwhile, another elevator arrives and a current develops in the gathering crowd around us. People funnel like sand grains through the neck of an hourglass.

"New?" Luther says, momentarily puzzled. "Nothing—same shit, different flies. Just come over to wish youse luck is all."

I say nothing because we both know it is a lie. Something is on his mind, and he sizes me up with his disconcertingly pale blue eyes. Alaskan-husky eyes. He says nothing for a moment and shows no discomfort at being with me. He chews his Juicy Fruit, or rather, clenches his teeth on it so that his ears move. He darts a second glance in Laurel's direction, and then he pivots lightly on a pointy shoe and gestures that I should follow. I do.

"What do you want?" I ask him and shift the Pool file from one arm to the other.

"Something I wanna tell you," he says, cutting the friendly routine now that Laurel can no longer hear. Standing next to him, I imagine this is how Laurel feels next to me; she thinks of me as I think of Luther. "For your own health, if you know what I mean." He quickly bends and drops his chewing gum into his palm. In the process, he allows me a view of his tanned head. He winces and gets closer.

"Listen, Giobberti. You and me, we had our differences over the years, but I always liked you."

"No, you never."

He smiles, this time a genuine smile. "All right. Maybe I never, but let's say I know you can do the job. Hmm? That fair? When you ain't going off on some tangent, I mean. That's why I told Whitey, you know—bring you in on this one when—you know—" He waits, and when I let him get away with it, he continues, "The, ah, the girl Laurie over there—she's smart, but a different kind of smart than you. She ain't from around here, you know what I mean? You and me, we know—"

"That's why you pulled her?"

"Whoa. Wait a minute. Nobody pulled nobody—"

"What's the story?" I say, interrupting him.

"What story? Your guy killed some sad fucker. So put him in jail. That's the story. Come on."

"So why you here?"

"I told you—to say *bon chance, mon ami*!" Luther snaps me a salute with an open palm, Legionnaire-style. I turn my back, but when I am already four paces away, I hear him say, "That . . . ," in a conversational tone. I stop. "That and Whitey wanted me to mention . . ." I turn to him but not entirely, thinking, *Here it comes*. "You know that sonofabitch Cully, right?" he asks. "On the *News* courts beat, right?" I nod. "Just give him the finger on this one," Luther says, illustrating with his own. "I mean if he comes by."

"Any reason? Other than Fister doesn't like newspapers?"

Luther drops his hand and gapes in mock disbelief. "That ain't so, Giobberti. He likes 'em. The fair ones, anyway. The ones that don't always go . . . twisting the story all around. Grinding the old ax, you know? This guy Cully, though. He has some . . . oddball ideas is all." Luther starts smiling again.

I leave him there. While I do not wait for her, Laurel walks beside me, no longer lagging behind. As we walk away from the crowd, I make a private curse for Luther, and then louder I say, "Shines Fister's ass for him."

"I hate him," Laurel says, as if to herself.

"Which?" I ask her, forgetting that we do not talk to each other like this, or at all. Beside me, still walking, she seems to remember that, too, and in my periphery I see her head turn to me in surprise, as if I read her mind. Maybe she thought she had not said it, only thought it.

"Forget it," she says, but her voice is different now—less reedy, less strident and wounded than it has been all morning. She did not know that I am like that with Luther, I realize. She probably believed us cozy as lice. *Letch Luthor,* we called him then, among other things. That was before he became political, back when he was a toad like the rest of us, sharing an office with five other toads. We were so new, with our white shirts and ties, we knew nothing. Yet even then you could tell Luther had ideas about Luther. Already he was bestowing his dubious favors and backslaps on anyone who could get him off the front lines, anyone who could get him upstairs.

I lead Laurel Ashfield to a back corner. She does not ask where we are going. Back we go, deeper into the building, through an argosy of swinging doors and narrow drywall hallways lined with decisional law, bound in green and black with gold letters. Back I take her, to a wooden door with a window of meshed glass at eye level, through which a barred gate can be seen. I open the door, then I pull the clattering gate aside and step into the private elevator.

"You're not supposed to be in there," she says to me, and does not get in. "It's the judge's elevator."

"You want to be late or what?"

She gets in. I let go of the gate, and it closes on springs after her, making a racket, making her wince. Close to her, I smell her perfume and it reminds me of something until I realize it reminds me of her, of last night, of her telephone—

"Now what?" she asks, and I press the ten button once again, round and worn, like an old typewriter key. Nothing happens. "You need a key," she says, pointing out the cylinder in the panel.

"Which I," I say, taking out my key ring, selecting one, and showing it to her with an unreasonable sense of triumph, "just happen to have."

"Do you mind if I ask how you just happen to have a key to the judge's elevator?"

"Because I just happened to swipe one," I tell her, inserting it. "Ten years ago. When you were still in the convent."

We wait and nothing happens. I press the button again and nothing happens.

"Hang on," I tell her, and then I smack the panel with the heel of my hand. The gate rattles.

"What are you doing?"

I smack the panel once more, again to no effect. Annoyed— perhaps more embarrassed than annoyed, embarrassed at showing off for the girl, as if this were grade school—I throw open the gate and then the outer door. I walk off with Laurel behind me again, asking me where I am going now. I kick open a door into a cinderblock stairwell lit only by slit windows and smelling like an ashtray. "You game?" I ask. I show her my watch, meaning that we are ten minutes late already. She seems to brace herself, then she slips her long black coat from her shoulders and drapes it over one arm. She spins away and up the first flight. Already she has turned the landing and doubled back above me before I have pulled the door shut and begun to follow her. I hear her light elfin footsteps above me but cannot see her except as an intermittent shadow in the wan light that comes and goes. On the third-floor landing I pause to rest. "Slow up, will you?" I say. "Holy Mother."

No one else is in the stairwell, graffitied and butt-littered. The overpainted walls are pocked with little circles where smokers have pushed out their cigarettes before hurrying back to court. I switch the file from one hand to the other and resume climbing with my heavy feet. On the sixth floor, I shout up to her, "Hey, Ashfield. Why do you hate Luther so much?"

I keep climbing. After a moment during which she says nothing, I call out, "What about Fister? Hate him, too?" Still she says nothing, but I hear her clipping along somewhere far above me, her pace unslackened. I continue, our footfalls at different rhythms, making odd syncopated echoes. "You ever meet him?" I say, wondering if she can even hear me. "Whitey, I mean?" Again nothing. I pause. Take off my overcoat. The Advils are wearing off, and I run a hand over my brow and realize I can no longer hear her. I crane my neck upward, but there is neither sight nor sound of her.

"Once."

Her voice comes down absurdly loud and close, but she is not close. Just a trick of this chimneylike space, a weird parabolic effect.

"Yeah? Yeah, when was that, Ashfield?" I stand and do not move, thinking that it might spook her if she were to see me, and I want to know her answer. I am waiting, looking up through the narrow opening that runs between the staircases in an ever diminishing symmetrical progression, like an image caught between two mirrors. I want to her hear talk, even like this—especially like this, for this cinder-block space has the private intimacy of a confessional. I will forgive all her sins, for I am a great sinner myself. I want her to impress me with hers.

"When he interviewed me. For the job," she says. "Four years ago. Five, I guess."

"What'd you think?"

"What you would expect," she says. "Open, scared, you know— a politician."

"Hey, Ashfield," I say, and I start stealing up the stairs. "Did he—did he ask you that hypothetical question about the witness dying? During your interview?"

"You mean, um," she says, thinking. "If your only witness dies before trial? And the defendant doesn't know about it but, ah—but he tells you he wants to plead guilty?"

"That one," I say. "He asked you?"

"Yes. Yes, he did. I forgot."

"So. What was your answer? Would you take the plea?" I ask, still softly walking. "Or would you tell them your witness kicked off?" I turn the landing and there she is, a half-flight above me on the tenth-floor landing, standing just inside a band of light with a smile playing lightly on her face.

"Funny," she says. "That seems so long ago. I was such a—"

And as I come near her, she turns, caught unaware. Her gaze is pliant and her complexion fresh from the climb.

"What was your answer?" I ask her.

"I'd tell them my witness was dead."

"Why am I not surprised?" Her other expression is gone, re-placed by the one I am accustomed to—one of sullen reserve. For that reason, perhaps, I hear myself saying with more vehemence than I intend, "Fucking guy wants to cop a solid plea? And you're gonna send him home?"

"I wouldn't lie to get a plea."

"What lie?" I ask her. "Guy said he'd cop out. You didn't lie."

"He wouldn't plead guilty if he knew the truth."

"So?" I ask.

"So. That's wrong."

I laugh at her and she does nothing. "That's crap," I tell her. She shrugs and does not argue. Instead she turns away and walks through the stairwell door into the lobby outside the courtroom.

"I think it's a character test, that question," she tells me as we walk together toward the courtroom door. "How you answer it depends on what sort of person you are." The click-clack of her black polished shoes over the fissured terrazzo exaggerates the atmosphere of the vacant lobby. Mine, still damp, only squeak.

"Maybe," I say. "But listen, one thing about this job is, what can I say?—living with a certain amount of moral ambiguity, I guess."

"What does that mean?" she asks without interest, without stopping. *"Moral ambiguity."*

"Forget it. Let's have this same conversation when you've seen something of the world. After you get a little dirt on your ideals. And your shoes."

She stops at the courtroom door, where a sign handwritten in bubble letters reads NO KNIFES OR CELULER PHONES ALLOWED IN COURT. She puts her hand on the door, turns to me, and says, "Don't patronize me." She means it. I face her. Her transparent brown eyes snap at me and she does not look away. After a long moment passes, she turns to walk off but changes her mind.

"You'd take the plea, then," she tells me without certainty.

"Yeah," I say. "Yeah, I would."

She nods and does not say anything more, thinking privately about something. Then at last she pushes open the courtroom door and tells me, "As I said, there's no right or wrong answer. It's a character test."

"What can I tell you? I'm a character."

CHAPTER 7

"There's no one here."

Laurel Ashfield stops short inside the courtroom and states the obvious as I keep walking past her to the prosecution table, where I drop the file at last. The courtroom is mostly wood, the wood mostly man-made: the prosecution table is a peeling veneer reminiscent of figured walnut, the defense table is the same except bolted to the varnished linoleum floor; there is the laminated flag-pole behind the bench, and there is the bench itself, which—like the rows of pews in the gallery and the linenfold wainscoting and the jury box and the balustrade between the gallery and the well—is oak, once fine oak but now purpled with lacquer to the point where it is indistinguishable from plastic.

"There's no one here, Giobberti."

"Thank God," I say and walk to the gallery and lie down, stretching out on a purple pew in a row of purple pews, all of them scratched over with tags and clever obscenities, even the one where I now lie, affixed to which is a stenciled sign: LAWYERS POLICE & PRESS ONLY. I put my hands behind my head and say, "That's trial work for you, Ashfield. A lot of waiting and work and aggravation. You wash your hair. You brush your teeth and put on nice clothes." She comes closer while I talk, but I keep talking at the ceiling, saying, "All of it for what? For one little word. Christ, what you do for sixty seconds of joy. Lot like sex, don't you think?"

"I suppose you roll over and go to sleep after the verdict," she says, a little too late for a spontaneous riposte. She *decided* that she would be spontaneous, but that is okay. She is feeling her way around, still uncertain how to be with me; already we are better together than last night, better than an hour ago. I turn my head, but it is hard to read her from this angle. Her hands are on her hips, but that could mean anything.

"No," I say seriously. "No, I usually get profoundly drunk."

"And what do you do if you lose?" she asks. She smiles artlessly.

"I've often wondered that myself," I say, affecting a philosophical tone, but she clicks her tongue and walks off. She walks to the prosecution table and sits in a broad shaft of yellow sunlight segmented by a venetian blind cocked at an odd angle in one of the three tall, arched windows along the left wall. Everything is still. The sole movement is the slow swirl of dust wheeling in and out of slanting window light. I watch her and decide that through the severity of her expression, beneath her black suit and right-angled shoulder pads, she is not as hard as she tries to put across to the world at large, or to me.

"So Darnell's a liar," I say, my words sounding hollow beneath the forty-foot ceiling.

"Excuse me?"

"Our witness. Darnell."

"Dellroy." Her back is to me. She is sitting in a black slat-backed banker's chair and does not turn or say anything else. She is perfectly still, as if waiting for me to shoot an apple from atop her head.

I ask, "What do you think?"

"Why—what?" she says, inclining her head a little to the right, although she does not turn wholly around. Then she faces forward again and seems to tense but says nothing.

"It's coming out, so I'd like to bring it out first," I say, standing and walking toward her in my squeaking shoes. Puzzled by her reaction, I want to see her face, not her back. Perhaps she suspects I am being disingenuous in asking her advice, and I am. I do not need her advice, but I want to know her answer. If she is going to be sitting next to me for the next two weeks, I need to know how her mind works on trial. "Do we open that up on jury selection? Or we could save it for the opening statement—"

She smacks her pen onto her legal pad and spins in her seat to glare hard-eyed at me. "I don't think you're very amusing. If that's what you mean—by asking me—"

"No."

"Then what is your point, exactly? Because I—I don't think you're—you appreciate that you're—you're constantly—" she says, not meeting my eyes and becoming uncharacteristically inarticulate. She has stopped making sense, and her loss for words feeds upon itself until she shuts up, while I wonder what the hell just happened. She sits there breathing.

"Laurel, look," I say. "Let's say I don't know you. I want to—"

"You want to pretend. Fine. But please. Please stop always—" and she does not finish. Her voice is ragged and weary, and I feel I must keep her talking, as though she swallowed a bottle of pills and if I do not smack her wrists and pour coffee into her, she will slip away from me into a silent coma.

"No," I say, "I mean I know you can do this. You got the pen set and everything." She does not stir. I say, "When'd they start giving out pen sets, by the way? All I got was steak knives." Nothing. "Which doesn't make a lot of sense, because on the salary, you can't afford steak." Nothing. "And you can't bring them to court—"

"Please stop," she says, interrupting in a small voice.

"All I meant is—" I shake my head. "Laurel, before you stand up on my trial, I want to know—"

"Stand up on your trial?" she says, and the force of her astonishment knocks her head up. Her eyes are lively and amused.

"On *the* trial," I say, thinking she objected to my tactless possessive pronoun.

All she says, quietly emphatic as she shakes her head, is "I'm not standing up on it, Giobberti."

I thought that we had gotten around at least this nonsense by now. I even think she may be sending up herself for last night, and for that reason I say, "No, of course not."

Her expression does not alter and, if anything, gels. "I told them—you—already," she says. "I don't want any part of this anymore." She articulates her words so there will be no possibility for me to misunderstand them.

I hesitate, and then all at once I feel color rush to my face. Anger, yes, but what I feel mostly is unreasonably betrayed by her; twice now she has refused to let me give her back her case, or as much of it as I can give. Moreover, I had believed that something passed between us, something private, somewhere between the lobby and the tenth-floor landing. Not much, perhaps, but enough to make her stop beating me with her misdirected anomie. She must register that, for she exhales a long silent sigh, and while she still observes me coolly, she continues, albeit with less assurance than before. "I was thinking, actually. I was thinking that I wouldn't sit at the prosecution table. I could sit in the gallery and—"

"Cut this shit. Right now," I say, my voice low and cold. I advance toward her, and the abrupt change in my demeanor catches her off guard. She recoils a bit when I come up to her. "I don't like this any better than you, Ashfield. You think I don't know why you're here? I know. You think I don't know you're here to watch my ass?"

"What?"

"I said cut the bullshit." I am standing over her. "I know what's going on, but you know what? I don't care. I have a homicide, and I'm going to try it. And you're going to stand up. Like it or not, you're going to stand up." Everything about her is delicate and tremulous under me, except her eyes, which have gone flat with disdain and defiance. For that reason, and for another, I tell her, "And you know what else? You're doing the first round. Jury selection, Ashfield. You're talking to them first."

"I'm not—"

"Hell you're not."

Twenty minutes later, I am standing at a window open to the winter air as the sun waxes over Brooklyn on its flat January trajectory. I imagine Laurel behind me sullenly staring at the prosecution table, hating me anew.

The back door opens. In walks Yost. Martin J. Yost, 26 Court Street, Brooklyn, New York City. He enters without his client, Haskin Pool, the guest of honor, who is somewhere downstairs waiting, sitting by himself on a cement bench, inhaling the shit-and-Clorox smell of the pens—the smell of subway stations on Sunday mornings. Yost sees me and comes right over, shedding his overcoat and briefcase onto a pew. He looks the same as my memory of him. Shapeless blue suit. Thick tie. Smoker's skin and uneven sideburns. His groove has not changed a lot since 1974. We shake hands, and he tells me he has not seen me in a while. He tries to remember the last trial we had together. I cannot remember it, either. Then together we realize we were not friends before, so why pretend now? He says something polite. I smile, and he walks off to await Pool at the table.

The courtroom begins to awaken. A few court officers come in. Stand around. Yawn. Look at a newspaper. They drift out the door behind the bench; I can hear them talking back there, laughing. Yost is on his cell phone. Something about a missed appointment. The court clerk is at his file cabinet. The right cuff of his corduroy pants has caught on a small handgun strapped to his ankle. Some civilians sit, after huddling and whispering by the back door, trying to decide something. They are women in Phat Farm jackets and stocking caps. They sit in the back row, as they did in school. They sit talking to each other and throwing scowling glances at everybody else and pointing. Haskin Pool's kith and kin, I decide. Sisters and cousins and aunts. Perhaps even a mother or two. He has no men here. They never do.

I turn back to the window and, for the hell of it, start counting church steeples, the only features of the Brooklyn panorama to catch the eye, apart from the thrusting phallus of the Williamsburgh Bank building. *Seventeen, eighteen*—but also in my mind I get ready to stand up, in case Laurel does not when the time comes. I try to remember some of my usual dog-and-pony for the jury, but I wind up counting steeples instead, trying not to worry that I cannot remember what I used to say. Last night's lonely butterfly starts beating its aluminum-foil wings in anger, and I lose count. *It's like riding a bike, isn't it?* If I were to stand up—if Laurel does not—then everything will come back to me, *just like that*—right? And in a deep lobe of my brain, a dirty thing that I kick down almost as soon as it bucks up, I privately wonder if I am making Laurel stand up not to slap her from her funk, not because she pissed me off, but simply because I am not ready.

"All rise," the clerk says, startling me in the midst of that fine thought, and I turn as Justice Jonas A. Gewirtz steals into his courtroom through the door behind the bench. He is pulling on his robe as he walks, hunched over, a pinched expression on his face. But for the off-kilter robe, you might imagine he had come to empty the trash cans. No one else appears to notice him except Laurel, who popped up like a martinet when the clerk called for order. I stroll to the prosecution table but pause midway to glance at the bottom of my shoe to see what I stepped in. Only gum, I think. Yost is still talking on his phone. "Well, I don't know where he put it!" he is saying.

"Goddammit!" Gewirtz says at last to no one in particular. Laurel looks quickly at me, but Gewirtz raises his arms and says, "Where's my stenographer?" He stands there running his palm over his head, rearranging the salt-and-pepper threads. "Who said we were ready? We're not ready."

"She maybe can't get an elevator," Yost offers, snapping shut his cell phone. Gewirtz ignores him, but Yost tries again: "Elevators slow today. Sure it ain't her fault."

"Will someone call downstairs?" Gewirtz says, still ignoring Yost; the clerk is already on the phone. Gewirtz puts his fists on his hips and gazes at the back wall of his courtroom, at no one, at a brass-bladed fan immobile for fifty years, with the dust to prove it.

"I'm sure she's on her way," Yost says.

Gewirtz at last turns to Yost. "She one of yours now, Yost? You don't represent her." Gewirtz shakes his head and tugs his robe, which hangs unzipped, exposing his maroon knit tie, plaid shirt, beltless trousers. "Where's the defendant?" he says, noticing the empty seat. "Sergeant, will somebody bring the defendant up? Will—" His phone rings. He answers it. "Yeah," he is saying. "Yeah . . . no . . . no, goddammit."

Now everyone is waiting again, no one is talking at all except the women in the back. The women are still scowling and pointing and whispering, but I cannot hear what they are saying. Gewirtz sits at last, and everyone follows suit except Pool's women, who never stood up to begin with. Yost opens his phone. The clerk is banging shut his filing cabinet. Two court officers walk languidly from the door behind the bench. Laurel watches with a skittish, feline expression; she leans forward with her hands caught between her knees. I start picking at the walnut veneer on the prosecution table, where an edge has begun to peel. I notice something tucked underneath. I tease it out with a fingernail. A note folded from a torn triangle of white ruled paper.

We're fucked, it reads.

A note from a onetime occupant of this very table to his second-seater, no doubt. Hastily, covertly written during trial, after the iceberg had been struck but the ship not yet sunk with the loss of all hands. The note had been read, silently acknowledged with a nod, then folded and deposited under the Formica for the same reason that men blow paint on cave walls and scratch their tags on subway-car windows and elevator doors—to say, *I was here once and now you know.*

I show it to Laurel as a peace offering, but she gives me a queer, questioning look and says nothing. She thinks I wrote it.

Five minutes pass and nothing happens.

Then the back door swings open and the stenographer comes through the middle aisle as quickly as her shoes allow. Everyone watches her except Gewirtz, who has sunk from view behind the high bench. The women in back point at the stenographer and scowl and whisper. She is about fifty, with conical breasts and elaborate makeup. I recognize her from before, but I do not remember her name. "Sorry," she whispers—to me, for some reason—as she enters the well. "The elevators are absolute *hell*," and Laurel and Yost, who is shrugging *I told you so,* exchange glances. As the stenographer unfolds the legs of her machine, she smiles at me and winks. Without speaking she shapes the words *Long time!* with her lipstick mouth.

I am smiling, too, a little. *A long time,* I think. Here I am sitting on my wooden seat, hoping it is a bicycle, waiting for it all to come back. So far it has not. Everything is the same as I remember, but it is the same as everything is the same in a recurrent dream; you know where you are, and the landscape is familiar, but when you wake up, you wonder what the fuck that was all about, and you have no idea. I turn to Laurel for some clue as to whether she is with me or not. She is writing notes on a legal pad.

"Number one on the trial calendar," the clerk says, and for the second time this morning, I jump and wonder if anyone noticed. I wonder if the women in the back are scowling and pointing at me. "People of the State of New York versus Haskin Pool. Note your appearances, please!"

Laurel is on her feet again, saying, "Laurel Ashfield representing the Government." She has already said it by the time I push back my own chair. Yost and I look at each other in unison. He shrugs and I shrug back, then he says, "Martin J. Yost. Twenty-six Court Street, Brooklyn, New York City."

"Andrew Giobberti for the People."

"Counsel approach," Gewirtz says, and we do. The stenographer takes her hands off her machine, examines a nail.

En route to the bench, I tell Laurel, "One thing, Ashfield. Yost puts his appearance on the record first. And we represent *the People,* okay?"

"That's two things."

"I threw in the second for free."

"Well. The Government is the People," she says, sounding puzzled and innocent but looking anxiously between me and the bench, where Yost already stands.

"All right, James Madison," I say, "but you tell a Brooklyn jury you represent the Government and—"

Gewirtz interrupts, "Whenever you're ready, People."

Laurel gives her attention to Gewirtz, who softens his expression in response. As he settles his gaze upon me, his narrow face misshapes oddly as it reverts to its more familiar attitude, stuck between two antagonistic states like refrozen ice cream. "Miss . . . ?" is all he says, turning back to Laurel.

"Ashfield, Your Honor."

"Miss *Ashfield*. Well." Gewirtz is casting about for something to say, something pleasant, and the effort nearly overwhelms him. "Well. Welcome." He spreads his hands.

"Thank you, Your Honor."

Gewirtz turns now to Yost, purposely taking his eyes off her so that he does not stare. I suppose he cannot be blamed too much. In the morning he drives his Maxima or whatever from Astoria or wherever to the Brooklyn-Queens Expressway and then to Schermerhorn Street, and then in the private elevator he uses his key to bring himself here. And here, from ten until four, he sees what he sees—lawyers and worse—his only respite being two hours for lunch with men who look exactly like him. And now, interposed in his day, is Laurel.

Again he turns to her, but he becomes brusque with her on purpose. "Well, Miss Ashfield. Mr. Giobberti knows my rules. So does Mr. Yost, but I don't think you've ever been before me."

"No, Your Honor." The honorific comes as a surprise to him every time. He straightens his posture when she says it.

"You— How long have you been in Mr. Fister's office?"

"Nearly four years, Your Honor."

"You're second-seating Mr. Giobberti here?"

"Yes," she says after only the slightest hesitation.

"Have— You have tried some cases of your own, yes?"

"Yes, Your honor. Eleven."

"Fine, fine," Gewirtz says. "But you, you're not from, ah, Brooklyn?"

"I beg your pardon?"

"Your—what do you call it? Your enunciation, your dictation, Miss Ashfield." Gewirtz's gray eyes glaze with concentration— *dictation* is not the word he needs, but all he can do is smile awkwardly and pray that she helps him out. As this unfolds I wonder at the effect she has on people, making them want to be better than they are but instead making them seem worse. I thought it was only me. I nearly volunteer *diction,* but I end up saying nothing. Turning to her, I see that her face is empty of humor, her smile a husk. Even Gewirtz seems to register that he said something wrong, although neither he nor I know what. At last he waves a hand. The moment passes.

Looking now at me, and at Laurel only in darting hooded glances, Gewirtz is explaining, "So it's really very simple. I bring in the full panel, and we start with sixteen in the box. I ask them a few questions myself—*What do you do? Where do you live?*—that sort of thing." He turns to Laurel, trying again despite himself, hoping she will favor him with a nod. She obliges, evidently recovered from whatever that was a moment ago. Gewirtz cheers perceptibly, continuing, "Then I shut up and you get your turn. You have thirty minutes to question— *Oh! Oh!*" He rolls abruptly backward in his big chair and stands faster than you think he could. "God in heaven!" he says, peering under the bench. The clerk comes over with the sergeant. They stand behind the bench, bent at the waist, watching, waiting. "I felt it!" Gewirtz tells the clerk, spitting the words. "This time I goddamn felt it."

Laurel turns to me for an explanation, as if this happens all the time and I would know why. I step up, and Gewirtz says, "We have a sort of—wildlife problem here." Laurel remains calm and even politely curious at the news.

She says, "Oh."

"Rats," the clerk says to her. He lowers himself behind the bench. He goes down arthritically on one knee, then the other, then I cannot see him anymore. The sergeant—who, unlike the clerk, is unarmed—stands by impotently with a doughy expression. Gewirtz is far back, ready to leap into his chair and raise the hem of his robe like a cartoon housewife.

"Had a pigeon in here last month," Gewirtz says, flushing. His voice has now pitched up a half-octave. "Terrific craps. Craps like black-and-white cookies." He makes a circle with both hands to illustrate. "All over my— You see anything, Bobby?"

"No-o," the clerk says, pulling himself up.

"Shoot it," I suggest to him.

"Right!" Yost says, getting into the spirit. "What happened to the last rat I saw in court. Day after he took the stand. Ka-pow."

Unnoticed by any of us at the bench but me, a court officer quietly leads Haskin Pool into the courtroom, to a wooden chair at the defense table. With his hands cuffed behind him, Pool has to lean forward in his chair when he sits. Before he sits, he raises his chin in greeting to the women in the back row. One of them puts a hand on either side of her face, as if she has a toothache. Pool is smaller than I imagined from his mug shot, a wispy little shit dressed all in black clothes falling off him, his sleeves covering his hands, his pants making a saggy bucket at his crotch. I want to know if Pool looks like a perp or like a kid. To me, he is both.

"Defendant present in the courtroom," the clerk says. To no

one he says, "Are we on the record? I don't know." Gewirtz seems not to hear, but the stenographer—implacable throughout—puts down her magazine of word jumbles and her pen and makes a few silent strokes on her machine. She smiles again at me, and the clerk shrugs. Yesterday at this time I was thinking about where to get a brisket sandwich and not much else.

A couple more court officers are behind the bench, searching. One has an enormous flashlight. Another gazes at the ceiling for the pigeon. In the back of the courtroom, the woman is crying unobtrusively, shaking her head with her hands still holding it. The others are rubbing her back. Pool sits there, a slip of nothing, but all of this is about him.

"Jury in the hallway," someone says.

I feel my insides sink before I turn automatically toward the voice, to the rear of the courtroom, to the back door, where a court officer stands. "You want 'em?" he says, and the silence is instant. We all stop where we stand, as if Mom just got home early; after a moment we wordlessly settle into our places, Yost at his table, Laurel and I at ours. The court officers peel away to the side, and the clerk steps down to his desk. Gewirtz, too, seats himself, but not without a final cautious check under the bench. "Yes, Officer," he says. I watch Laurel's slim hands curl into fists on the tabletop, and I still do not know if she is going to stand up.

Three court officers begin to shepherd seventy-odd potential jurors into the courtroom. They are a noisy bunch with their shifting around, and their winter jackets rubbing against one another, and their coughing and bitching and throat clearing, and two or three already are giving grief to a court officer in the corner who opens his palms and tells them all to sit down because he cannot do anything about it anyway. With a purposefully impassive expression, I begin to sort them in my mind. A librarian in the front row smiles politely at everyone; she has the soft, indistinct features of someone who owns cats. I make a mental note to get rid of her. Another guy: white, hale and hearty with clear skin, and new in town. Beneath a neat denim jacket his T-shirt reads MICHIGAN, and that would have been my guess. Get rid of him, too. Same for an earth mother from Park Slope sitting in the back row wearing unnecessary scarves. Now a rosy-cheeked woman, old, paces heavily to the front of the gallery and raises her hand. I smell her perfume, the heavy sweet tang of church and relatives from Massapequa. "Mister!" she is saying to the judge. "Mister! Mister, I have a doctor's note!" She is waving a worried slip of paper above her head. "From the doctor's office!"

At once I am back on my bike. I am coasting downhill with my feet jutting like pectoral fins. I can do this, I realize. And I want to do this. I am already doing this, winnowing them before they even sit down. Until this moment, until the jury panel walked through the back door and began bitching and sneezing and waving notes at the judge, there was no trial. Until now it has been all about the file, about reading it and getting paper cuts from it. Now it begins, and I want to talk to them. I want to stand up and to ready them to say that one word.

Gewirtz introduces himself and then Yost, who stands and turns to the gallery and, in the process, spills to the floor several papers he had forgotten on his lap. "And to Mr. Yost's right," Gewirtz says, "is his client, Haskin Pool." I turn my head to see Pool, but Laurel does not. She sits with her fists on the table, clenching and releasing them. "Stand up, Mr. Pool."

"Stand up," Yost whispers too loudly to Pool, and he stands. Without turning entirely around, he angles himself enough so that he can see the jurors and they him. He does not smile or say anything. He is dead-eyed. He displays himself to them as if he were for sale. One shoulder slumps. *Thank God,* I think. The first look is important. If your guy does not look like he could pull a murder, if he looks like a rabbit, if he waves at the jury and says *Hi!*, start writing little *We're fucked* notes to your second-seater. Because you are.

"I love ugly killers," I whisper to Laurel, whose eyes have gone as blank as Pool's.

"And on my right. That's your—*left*? Your left," Gewirtz says, "is Andrew Giobberti and Laura—*Laurel* Ashfield. Miss Ashfield is the pretty one. Ha ha ha." We stand and Laurel's eyes dart at me with startled annoyance when Gewirtz says, "They represent the Government."

CHAPTER 8

Afterwards, after the courtroom is emptied and Pool is put on his feet by two court officers and cuffed again and Gewirtz has stood and yawned at us and said, "Two o'clock," Laurel sweeps from the prosecution table to the coatrack, where she stabs her long arms into her long coat and leaves on clicking heels without me. We do not talk on the elevator, or while we wait for it, and when the doors open in the lobby, she bolts, a greyhound from the gate, away from me and out onto Schermerhorn.

This is what happens two hours after seventy civilians filed warily into Gewirtz's courtroom, after he called sixteen forward and sat them in the jury box, after he asked them their names and where they lived and what they did for a living. Most of them answered those questions without too much trouble. Then Gewirtz turned to me and said, "Mr. Giobberti, proceed."

Laurel Ashfield stood instead. But not before hesitating an excruciating fifteen seconds, during which she appeared oblivious to Gewirtz, lost in some private dialogue. Everything grew quiet. I felt everyone's eyes upon me. During that quarter minute I silently willed her to refuse, to stay in her seat. I wanted that, and not simply because I wanted to stand as much as I have ever wanted to stand before a jury. I wanted her to refuse because I was making her stand. I wanted her to say *To hell with you* as she had to Fister. I wanted her to refuse because of the glorious pointlessness of making her point, and also because I see in her a familiar ghost of myself. I was recklessly principled like that once; I was rich then and, with the arrogance of the rich, believed I would never be poor.

She stood. With a polite nod to Gewirtz, she thanked everyone, including *Mr. Pool,* making me bite my tongue, and she approached the jury box holding on to her legal pad for dear life. For thirty minutes I watched her walk back and forth in front of the jury box, putting one foot directly in front of the other as she had learned in ballet class twenty years ago. *She knows how to do this,* I admitted to myself. She asked the right questions. She never faltered. Even so, I twisted in my seat, loosely dissatisfied. If I had to articulate what she did wrong, I could not—except to say that there was a rote, mechanistic quality to her voir dire, as if she had memorized it all; it was as if she were watching herself from the gallery while everything came out in perfect order. One two three. For thirty minutes her measured voice spread over everyone like a clean white salve absorbed entirely, leaving no scent, no feel. The jury watched glassy-eyed. Someone yawned. A toothy uncovered yawn.

Now she walks ahead of me up Schermerhorn Street. Her

back is straight, her arms in motion. She is strong, not from muscle but from leverage, from the length of her bones, from the placement of the fulcrum of her knees, hips, and elbows: all of it fueled with anger and I do not know what. I follow with the file under one arm, and what I see is the back of her.

Where Schermerhorn crosses Boerum Place she has to wait for traffic. I come abreast of her, and we say nothing. A pigeon, blurry and gray, pecks at a dry chicken bone in the gutter. A cold-cuts truck passes. Affixed to its radiator is a Christmas wreath encircling a stuffed bear, its head bent as if lynched. In a momentary lull of cars, Laurel runs into the road, but traffic pins her within the concrete median. From the curb I see her in strobe effect, between passing cars. Now traffic lightens on her side, and she is off again. In another ten seconds the light changes and I follow.

After two blocks she turns onto Joralemon Street, and there I catch her. As we turn the corner together in silence, a shapeless pile of rags with an antique beard looks up hopefully at us. Laurel is momentarily nonplussed by his extended cup. I see his sign— HELP FEED MY PUPPEY—and his forlorn spaniel lifts a milky eye at us. A routine tableau of filth and want, but I sense she would have dropped in some change were I not here. I say to her as we move on, "If you're homeless and starving, I wonder if you should have a goddamn pet."

Wrong wrong wrong. I know it the instant I open my mouth, but something makes me want to poke and prod her for a reaction. After the jury recessed, for instance, I needed to give her my opinion of her voir dire. She listened. She nodded. She pursed her lips, then darted to the coatrack after she asked whether I was done. I said yes.

We walk another block to the Municipal Building, a block of mostly one-syllable answers to my questions.

"Darnell's coming down today, right?" I ask.

"Dellroy."

"Is he? Coming down, I mean?"

"Yes."

"When?"

"Now. Noon."

"Did you subpoena him?"

"No."

"Why the hell not?"

Nothing.

"What about the case detective?" I ask. "Who is it again?"

"Heatly."

"He coming? Did you notify his command?"

"No."

"Why didn't—"

"Just—*stop,*" she says, turning to face me. Her coat sweeps around her as she turns, like a cape. "Just stop, okay? Stop telling—and treating me like—"

We are in front of the Municipal Building. Across the street some sort of squalid, impromptu fair is going on, and the place smells like a carnival with noisy children running and vapors hanging around tents and trailers selling funnel cakes and sausages and sticks of greasy cubes where old women with sunglasses and rubber-tipped canes obediently line up. The cold wind cuts flat down Joralemon, and I am already tired of this gray city winter and I long for summer when I can sit on my wooden bench and eat my lunch and watch pigeons dance on the hot cement. I am thinking about Laurel's reaction, and I do not know why everything is so difficult with her.

"Laurel," I say, and she turns away. "Laurel—this afternoon—"

"I know."

"I'll do the next round."

"I know."

"It's not that," I say. "You did good. The rest of it—everything I was talking about?"

"The *psychological whatever?*" she says, quoting me, and I smile, knowing I should have been more articulate than that if I were to offer her my opinion. Still! At least she is throwing something back at me instead of rolling over on it.

"Yeah," I say. "All that. It'll come, Laurel. That's what I meant."

"That's not what you meant."

"No," I say, smiling again. "But I mean it now. You can do this."

"Thank you." She is pleased despite herself. That is what she was waiting for, although I cannot imagine my opinion carries much weight with her. I think she may say something more, but all she does is walk to the Municipal Building. I hold the door for her, and for a man coming out. "Help yourself," the man says, and I say, "Go ahead," and he motions me on, and then we both move simultaneously and get jammed up in the doorway.

"See that?" I say to Laurel as if I had already told her. "It's easier in Brooklyn when people are rude. When you try to be nice, everything just gets all confusing." She keeps walking toward the elevator bank, through the crowd of people across the dimly lit, high-ceilinged foyer of the old building. She says nothing in answer. As usual, I do not know what that signifies, if anything.

"Where's the kid?" I ask Laurel. Twelve-thirty, and we stand facing each other in the bureau's reception, really a desk at the terminus of a fourth-floor hallway and an empty row of metal chairs for the comfort of visitors: witnesses, cops, relatives of boys shot and killed—where Dunn should be sitting right now. Instead there are only the two of us and the receptionist eating Sun Chips at her desk and licking her white fingers one by one and then brushing the crumbs onto the linoleum with the blade of her hand, all the while gazing at me in mild wonder. On the painted drywall beside her is a tourism poster, hung so long ago that the tape has yellowed. WELCOME TO BROOKLYN! ENJOY THE VIEW! And the view, of course, is not of any Brooklyn vista but of lower Manhattan rising across the East River like Camelot.

"Where's Darnell?"

"Um."

"Pearl. Pearl, you got a guy here for us? Witness?"

The receptionist shakes her head, swallows, then says no.

"You served him, right?" I ask Laurel.

"No, I told—"

"No?" The way I say it makes her face me. "Didn't you say you subpoenaed him?"

"No!" she says, making herself angry to choke out whatever other emotion she is feeling. "No. I told you—*Dellroy*! You keep—"

"Why didn't you?"

"We're not putting him on the stand today." She moves away from me. I follow Laurel to her cubicle, where she is already leaning her torso over her desk, jabbing her finger in a paperback *Criminal Procedure Law*. She is moistening her fingertip and turning pages noisily until she finds what she wants, and I know what that is.

"Here," she says, offering me the book with her face all lit up. When I do not take it, she reads to me, " 'A district attorney in a criminal action may issue a subpoena for the attendance in such court of any witness whom the people are entitled to call in such action.' "

"Yeah."

"Attendance *in such court*—I can't subpoena him to my office."

"You subpoena him to court," I say, "but you tell him to come to your office."

"That—that's not what the statute says."

"That's what you do. That's how you get it done."

"But that's—" she starts, but she stops short of telling me that it is *wrong*.

"So's killing people," I say, angry myself. "Remember what we're trying to do here." Down the hall a man is shouting—shouting and spitting out a string of curses. Then he starts laughing, a high shrieking laugh, and I realize he is quoting someone for someone else's benefit. Still it makes me realize I cannot be that way with her. I sit on a metal chair and think. "Did you reach out to him?"

"I talked to his mother," she tells me in a conversational tone, no longer so defensive. "His grandmother, I mean."

"His *grandmother*? You kidding me?" She nods. "Well, Christ," I say, almost laughing because it is funny to me. She says nothing else, and I am not thinking about her but about what I need to do. "We'll have a full jury tomorrow—I'm not opening until I hear from this kid. He's the case."

"He knows his story."

"I want it from him, Ashfield. And I don't want to hear it as I walk him to court."

"He knows his story, Giobberti," she says again, flat and low. "He knows what this is."

"You know the hardest part of trial, Ashfield?" I ask her without rancor, just to let her know.

"I don't know," she says in the same voice. Her desk is between us, and my eyes are fixed on the *CPL* atop it. She is right, of course, in the same way as she was right with the jury this morning, and the one is much like the other. I want to tell her that there is a difference between drawing neatly inside all the lines and making a picture, yet I believe she would not understand. She is so very—*right,* so altogether *right*. But right or not, I have no witness.

"Hardest part of trial," I say again. "What do you think?"

"I don't know." She is in no mood for a parlor game. She uncrosses her arms, recrosses them. "Doing a cross-exam on the defendant? Summations, maybe?"

"Getting your witnesses in. Just getting Elvis in the goddamn building."

Still unapologetic, not listening and again defensive, she tells me, "Giobberti, she wrote down the message!"

"Who? Grandma?" I say, smiling at the idea and at her, although I know better than to smile at her like that. "He's a kid in East New York. He is a witness to a murder—he's not coming in because we ask him nicely. Or ask Grandma."

"He'll come in. He knows he has no choice."

"Maybe," I say, doubting it.

She softens. "We can get a material witness order, if—"

"An MWO," I say and am nearly sarcastic with her once more. Enlivened by her idea, she starts paging through the *CPL,* again looking to tell me something I already know.

"Yes," she is saying. "If—if we have to, we can. Here." She reads with her fine voice: " 'A material witness order may be issued upon the ground that there is reasonable cause to believe that a person whom the people desire to call as a witness,' ah, 'possesses information material to the determination of such action.' " She raises her head hopefully, but in the unforgiving gray daylight from her window, her expression is worn and tired, like a young mother's.

"Read the next line, Professor," I say. " 'And will not—' "

" 'And will not be amenable or responsive to a subpoena.' " Her face is puzzled. "What?"

"How do we show Dellroy won't respond to a subpoena?" She waits. Careful not to allow any expression, either, I ask her, "You think Gewirtz is going to sign your MWO because you left a message with Grandma? With a shady witness, the best way to show he won't obey a subpoena is you subpoena him." I stand and walk to her window. "Then you go cuff him when he blows you off."

Neither of us speaks. The sky has taken a metallic cast, like burnished aluminum. I am thinking how much I hate this shit. I hate the elevators that do not work; I hate the judges who show up late and the jurors who want to go home and the witnesses who want to be left alone. I hate it all. I tell myself I hate it, but none of it generates any real heat. All of it is the stuff of trial work, and all of it, through the perverse alchemy of association, is secretly, oddly wonderful to me. As the cold, sopping bath mat is Ann, all the bullshit of being on a murder trial means you are on a murder trial.

I am on trial. There were a hundred mornings during my big vacation when I opened the metro section and there was something, a photograph, an item. Someone was dead. I used to know about it before the body left the scene, and now I was reading about it in boxer shorts, dripping milk on the newspaper from my spoon. I would read every word, but I never believed that would be mine again.

Laurel says, "Now what?"

I do not turn from the window. Helicopters begin slowly to gather like fat bumblebees above the blue spires of the Manhattan Bridge a mile distant. "Another post-holiday suicide," I tell her instead of answering. " 'Tis the season."

"Now what?"

"You know that suicide is a crime punishable by death?"

She makes a small noise, a drawn-out sigh that causes me to think involuntarily, instinctively, biologically, what she would be like. And I realize that I have not, until now, thought about her that way. At least I have not thought about her as much as you would think. She has that sort of clear, crystalline beauty that renders her unassailable, secure against even a fleeting elevator fantasy. If a hair were out of place it might be another story altogether.

I face away from the window to see that she has turned in her chair, her brown eyes gone liquid with emotion. I try to imagine Mark Luther atop her, grunting and pawing. I try to see her holding her breath and grabbing at the bedpost in a sordid downtown hotel or the backseat of his office-issue Crown Victoria in a cement-wall parking garage. I cannot. But if not that, what? Even with her pen set and her charming dictation, eleven trials are not enough. She needed eleven more, yet they sent her to Homicide. She rode the case with Luther and the next day she was here. Before that she was a line assistant in the Investigations Bureau—one of forty line assistants. *Why her?* The question she asked about me. *Why Giobberti?* Neither of us should be on Haskin Pool, yet here we are.

I come to her desk, close enough to catch her perfume, and pick up her telephone. I ask her for Dellroy Dunn's phone number. She complies without understanding. I dial. She has taken off her black suit jacket and is sitting in a plain silk shirt the color of cream. She is smaller now, smaller than she seemed in front of the jury, walking with her shoulders back, jacketed and upholstered. From above I see the thin line of shoulder bone beneath the slippery material of her shirt and feel an absurd impulse to put my hand on her there.

"Why'd you run out of here last night?" I ask her, and she pretends not to hear me. Then someone picks up the phone. "Hello?" I say, and several seconds pass before I hear something sounding like *hello*. "Hello?" I ask again, and again the same distant voice— man or woman, it is impossible to tell—says something I cannot understand. "Hel-lo?" I say, enunciating both syllables. "I am looking for Dellroy. Dell. Roy." But I hear only a TV and the mechanical sound of studio laughter. Then the voice, now clear, asks, "Who is this?" and before I can answer, the phone on the other end falls. Into an aquarium, by the sound of it. I look at the receiver in disbelief before banging it onto Laurel's desk, saying, "How hard is it to answer the phone?"

She smiles apprehensively but says nothing. I try again, and purse my lips as the line rings and rings. I hang up a second time.

"All right. Let me ask you this, Ashfield. What if Dellroy had answered the phone, and what if he told me in no uncertain terms to go fuck myself?"

"He wouldn't," she says, but now she is not so sure. "He knows he can't—"

"Just what if?"

"Then—then you could get an MWO," she says with caution.

I point a finger at her like a gun to show her she is right, and as she watches, I replace the phone to my ear. Without dialing, I say in a very polite voice, "Hello, Dellroy? Andrew Giobberti here. Oh, you don't want to come down? Oh, you have better things to do? *Fuck me?* Well, all right. If you say so, Dellroy. Have a nice day." I drop the telephone lightly into the cradle and shrug. Laurel is watching, uncomfortably amused. "Well, there it is," I tell her. "Kid told me to eat my shorts."

She laughs slightly, then stops laughing because I am not. She starts to get it the instant before I turn and walk from her cubicle. In half a minute I return with a blank form from a cabinet down the hallway full of blank forms: time sheets, lunch vouchers, discovery requests, and, of course, material witness orders and affidavits to support them. I set the paper on her desk and sit across from her.

"What are you doing?" she asks in a voice that suggests she does not want to know.

"Oh, you want to do it? Your handwriting is nicer."

"I'm not— I told you," she says. Her expression changes from worry to hurt to anger, although her physiognomy hardly alters at all. Everything happens within her eyes.

"Do you know what happens if Dellroy is in the wind?" I ask her. "And we can't find him? We all go home, Ashfield. Mostly Haskin Pool goes home."

She does not say anything, so I reach over and take a pen from her pen set. I start to write with it, but it does not work. "You should've asked for the steak knives," I tell her, shaking the pen and trying again with no luck. I offer it across her desk to her. She will not take it.

She shakes her head. "No more," she says, barely above a whisper. "No more of—this!"

"Just give me a pen."

"You never stop, do you?" she says. "You're just like them. You're just like them after all."

"I'm asking for a pen. Christ!"

She yanks open her drawer and smacks a pen onto the metal desktop. I say thank you and do not argue with her but instead start writing the affidavit in my moronic scrawl—swearing under oath that I telephoned one Dellroy Dunn whereupon said Dellroy Dunn informed me to eat my shorts. After a minute the fire alarm goes off, as usual for no reason, and I keep writing. I write the whole thing out, which takes five minutes. She sits there and the fire alarm dies away presently and there is no general clamor to escape the building. Cops keep pushing prisoners up and down the hallways, and paralegals keep spreading rumor and innuendo in corners. I hear shouts and curses and laughter and tears. Everything goes on as before.

CHAPTER 9

Inside the teeming courthouse elevator, humid with human heat, I press involuntarily against Laurel, who is pressed into a corner, and the panel buttons go dead. Someone is cursing and banging them. Then the overhead fluorescent tube flickers a white-green light, light the color of nausea, and the car moves upward in an abrupt jolt.

"Hey, I know you," a guy tells me in the polite quiet that ensues during the elevator's undetectable climb. I was studying the haphazard display of floors (three, nothing, five), but now I look at the guy. His baby dreads are tied up with a rubber band, spraying from the top of his head, a nightmare dragoon, and he is giving me a scowl of recognition. I have no idea. Everyone around us does nothing, unwilling even to look, unwilling to seem wary of trouble, as if that would bring it on, believing thugs—like dogs—smell fear.

On the sixth floor the elevator doors open and the car empties, leaving the guy alone with me and Laurel, who does not move from her far corner. The door closes with a death rattle. The car lurches up.

"Yeah. That's right," the guy keeps saying, half to himself. "That's right—I know you." I smile politely, the same smile Laurel gave me once or twice when I thought I was being funny. He snaps his fingers and the scowl disappears. "You was my D.A. That's right. I knew you was familiar when I seen you."

"Yeah? No kidding. Who're you?"

"Burton. Valentino. But you probably ain't know my name, 'cause all you ever call me is *the defen'ant*. Like, *then the defen'ant did this, then the defen'ant did that*. Nah mean?"

"Valentino Burton." I cannot place him, but then I always remember the dead better than the living. "Sorry, brother—who'd you kill?"

He laughs. "I ain't kill nobody."

"Sure."

"Naw, man. For real. You got me on a robbery. Arm robbery. I just get out like a year ago. Attica," he says. "Before that, they have me at what do you call it?" He snaps his fingers and his eyebrows join with thought. "Auburn."

"Nice place?"

"You know," he says and shrugs. "I ain't like miss it or nothin. But I remember you, man. I remember you 'cause you was *fair*. You keep it fair, nah saying?"

"Another satisfied customer."

"Yo, you funny, too." He laughs again, a big chesty laugh.

"So why you down here?" I ask him. "They got you on something new?"

"Just—bullshit, man," he says, and he smiles so I know that it means nothing to him. "I mean, I *done* it and shit, but it's just—" Then he hits the panel. "I miss my floor. Dang!"

A moment later the elevator door clatters open onto the tenth floor, or close enough that we have to step up only a half foot to the landing. Laurel starts walking immediately past prospective jurors gathering in the hallway, eating, sleeping on the wooden benches. I follow, and Valentino Burton says he will see me around.

"You hear that, Ashfield?" I ask her at the courtroom door. "I'm not so very wicked."

"He must have known you before you started—stealing elevator keys," she says as if thinking of saying something else. She pushes open the door.

Behind her high heels, I say, "All those fine ideas of yours, Ashfield? What are you gonna do with them if you can't even get to court?"

She keeps walking to the prosecution table, making no acknowledgment. Inside, Yost is pacing around with his cell phone to his ear and the other hand in descriptive motion. He is alone in the courtroom except for a man seated in the gallery with his back to me. I ignore Laurel ignoring me and shout, "Hey, Yost. No phones in court. Or knives." I have to shout because the air conditioners— there are three, one in each window—are blowing inexplicably. Yost waves his free hand at me, unperturbed, and continues his conversation. The other man stands and walks to me.

"Roger Cully," I say. "I'll be damned."

"And deserve it, too."

We shake hands, and I remember what a sly, altogether likable character this Cully is. We smile, pleased out of all proportion to how we knew each other before I left. He looks like hell, though. Worse than he was then, and even then he was bad with whatever was killing him. Now he is circling the drain. Skinny, and purple and black beneath his eyes. His sallow skin looks as if he had a beard but shaved it. His hair is hardy enough, growing out defiantly in a great tangle of brick red. We stand there shaking hands and neither of us lets go. We are both still around, I suppose, and that explains it.

I say, "Mark Luther tells me I can't talk to you about this caper here."

"So naturally you want to."

"As soon as possible."

Cully smiles. "How you been, Gio?" he asks me, knowing everything and wanting a real answer.

"Better," I say. "Better. You?"

"Dying," Cully says, truth for truth. On cue he wheezes asthmatically for twenty seconds. Laurel turns in her seat. When he is done, Cully runs a venous hand over his mouth. "So. What's wrong with it?"

I shrug. "The usual fun."

He does not press for more than that. His eyes go to Laurel, who turns away. He bites his hand. "Yipes. Fuck her yet?"

"She comes with the case," I say, shaking my head. "Besides, not my type."

"Luther, maybe?"

"Not my type, either, Cully," I say, but neither of us feels like laughing all of a sudden. I ask him, "Why? You heard something?"

"No. Like you say, she came with the case. She rode out with Luther the night your witness came in. You give me his name yet, by the way? Your guy in the back room?"

"Sure," I tell him. "He's Confidential Witness Number One."

"Thanks, friend."

"I'd like him to stick around, at least until he testifies. Besides," I say, "not supposed to talk to you at all, remember."

"Right, but someday you're going to need me and—"

"What did you hear—about her?" I ask, and I know it is a mistake to ask twice. He knows it, too.

"Not a thing," he says very slowly. "Guess Luther liked her work is all." He shrugs, noncommittal. "You ask me, that's all it was. I don't see anyone wanting into Homicide that bad."

The clerk calls order. I turn away from Cully and am nearly at my table when I hear him over the blast of the air conditioners: "But then I'm done being surprised by what goes on around that office a yours."

I do not answer or turn around. I sit next to her and think. Nothing happens. Gewirtz has picked up his telephone, and the conversation evidently is social; he is smiling wickedly. Laurel says nothing to me, sorting and writing, writing and sorting. The stenographer is reading *Glamour.* The clerk at his desk shows something to two court officers. The three of them start laughing, and Gewirtz is still leering, and the stenographer puts down her magazine and retouches a fingernail. Already Yost and Pool hate each other so bad they do not even talk. They sit at their table and stare straight ahead, a married couple in a fight. I cannot sit still anymore.

"Here," I tell Laurel, standing abruptly. I gesture to the empty third chair at our table. "Sit here. Closer to the jury."

"Why?"

"It, you know. Sends a message."

"What message?"

"It says, *We're friendly. We don't bite. The dangerous man is over there. Just the friendly D.A. over here by you, ladies and gentlemen.*"

"That's part of the psychological whatever, too?"

"Fuckin-A right," I say. "And he's not *Mr. Pool*. He's always *the defendant*. Okay? Don't be courteous to a killer. You're not *The New York Times*. Don't say *Mr. Yost,* either."

"What is he?" she says, a residuum of annoyance from this morning coloring her voice, darkening it. *"That guy?"*

"He's the *defendant's lawyer,*" I tell her. "That's what you call him. Two cuss words, Ashfield. You're saying, *Hey folks, he's not just a lawyer—*"

"He's the defendant's lawyer," she says, smiling against her will.

"Um-hmm. You're saying, *That's why he's sitting over there. He's the killer's lawyer. He could kill you, too!*"

"You have it all figured out," she says without giving the impression that she has taken to heart any of it. From a leather portfolio she is unpacking folders, and pristine legal pads, and pens, and yellow and blue sticky pads, and highlighters, and little charts that she made with a ruler.

"Hell is that?" I ask after watching in fascination as she arranges everything. "Holy Mother. Get rid of all that crap."

"No," she says. "I need them."

"Look over at Yost's table. Look at what a goddamn mess he's got over there. Papers. Con Ed bills. Looks like he slept on that table. I mean, the table looks like Yost."

She turns her head to the defense table. Haskin Pool turns slightly. Yost, too, and he uses the pretext of Laurel's glance to get away from Pool. He comes to our table, eyeing Laurel's assortment of necessaries with unfeigned interest. The blue of his pants and the blue of his jacket do not quite match. His tie has gone belly up, a dog wanting a scratch.

"See that good enough, Yost?" I ask him, holding up one of Laurel's legal pads. "See—it's our *secret evidence.*"

"Pretty," he says to Laurel. "You wanna know somethin? You got nice handwritin. Like my mother."

"That's what I said," I say, smacking my own forehead. "Like somebody's mother."

"She made gloves, my mother," Yost tells us. "It was, whadaya call it? Piecework. They sold at the A&S, which was down on Fulton before they opened up the projects there and the whole neighborhood turned into a place where you can't walk with your kids no more. Without you wantin them to get shot at, I mean."

"By one of your clients, for instance," I say.

Yost shrugs. Gewirtz has hung up on his girlfriend and is standing at the bench with his fists on his hips, his robe asunder, a man who awoke in a strange land. "What—what's that noise? Sort of a—" Gewirtz says, and a court officer starts walking to the windows behind the jury box. Everyone watches him. I turn and see Pool's women scowl and point from their corner. The officer shuts the air conditioners off one by one, until a buttery silence descends, making it hard to move or think. I hear Gewirtz ask if we are ready and I hear Laurel answer yes. I should have had a better lunch than a Coke, but I was too occupied with my petty perjury, too busy writing the folded paper of white lies that digs its pointy staple into my flesh from my right breast pocket. Laurel pretended not to notice me writing. All the while she ate her own lunch, fruity and yogurty, with a plastic spoon.

Behind me I hear the jury being led in. They are this morning's leftovers, and now we must reheat them. The thin novelty has already worn off for them, and they do not even bitch anymore. They file in, and all I hear is the creak of the purple pews behind me as they sit, along with their sighs. Laurel sits upright, hands folded. I wonder if I should have looked in a mirror, but at least my shoes are dry and will not squeak so much. "Come in, everyone," Gewirtz says. "Welcome!" He is feeling expansive this afternoon and happy to be living in a democracy. He tells them to cheer up because this is not Russia. "They don't have jury duty in Russia!" he says, smiling at one and all, and holds his arms out wide. He is full of joy. Maybe even a little drunk.

"I have good news!" Gewirtz says, but no one believes him. "We already picked five jurors this morning. And a full jury is— how many people? Anyone?"

"Class?" I whisper to Laurel.

"*Twelve* jurors," Gewirtz says. "That means we need *how many more*? Anyone?"

"Class?" I say again to her. "Bueller?" But she was probably fourteen when that movie came out, and her hands stay folded on the tabletop that she has cleared off except for a legal pad.

"Anyone?" Gewirtz asks, still smiling.

"You know why he's asking, don't you?" I pull myself up and say into her ear. I smell her sweet jam smell. A school-lunch smell. "Because he actually wants to know." She blinks once. I sit back after a few seconds.

"Anyone?" Gewirtz asks, still game. A guy with a clipboard and a baseball hat raises his hand. I underline my mental note to get rid of him. "*Yes-s?*" Gewirtz says, pointing.

"Seven," the man says proudly.

"*No!*" Gewirtz shouts, still smiling, looking across the jury panel. "No!" he shouts again. Everyone is looking at him. "Nine," he tells them. "We need seven regular jurors and two alternate jurors. Ha ha ha." No one laughs.

"Funny," I say to Laurel, "but most of them probably think—"

"Please be quiet," she tells me, giving me nothing more than her fine profile. *Okay,* I think. *Okay.*

Gewirtz continues. The stenographer is typing. The clerk is wearing white tube socks. I sense Pool's eyes on me all at once. I think he is a ballsy little prick for giving me the old stare-down here in open court, but when I turn I see that Pool could not give a damn about me. His eyes go past me, to Laurel maybe, who faces straight ahead. Yes, definitely at Laurel.

Gewirtz is telling a story about a fish. Maybe it is a parable, but I have not paid enough attention to know. Probably it is just a story to show them he is a regular guy, in case they had any doubts. Yost is writing checks. Con Ed. Bell Atlantic. Brooklyn Union Gas. I look at my own table, where on one of Laurel's blank legal pads I have unthinkingly drawn fifteen circles in black pen. I recall my sophomore psychology class: doodling circles signifies sex on the mind, or so they said. The evident bullshit of that hypothesis confirmed my budding realization that psychology is nine parts crap. *Circles?* At sixteen, what did not signify sex on the mind? Everything underscored the nature of girls and that I wasn't getting any.

Circles.

I give Laurel a covert glance, and she seems aware of it. She does not alter her posture, but I notice the slightest movement at the corner of her profiled eye, a flutter of lash. She knows.

Circles. Part of the psychological whatever.

Here, does it really matter if the prosecution table is swept clean? If Yost is the *defendant's lawyer?* If we represent the *People?* If we sit close to the jury? What do I know? Just something to tell a second-seater, to convince her that I still know a little about this job, that there is more to putting a guy inside than dumb luck, that you are not merely taking tickets and showing twelve strangers a show. All of it: an accumulation of lore that one prosecutor hands to another, as irrelevant to hearing *guilty* as a guilty heart. Juries do what juries do. In the end Pool will go down because he has a thug's face. If he were better-looking, if he wore better clothes, if he did not have a gold tooth, if he had waved to the jury, smiled, and said, "Hi, everybody!," he might have walked. He might have gone home next week with his sisters and cousins and aunts. And I would say, *He'll be back.*

"Proceed, Counsel," Gewirtz says, interrupting me from my thoughts.

I stand and button my suit jacket. I walk to the jury box, and it is nothing. It is what I do. As it always was.

"Step up."

I thought Gewirtz had already left. Laurel is at the coatrack, and Yost is throwing loose paper into a lit bag: coffee-stained legal pads and electricity bills. A court officer, yawning, puts a hand on Pool and brings him to his feet. Pool complacently puts his hands behind his back, and the handcuffs ratchet sharp and metallic as they close around his skinny wrists. The women watch from the back, waiting for him to turn around before he is taken away. The jurors are gone. Cully has left, bored. Four o'clock and the day is over, so when Gewirtz says *step up,* everyone looks. We three lawyers stand in front of the bench, which comes up to my chin. Gewirtz is sitting in his seat, hands folded into a church with his chin on the steeple, as he says, "Where are we with this thing?" He is lethargic from sitting two hours while the three martinis from Gage & Tollner settled slowly into his ass, and his eyes are yellow. He yawns. "I want to finish picking tomorrow. Start this thing Thursday morning. Problems?"

I put my hands in my pockets, shrug.

"Judge," Yost says, "I still don't got a witness list, even. I still don't—"

To me Gewirtz lifts an eyebrow and says, "People?"

"He's not entitled to—" Laurel starts to protest, but Gewirtz shuts her up with an upraised index finger. While she is right, while Yost is not entitled to our witness list—not yet—Gewirtz does not care. I do not care, either, not enough, anyway. Gewirtz is rolling his eyes with impatience.

"Just give it over," he says. "Let's go."

Laurel hesitates. I nod to let her know it is all right, and from the file on the prosecution table she withdraws a folder and produces two sheets of white paper. They are identical: a neatly typed list of seven names beneath the case caption at the top of the page. I nod again, and she hands one up to the bench. The other she gives to Yost, who opens his reading glasses.

"There's your list, Mr. Yost," Gewirtz says, standing. "We're going to start this thing Thursday, so I don't want—"

"Dellroy Dunn," Yost says. "That's the kid? The kid in the back room? He's the only civilian you got on the list here." Gewirtz starts to move toward the door. Yost snaps off his glasses. "I don't see the woman—the woman across the street." Yost turns to Gewirtz, who stops walking. "Judge," Yost is saying. "Just— before you go—just to put everyone on notice. I'm gonna ask for a missing witness charge if—"

"Mr. Yost," Gewirtz says before I can. "Mr. Yost, the People haven't opened yet. We don't even have a jury, and you're asking for a missing witness charge?"

"There was a woman, Judge. By the name of—ah—"

"Marjorie Henkis," Laurel says.

Yost snaps his fingers. "Marjorie Henkis, Judge. Seen someone runnin down Sutter about the time of the incident—"

"So what, Mr. Yost?" Gewirtz asks.

Yost opens his hands as if the answer were there. "She called him a beanpole, she said. A beanpole, Judge. Look at my client!"

Gewirtz closes his yellow eyes. "Was this person—this beanpole—ever ID'ed?"

"No," Yost says. "She did a lineup with the detective, right? A day after the incident!"

"She no-hit, Judge," Laurel says.

"There you are, Mr. Yost. If she never identified anyone then, ah— By the way, who was the subject of this lineup?"

"Lashawn Sims," Laurel says.

"Why?" Gewirtz asks her. "He was never arrested—yes? No? Why put him in a lineup?"

"He's a beanpole," I say, guessing.

Laurel nods, and Gewirtz is satisfied. "No arrest?" he asks her, not me.

"No, Your Honor," she says. He waits for more. She says, "My understanding is that the assigned detective asked Mr. Sims to stand for a lineup because he fit the description provided by Ms. Henkis. Mr. Sims agreed, but Ms. Henkis failed to identify him, so he was released."

Gewirtz is paging through his file. "I see it now," he says. "And your Mr. Pool is arrested the next day, yes?" Laurel agrees. "Fine," he says. "And where is, ah, Mr. Sims today? Is it possible to, I mean, should it be necessary to—"

"He's dead, Judge."

"Ah," he says. "Ah—there you are, Mr. Yost."

Yost is wearing his reading glasses again, and they rest cock-eyed on his nose. From his expression, you would not think he had been listening, but he asks who killed Sims, whose name strikes a note with me but does nothing more than that. Gewirtz has unzipped his robe and is standing behind the bench in his plaid short-sleeved shirt and knit tie; he is the janitor again.

Laurel tells him, "There's been no arrest, Your Honor."

"There you are, Mr. Yost," Gewirtz says, but already Yost has walked to the defense table, not listening anymore. Gewirtz shrugs and leaves through the door behind the bench. I walk with Laurel to our table.

"See that?" I tell her. "Never bring on a motion when the judge has to use the can." She isn't paying attention. I hear Yost talking to Pool without hearing the words. Laurel asks me what I said. I raise my arms to stretch and—

"Motherfucker!"

I turn.

"Motherfucker!" Pool is saying, and the officer behind him is wide-eyed and pulling on Pool's arm as he tries to break the hold. Two other court officers rush over from different directions. They all take hold of Pool and push him through the door behind the bench. All the while Pool is twisting his lithe little body and saying the single word, repeating it again and again.

"The fuck?" I say to no one, but Laurel answers me.

"So now he knows."

"Knows what?"

Her face tells me she thinks the answer should be obvious, yet she says, "Knows it's Dellroy."

CHAPTER 10

Already, after one day of this, I feel the familiar weariness, the lethargy that creeps upon you at the end of a trial day. Exhaustion from a day spent being observed. I want to go somewhere alone. I want a door to shut. I want to walk around in my underwear. I want to scratch my ass if I feel like it, and slump. Trial is dinner with your girlfriend's mother.

Instead I am in the barber chair, a head atop a plastic cape under fluorescent lights. The barber depresses the foot pedal and I sink. Laurel is home, I imagine. She lingered in her cubicle doorway before she walked out at five minutes before five, beating the secretaries and paralegals. I said nothing about that, but before she left she asked what I was going to do.

"Make some phone calls," I told her.

"I did. Already—you mean for Dellroy?"

"Yes."

"I called the Seven-Five."

"Okay."

"I gave them your number. In case."

She watched while I stood and took my coat from the back of the metal chair. I did not know why I was standing. When she asked, I told her I was going to get a haircut. We both stood there in her cubicle, and then she said, "Bad luck—getting a haircut on trial."

I smiled, because it seemed an unlikely thing for her to say. "You believe that?" I asked her.

She said no, and then she left. I waited until I heard the elevator take her away, and then I walked out of the bureau, to the elevator, to the dark and empty street.

In the barbershop I sit now thinking disorganized thoughts, one of which features the MWO affidavit still folded in my jacket. I never asked Gewirtz to sign it. I put a hand under the plastic cape and withdraw it from my breast pocket. For a half hour as I walked in front of the jury box, asking sixteen strangers if they could serve as jurors, if they could follow the law, I felt the staple in the affidavit biting through my shirt like one of Laurel's white incisors, biting through my T-shirt and into my skin. Goddamn her.

I tear it into two halves, and the paper makes an inadequate sound, not enough to monument this occasion. So I ball the paper and shoot it toward the corner basket, miss. The barber says nothing.

Goddamn her.

Everything about the woman. She would have me better, healthier, happier, neater, cleaner. Soon I will be drinking carrot juice and milk without hormones. I will move to Manhattan and put Q-tips in my ears. I will wear leather shoes and underwear without holes. I will join public television. And perhaps, if Ann's biological clock allows, I will have children—several blond babies, and we will send them all to private schools I cannot afford. Thinking about what I am in relief against what I am not, viewing myself in high contrast under the light Laurel shines on me, I recall an isolated stanza from high school English. Or was it high school history? Some classroom in Bay Ridge where I sat with an open notebook written over with doodled circles. A verse from a Romantic poet, perhaps, or a statesman, that gave me the first idea of myself as I wanted to be: *Wert thou all that I wish thee, great, glorious, and free!*

Great, glorious, and free. Wert thou no shit, Giobberti. How the hell did I end up here?

I look up and see myself looking back between a stack of towels and a jar of blue Barbicide, black combs suspended inside like demonstrative organs or spiders. The barber is holding a mirror, showing me the back of my head. I nod, and with a small flourish, he whips off the cape. I stand and feel hair inside my collar. Immediately my beeper sounds, and I recognize the number but cannot associate it with anyone. Then I do, and I ask the barber for a phone. He points, and I fish a quarter from my pants and call the Seven-Five.

"Moss," I say. "That you?"

"Who's this?"

"Andy Giobberti."

"Giobberti. Christ," he says, but not much else about that. We talk about nothing in particular. In the background is the familiar sound of a precinct detective squad—typewriters and men. Then he tells me he has Dellroy Dunn, if I want him.

"Where?" I ask, feeling myself smile.

"Here. At the house." He tells me Dellroy wants to go home.

"And there ain't nothing we can do about it," Moss says. "You shoulda got me an MWO, counselor."

"Yeah, yeah."

"So. What should I do with this kid a yours?"

"Give him cigarettes" is my advice. "Get him laid. I don't care. I'll be there in half an hour."

"Giobberti, you fuck," one of eight detectives calls out the moment I push open the swinging half-door to the Seven-Five detective squad room, East New York, Brooklyn. *"Oh-h,"* they all say, all of them remembering me and why I checked out. I see it written on their faces. They are a cold crew, the old four-to-twelve mob. I breathe the familiar air of this place, and their reception, the rough-edged hello that comes across with real affection, touches me strangely. I had not known I missed them all until I walked in.

"Gio G. Giobberti," says another. "About fucking time you got off your ass."

"Boys," I say in acknowledgment, smiling despite myself. "Slow night?"

"Oh-h!" they all say, taking offense on purpose, yet they are all here, and that means no one in this neighborhood has been robbed tonight, or stabbed, or shot, or killed. While they wait for it, they wait with their jackets off. Their ties remain undone around their necks and tucked into their belts. Cracked shoe leather rests on an odd assortment of metal desks shoved together in the center of this long room. The walls are baby-blue cinder block, and the doors are blue, and everything vertical is covered with posters and flyers and hanging clipboards. Everything horizontal is covered with papers and pencils and aquariums.

"Slow?" one says. "Naw, we're just doing a little, what do you call it? A little experiment."

"Yeah, an experiment," says another. They are all smiling,

with their arms crossed. Someone is typing with a cigarette hanging, and ashes are falling into the keys, and he is smiling, too. When I walk over, this one shakes my hand and winks knowingly at me. *We all have a closetful of shit,* the wink tells me, *and your closet ain't no more full than mine.*

Someone else says, "What we do is, we're just not taking any calls for a while. You know? See if it makes any difference. An experiment, like he says." In fact a phone is ringing somewhere, anywhere. There are phones everywhere. Black phones with gray buttons, phones repaired with duct tape after falling from desks and being thrown a lot in anger. No one is answering. The phone goes on ringing and ringing, and Lieutenant Al Moss walks over through this scene to me. He wipes his hands together, then gives me one. He starts talking to me about whatnot and is friendly enough, but his gaze sheers off in the direction of the lockup behind me.

"Heatly ain't in," he says, meaning Bill Heatly, my case detective. Moss tells me Heatly is not in without my asking and proceeds to tell me exactly where Heatly is and why he is not here. I peer inside the unlit cage, where I see a dark shape that could be anything, even a seventeen-year-old boy. "Door ain't locked," Moss says, again without my asking.

"He know that?" I say, and then I shout toward the cage, "Be with you in a minute, boss."

"Next time get me an MWO," Moss says. "You're gonna get some goddamn defense lawyer crawling up my ass, saying why'd you put my client under and et cetera." He pinches the skin on my shoulder with his thumb and forefinger. It hurts.

"He gonna help me, this kid?"

Moss considers the question. "I tell you, this one ain't wrapped too tight." He says it not as quietly as he should, and I look over my shoulder, but Dellroy Dunn has already moved back into the shadows. Moss says, "Seventeen going on eleven, you know what I mean? Got stabbed in the head when he was a kid, Heatly was telling me." Maneuvering behind me, Moss presses the blunt tip of his forefinger into the base of my skull. That hurts, too. He gets closer and says, "Like that." I smell sweat and aftershave—a good smell, a workingman's smell. "With an ice pick. Screwed him up, maybe."

"Yeah, maybe," I say, frowning.

"You heard none of this?"

"I just came on board yesterday."

"Ahh," Moss says, and that seems to explain something to him. "Anyway. Kid's mother bumped the father way back when."

"Over what?"

Moss shrugs. "Asking me? She had a beef with the guy, whadaya think? Have to get the whole sob story from Heatly. His collar, you know." He points at me again, this time at my breastbone, which he then proceeds to tap. "That's how he knows your boy." Moss pauses, and then he says, "Not a bad kid, all things considered. Coulda turned out worse."

"Or dead."

"Or dead." He nods in solemn agreement. "Been known to happen. Around here. Once in a while." I shake my head and smile weakly. Moss goes on, "You got the other piece, though. It's his partner that's the real scummer."

"Pool?" I say.

"Right. You put that one in jail, Gio. You do Brooklyn a favor."

"You said *partner*."

"What'd I say?" Moss says, shrugging before he walks off. "Partner, witness. Perp, victim. Twenty-three years on the job, and I can't tell the difference one day to the next."

CHAPTER 11

Dellroy Dunn, sitting in the leatherette swivel chair in Moss's cinder-block office in the far corner of the squad room, will not look up. I sit across from him on the other side of the desk, and Moss stands in the doorway, leaning against the door frame and watching impassively, a hand in a pocket.

One of my tricks: put the guy in the big chair, if you can. Cheer him up. Make him talkative. Make him feel, well—now I am no longer sure. Another part of the psychological whatever. Anyway, the chair does not help Dellroy Dunn. The big chair in the man's office, it underscores who he is and what he is not; it makes him feel small. Yet Dellroy Dunn is a big kid. Big and doughy, all curves, as if he has been scooped up and dropped into the chair with a spatula. He leans forward, sitting like you sit when you are cuffed. Mostly all I see of his head is his hair, unwashed, which collects moth wings and the like, dried white. The room smells like him, like fried food and the skittish nervy smell of cat breath.

"Dellroy," I say again.

"Dell-roy," Moss repeats after several seconds. He gives me a look, cold and obvious.

"Yeah," Dellroy says at long last.

"Dellroy. You wanna take a nap, maybe?" Moss says.

Dellroy thinks he is serious. "No," he says. "I ain't."

" 'Bout a coffee, buddy?" asks Moss. "Something to get you on your feet."

"No."

"You hungry, Dellroy?" I ask.

"No," he says. "Yes."

Moss shouts a laugh—*ha!*—so that Dellroy's face at last comes up, involuntarily. His eyes turn almond beneath fatty lids and when he lifts his head his neck is veined with creases. "Burger?" Moss asks. "Chicken salad? Go ahead."

"Chinese."

"Okay." Moss claps his hands once, and it seems very loud. "Now we're getting somewheres. Chinese."

"Shrimp fry rice," Dellroy says. "And a cream soda."

"That it?"

"And a Butterfinger," Dellroy adds.

"A gourmet," Moss says, walking over and slapping Dellroy on the back, hard. "A regular Julia's child." Dellroy winces and re-coils from the blow, although he is twice Moss's size. The lieutenant leaves, closing the door behind him, and then it is quiet. No one is talking. Behind Dellroy, outside the gated window of the lieutenant's office, a snowy rain falls.

I ask him, "You know who I am, right? They told you?"

"You the cop."

"No, Dellroy. I'm a D.A. I'm prosecuting Haskin Pool."

"Oh," he says, still avoiding eye contact but interested suddenly. "I thought you mighta— Nothing."

"What?"

"I dunno. Mighta 'rest me or something."

"Arrest you?" I say. "No." Now he sees me for the first time, really. He looks at me with one eye only, keen and bright, for the other is lazy and is aimed dully somewhere else, giving his awkward face a cubist effect. "No," I say again. Then I smile and say, "Should I?"

"I— Because of what happen with Gomez. When they come get me today, that's what I think it was, you know?"

"No. I told the police to find you. Because you didn't come down." He thinks without telling me what he is thinking. In the background, behind the door, I can hear the squad room erupt in sudden laughter. I say, "Dellroy, why I'm here is because I didn't talk to you yet. Before you testify, I want to talk to you about that. About what happened that morning. With Gomez."

"A'ight."

"What I want to do is this," I tell him. "I want to ask you the questions I'm going to ask you when you testify."

"A'ight—I mean, I already know."

"Know what?"

"How to tell it," he says.

"Good, but I—"

"Heat know I cool. You can aks him if you want to."

"Listen, whatever Heatly told you—" I start, then interrupt myself: "Forget about Heatly, all right? This is my job, okay?"

"Okay."

"Let's just talk. Let's just start at the beginning. Just— everything you remember, and we'll go from there."

"A'ight," he says, but he does not say anything.

"Go ahead," I say.

"You mean like what happen, or what?"

"Yeah, that morning," I say. "What I'll ask you—I mean, when you're on the stand—I'll say, *Did there come a time when you went to work that day?* And you answer . . . ? And you answer what, Dellroy?"

"A'ight," he says and nothing more, and I pass my palm over my forehead and sit up in my chair, realizing that it is going to be a long night.

"So. Did you go to work that morning?"

"No."

"You didn't go to work?" I ask mildly.

"I mean, yeah."

"Okay," I say. "What time did you start?"

"What you mean?"

"Just—what time did you start your work that morning?"

"You want me to say it like . . . ," he says.

"Let me ask you this: was the store already open when you got there, or did you open it with—with Gomez?"

"Yeah."

"It was already open?"

"Yeah."

"And what sort of work did he have you doing that day?" I ask.

He looks at me with the good eye. "I ain't—" he starts to say, but then he looks away and does not finish. "You mean—when are you aksing me?"

"Let me back up," I tell him. "How long did you work for Gomez? Like a year?"

"More. I ain't know, exactly. Long time, you know?"

"What'd you do for him?" I ask. "Stock shelves or whatever?"

"You know, this and that. You know. Whatever he need."

"But it was a job, right? I mean, he paid you."

"He ain't pay me money except sometimes," Dellroy Dunn says. "It's like he—he would give me food and shit. Bread. A sandwich. You know. I would, like, open boxes or whatever, and he would give me a sandwich for that."

"All right. Just say that, then. Just say you would work there from time to time."

"A'ight. Time to time."

"Now, that morning," I say, "you get there and you're working, right?"

He says nothing, then, "You want me to like—" He stops. "You want me to tell it like—"

"Just whatever happened. Just the truth, you know?" I smile and say, "That's all I'm telling you to say. That way, if they ask you, 'Did the D.A. tell you what to say?' what are you gonna say?" He does not answer. "Tell them I told you to tell the truth!"

"A'ight."

I put a hand up. "I have an idea. Let's do this another way. What I'm gonna do is tell you what I know, and if I'm getting it wrong, then tell me."

His expression does not change. His eyes throw me off: one looks at me knowingly while the other wanders off. I do not know which is Dellroy, so I do not know if I need to hold his hand through this, or if he could tell me more about this ruined edge of the world than I already know. The good eye has a caged bear's awareness: he sees me not as an enemy but as something foreign, a stranger come to gawk at him.

"So you get there, like, what, nine, nine-thirty?"

"Yeah."

"And Gomez is there. Right?"

"Yeah."

"And he gives you some work to do in the back."

"Like for real, or—"

"Just what happened, Dellroy," I say, an unease beginning to settle on me. "However you remember it."

"Man." For a very long time he says nothing more, and his head goes down. Then it comes up. And I have that dizzy dystopian feeling you get sometimes in an interrogation or in court when a witness takes an odd detour to an unexpected place. At those times you wish the guy would make things plain by telling you to go fuck yourself. *Go fuck yourself, because I ain't cooperating,* for a thousand good and valid reasons. I know how to deal with a witness like that, because I know every one of those reasons. I have heard them all before, and they all make excellent sense. But that is not what I am getting from Dellroy. He is not playing me, he wants to talk. He wants to tell me his story, but he does not know his story anymore.

"Dellroy, what the fuck? Talk to me."

"Man," he says. "I don' think you aware."

"Aware of what, Dellroy?"

"Aware of what the facts is."

"You tell me," I say. "That's why I'm here."

"Man," Dellroy says and leans back in Moss's chair. A sort of beard grows under his chin, like a mold. He leans back, and a single roach darts from his hoodie and up the chair; it twitches its antennae inquisitively, then is gone. "You got a smoke?" Dellroy asks, but before I can say no, Moss comes in with a white plastic bag containing one order of shrimp fried rice and a cream soda, but no Butterfinger.

I use the Butterfinger as an excuse to get out. The walls have begun to close in. I need to get out before I hear something I do not want to hear. I need a smoke and I don't even smoke. So while

Moss sets Dellroy up, I walk down Sutter Avenue in the sullen rain that turns orange under the streetlights on every isolated corner from the station house to the all-night bodega down the block. I walk with my hands in my pockets, without an overcoat, forgotten in my hurry to get away. A hooker calls down at me from a second-floor window. Naked, her tits bags of fat. Coming inside the bodega from the dark, I find it very bright, very fluorescent. I stand in the doorway blinking at two aisles of breakfast cereal and cans of beans and envelopes of Mexican rice. Just add water. Heat and eat.

"Butterfinger," I say to the Pakistani cashier sitting on a stool behind a Plexiglas window. "You know, candy bar?"

He shrugs, so I walk up and down the aisles. There is nothing here. Probably go out of business altogether if they didn't sell dimes of crack and Ziploc bags of weed in the off hours. I find a metal display of five sorry Clark bars and a solitary Butterfinger. I take it and ask the guy for a pack of Newports. He puts a finger behind an ear, and I say it again so he can hear me over the music through the window. I slide him a ten through the hole, and he gives me the pack and my change in a hand wearing a gray fingerless glove. On the floor beside him is a space heater, its five coils glowing like cigar ends.

Walking back, I pass a fire-escape platform where an old man sits under an asymmetrical umbrella watching his small world go by. The survivors, these old men in these bad neighborhoods. Shell-shocked. Quiet. A ghetto counterpart to the old men of my neighborhood: Windsor Terrace men who shuffle to the corner store in three-piece suits and hats, their feet never leaving the pavement, taking half a day to buy a dented can of evaporated milk.

Dellroy is wrong, I know. This case is wrong, but it is not as easy as that. I walk slowly back and feel the icy rain.

Upstairs the squad is gone, except for some white-haired character in the corner, typing with two index fingers on an orange Nixon-era Selectric that periodically buzzes like an angry hair trimmer. *Someone just came to a bad end,* I think. So much for not answering the phone.

"Detective," I say. "Where's my guy?"

"Head," he says after a pause.

I sit in a hard fiberglass chair to wait. I wait a couple minutes in this familiar place. Here, as in all cop places, there is a pervasive dull expectancy; as in a dentist's waiting room, there is the sense that people will soon be doing things to you. So I sit with the syncopation of the typewriter and stare at wanted posters Scotch-taped to the blue cinder block, looking for my own face, maybe. After five minutes I decide to roust Dellroy. I walk around the corner, past a small room where two undershirted cops face each other with playing cards fanned in their hands, past another cop alone with a black-and-white television set, past a hallway lined with lockers, past someone shaving at a stained enamel sink, past a curtainless shower, and into the narrow bathroom where there is no toilet paper and no Dellroy.

"Guess he ordered that fried rice to go," I say aloud in the empty stall.

CHAPTER 12

I **remember nothing of** the ride back from East New York. Or why I came immediately to Phil Bloch's office, but here I stand in his doorway, on the otherwise darkened fourth floor, watching him sing, and conduct, *H.M.S. Pinafore*. An aria of.

> *I thought so little, they rewarded me*
> *By making me the Ruler of the Queen's Navee!*

"Encore," I say from the doorway as Bloch winds up the number, and he leaps, to great comic effect, but I am in no mood to enjoy it. I go inside and sit and wait for him to get over it.

When he mostly has, he lowers the music with a remote control and eyes me. "Hell you doing here. Sneaking around," he says. "It's late—Christ, it's nine o'clock."

"I should ask you. Who's going to walk the poodle?"

"Bichon frise," he says defensively, annoyed that I startled him, annoyed that he owns a poodle, annoyed that I know about it. "And it's my wife's," he says in the same tone. "And I'm working, to answer your question. Got a meeting with Fister tomorrow and—"

"And you're scared."

"Yeah, I'm goddamn scared," he says, looking at me with road-map eyes. He reaches into a glass bowl of Snickers. Fun Size. He hesitates, and then he takes one anyway. He unwraps it and talks with his mouth full to make a point to someone not here. "What do you want?"

"Just talk, Phil. Relax."

In a moment he does. He lets his shoulders fall, and he slumps heavily backward into his upholstered chair. "Je-sus," he says, rubbing his eye sockets. "I don't know how you did this—goddamn paperwork."

"I didn't," I tell him, and he shakes his head and laughs at me because he knows it is true. "Don't be so hard on yourself, Phil. You're a born bureaucrat—and a damn fine conductor, too."

He gives me the benefit of the doubt and asks, "How's that trial going? You got a jury yet? Open tomorrow?"

"Thursday, maybe. Maybe."

"Yeah?" he says. "How about that Ashfield—she working out?"

"She's no Phil Bloch."

He has straightened up and is moving things around on his desk. "You made the papers," he says, finding what he is looking for and pushing it toward me: this evening's *Brooklyn Daily News,* already open to an inside page. A small item: JURY SELECTION BEGINS IN BODEGA SLAY. Circled in pen. Six sentences and that is all. No byline. "That's Cully, I bet," he says. "You seen him around court? Skinny guy with red hair?"

"I know him."

"Well?"

"What, I can't say hello to the guy?"

"Don't touch him, Gio."

I wave away the advice with a hand, as if it stinks. I read through the newspaper piece, then I push it back over the desktop to him.

"Let me tell you about that guy Cully," Bloch says. "He wants Fister out, that guy."

"Everyone wants Fister out. Except the people that run this borough." Bloch glances nervously at his door and the vacant hallway beyond. "Yeah, yeah, I know," I tell him. "He's a dope, but he's our dope. Punches your meal ticket."

"And yours." Bloch looks at me with sullen wonder. "Listen, Gio. I'd put a lid on that kind of chatter. Get you fired, in the first place. And in the second—"

"What do you know about this case, Phil?" I say suddenly, calmly.

"Bodega case?" Bloch asks with an open expression. His face tells me something. He knows something, or maybe he just smells Luther on it. I do not know which.

"You know the kid Dellroy. Right?"

"What kid Dellroy?"

"My witness. Kid in the back room."

"Well, I never talked to him," he says, not defensively. "If that's what you mean."

"I did. An hour ago."

"Yeah?" he says, shifting his weight on the chair. He fumbles for another Snickers and darts little looks at me under his heavy brow. The glass lid slips from his fingers and clatters on the metal desktop. "Kid gonna do some good for us?"

"Split in the middle of the interview."

"The fuck?" he says, eating.

"I mean, he wasn't under," I tell Bloch. "Wasn't handcuffed to the wall."

"Well, get an MWO next time. Lock his ass up." He swallows. "Can you tap-dance until you find him?"

"Sure," I say. "Sure. Couple days."

"But that's not why you're here."

"No," I say. "No, it's not," and in that instant I decide to talk to Phil Bloch about this. I decide to talk to him, not around him. "Reason I'm asking is Luther authorized the collar. Luther rode out when Dellroy came in with his story."

"Yeah."

"Since when does Letch ride homicides, Phil?"

"He took a ride," Bloch says, putting his hands out. "He's Fister's number one—he can't take a ride?"

"Letch has never been to the Seven-Five in his life. Couldn't find it with a map, and he's out there riding a murder?"

"Ashfield wrote it up, didn't she?"

"You know what I mean."

"What am I supposed to say when he tells me he's getting in?" Bloch asks me. "*No?* What's your point?"

"I don't know."

"Listen," he says after a full minute passes in silence. "You weren't down here when this thing hit. Just another bodega rob until your friend here decided to make it big." He pushes the newspaper toward me as if it is my fault. "Fister wanted it handled."

"And Luther handled it."

"Yeah, Luther handled it. Kept the heat on. This was last year, remember? Two months before election. Luther made sure the PD didn't let it go to Cold Case, that's all."

"And he got his collar."

"What's that supposed to mean?"

"Something's wrong," I say. "With the case. Something's wrong."

"What? Because your witness won't play ball?"

"No—Christ. What else is new? Look. I told you I don't know. The thing with the kid is, he's scared."

"Pool get to him?" Bloch asks me.

"No. Not that I know."

"Someone else, maybe?"

"Maybe," I say without believing it. I am thinking of the way Dellroy Dunn looked at me before I left the room. "He's scared of me."

"You?"

"Don't ask me what I mean, because I don't know that, either." I rub my eyes. Then I stand up. "Just answer me. Did anyone—you, Luther, anyone—ever give Dellroy Dunn a hard look?"

"I told you, I never met—"

"Listen. Here it is," I interrupt. "The day of, someone in the squad finds out Dellroy works at the scene and writes a pink 5 on him. The kid's got nothing to say. *I wasn't there,* he says. *I know nothing.* He's Sergeant Schultz, okay?"

"So what? He was scared. He's scared now. He was scared then."

"Snitches get stitches, that's the way I figured it," I say. "But if the kid's so scared, why's he come in a couple weeks later? Heatly's got an open felony murder. No witnesses. No fingerprints. Nothing for two weeks. All he's got is Luther sending him Whitey's love every five minutes. Then—a fucking miracle. Dellroy walks in the door with his story. *You're never gonna believe what I saw, Detective.*" I wait for Bloch's reaction, and he has none that I can see. I say, "I'm not saying it didn't happen that way. I'm just saying."

"Saying what?"

"*What if,* Phil. Just what the fuck if?"

"If what?" he says, understanding what I mean the moment he asks the question. He puts up his hands. "Whoa, slow down. You're scaring me now."

I come closer to him. "You said yourself Luther was on Heatly like stink."

"Come on, Gio. You're talking about a first-grader," Bloch says. "A fucking first-grade detective! Why—why's he going to—"

"He wanted a blue 5."

"That bad? That bad he wanted to close it out? You think he's—you think he's gonna make a witness out of your kid? Feed him a story to tell?"

"It's possible. You know that."

"Possible don't mean shit to me!" Bloch says, angry to have been brought into this, and I know him as too poor an actor to be showing anger only for my benefit. "Tell me why I should think different. What do you have?"

"Nothing. I got nothing, Phil."

"It doesn't make sense, Gio. Think. I mean, Jesus, why him? What's his name—your defendant? Pool. What, did they just pick his name out of a hat?"

"That's easy. Pool's a local wise guy," I say. "Walked on a murder a few years ago with a gun plea. Cops don't forget that shit. Hell, Pool's easy, the little mutt." I am thinking of Moss's words to me. *You do Brooklyn a favor,* he said. I think aloud, "What I want to know is why Dellroy."

"Yeah. Why Dellroy?" Bloch says, as if it were his question. "Why is he gonna agree to frame up Pool? What's his end in this?"

"I don't know. I told you I don't know."

"You don't know. So remember that before you go off half-cocked," Bloch tells me. Then he says, very cautiously, "You say you have nothing. I mean, you have nothing, right?"

"No, Phil. Nothing."

"This is all just you thinking out loud?" I nod, to his relief. "Then what?" he asks. "Help me out, because I don't—"

"I got nothing. That's why I'm asking you if you heard anything, or if Luther said something, or— Oh, Christ, I don't know what I'm looking for. I'm just trying to figure this out in my head." I stand and face the wall.

"What did—" Bloch starts to say, trying to understand it himself. "Did the kid—"

"No."

"His story's fucked up, or what? I don't—"

"No," I say, sounding angry because I am, because there is nothing there. I face Bloch again. "It's what I'm telling you: I got nothing. Even with Dellroy running out tonight, I don't make him as a liar. Such a thing as too stupid to lie. Kid's got the brain of a squirrel."

"But you're saying he's lying! That's what we're talking about here."

"It's Heatly's lie we're talking about. Not Dellroy's."

"Fine. The kid's lying, but he's not a liar," Bloch says, sounding dissatisfied, and I sheepishly watch him. He shakes his head. "Why him, then? Can you tell me that?"

"No." After a moment, though, I say, "Maybe because Dellroy's got a reason to be there. He works in the back. Heatly would have figured—"

"Can you prove that?" he interrupts, his voice brittle. "He work on the books?"

"No."

"So you don't have that, either." He smiles painfully.

"I don't have any answers. Maybe it's simple—Heatly thought he could get over on Dellroy. Use the dumb kid, you know? Also, Moss said Heatly knew the kid from an old collar." I try to remember if Moss said the kid's mother killed the father or the other way around.

"You talk to him?" Bloch asks. "Heatly?"

"I've had this case exactly one day, Phil."

"What if Dellroy's using Heatly, you thought of that?" Bloch asks me.

I had not. I ask, "You mean to frame him up? Frame Pool?"

"Right. Your witness have some reason to pin a murder beef on the guy?"

I shake my head. "They're on the same block, but I don't see these two hanging out long enough to start hating each other that bad."

"Pool make a statement?"

"No. Never," I say. "Lawyered up—he's been there before. Practically pays rent in the Seven-Five squad."

"They know each other, though? Pool and Dellroy?"

"Yeah," I say. "Pool shit today when Ashfield turned over our witness list. So I guess he knows Dellroy well enough."

Bloch nods. "She with you tonight?"

"Ashfield? No, this all happened after five o'clock."

"She moonlights." Bloch smiles, but the smile wanes quickly. "So, what about her? She was out there. That night. She indicted Pool, remember. Maybe you should— What?"

"No—Phil."

"You don't think you—"

"No."

"Well," he says. "You're goddamn choosy—about who you point your finger at, I mean."

We sit for a while and do not look at each other or talk.

CHAPTER 13

Everyone is looking at my hair, staring at my bad-luck haircut. Or because, for some reason, I put some stuff in it this morning. Some pinkish gel a barber gave me a hundred years ago that smells like France. I put some in this morning, calling myself names. And then I combed my hair for about five minutes, so there it is.

Mark Luther sees me. "Hey. Enrico Suavo. Looking good." He cracks himself up in the courthouse foyer where everyone is waiting for an elevator. He is wearing mirrored beetle-eye sunglasses on the pretext of having just walked inside. I push my way onto an elevator, Laurel following, and say nothing to him.

On the fourth floor a downtrodden man, say fifty, shoehorns himself aboard as the elevator door closes. Everyone inhales and a girl says, "Jesus. You better not get on." He does not answer, and the door is closing and hitting him, then opening, then closing and hitting him, then opening. "You better get off!" she says. "You got it, Pop!" says someone else, someone still in the hallway smiling encouragement with a mustached lip and bad skin.

Upstairs, the guy from Probation is hanging around, sitting in the defendant's chair with a thin leg draped over the balustrade between the gallery and the well. A court officer is showing him an article in the *Post*. Gewirtz is not here. Yost is not, either, nor Pool. I sit with Laurel at our table, neither of us talking. When we fall under each other's eyes, we look quickly away, as if embarrassed. Now I sit facing the linoleum underfoot, which is overlaid by a sediment of dirt and varnished. Antique filth, preserved like amber. A plaster flake wafts from the ceiling and alights on my shoulder like lucky bird shit, and I turn my head to the ceiling, thinking about Gewirtz's pigeon. Laurel notices and seizes upon it as a reason to interrupt my solitary silence. She turns in her chair and brushes my shoulder with the rough tenderness of a mother. I look at my shoulder, at her touching it with her long, delicate fingers.

"Look at you," she tells me. "You're all dressed up."

I am tired, of course. To bed at three after reading the file again, after bringing it home and setting it in the kitchen and ignoring it again while Ann watched the eleven o'clock news and I watched her. We sat on the couch in the dark and I ran my hand absently over her back and she leaned in to me as she does. I told her nothing about what I was thinking, although I wanted to. We sat there in the weird shadows cast by the television light. Later, in bed, I waited for the sound of her breathing to alter, then I slipped away to the kitchen. I read everything again, looking for— something. I found nothing except Laurel's handwriting, and I thought of Yost's mother making gloves in her own kitchen fifty years ago.

"You look nice," Laurel says to me now. My best suit, but I suppose she is just making conversation. "You didn't pick out that tie, though."

Amanda's tie. I had forgotten I tied it on this morning. I dressed automatically. I must have shaved, but I do not remember that, either, nor standing on the bath mat that Ann must have left sodden. Yet I remember kissing her goodbye on the stairs before I left and how she felt when she held me. I remember wanting to make her happy and feeling incapable of it.

"Zegna. I thought so," Laurel says, turning over my tie, her fingernails lightly scratching the material of my shirt, and by association I remember the Mass card and the unfamiliar name, one of a hundred thoughts. She is trying to draw me out; it is not in her nature to pursue, nor has it been that way between us these past two days. I have been pursuing her in one manner or another. At first because she was a problem to solve and then because I began to like her. Now I am pursuing her for another reason altogether, or should be, but for now I leave her alone. I am afraid of catching her, so I leave her alone. She senses that, I am certain, and while she would do better to leave me alone as well, she wants to know what I know. So I tell her what I know, but not what I have come to believe: "I saw Dellroy last night."

I say it quite naturally, and she reacts not to the words or their meaning but to the nonchalant sound of my voice. "Oh?" Then she pauses for a heartbeat. Her hand turns my tie over and smooths it onto my sternum, onto my stomach, which I automatically flatten. Preoccupied by other thoughts, she is unaware that she is touching me. Her hand remains longer than necessary until she comes to and takes it away. She waits for more, but I, too, have lapsed into a sort of stasis; I am watching her. We are each waiting for the other.

"He—he actually showed up?" she asks, impatient but hiding it well.

"No. The Seven-Five picked him up."

She nods. "On Gewirtz's warrant?"

"No. I threw it out, the MWO." I try to read something from her upturned chin, from her set expression, but like the file, she has no answers for me. I stand up and walk away because I want to make her worry for a while in private. Another trick of mine. If I had a big chair, I would put her in it.

At the window I look outside. The world beneath my feet is the same. There are people walking on Schermerhorn Street, men parking cars in a lot, buses spilling their gray poison over everything, and I see a billboard of faded paint on a building wall. On it, a handsome blond man rolls up his shirtsleeve to shake a fist at a cartoon lion. YOUR LAWYER, it says, and something else I cannot read, something lost to a thousand rainstorms and ten thousand sunny afternoons since 1967. Yost comes in, swinging open the back door and talking into his phone. Cully sits in a middle pew, and he nods when I turn but makes no move to come to me. Today, with his sickly complexion and his thin arm draped over the top of the pew, I do not want him here. Staring at me as he does, he is foreboding.

Pool is led in. He is so right for this caper that I think it all may be nothing—that I lost sleep and unnerved Phil Bloch for nothing, that after nearly two years I have become skittish and wary, imagining plots and conspiracies like an Idaho nutjob. This nourishing notion makes me exhale, and I try to muster some hatred for Pool, but as usual, I cannot. He is one more kid in the chair, a convenient proxy for something without a face. He's the Michelin Man; he's Tony the Tiger. Still, as I walk to Laurel, I notice something different about Pool today. Someone has gotten him a suit. He, too, is all dressed up. He swims in his suit, though. He sinks within the black cloth, and the collar of his shirt is too big. His head is like a swivel. With his hands pinned behind his back, his shoulder pads jut like cantilevered platforms.

"A suit!" I say to Laurel. "Pretty fly, Haskin!"

She writes notes to herself on her legal pad, her brow furrowed. Yost now sits, spreading papers over the defense table for no evident reason. Pool looks ahead. I turn around to the back of the courtroom, where the familiar women have gathered. Today a teenage boy is with them, top-heavy with dreadlocks piled under a ballooning sock on his head, a sock knit from black yarn offset with tricolored bands of red, gold, green.

"That's his defense," I say to her. "A suit and a family."

She does not immediately respond. I expect nothing, but then she puts down her pen and asks me, "What do you think the defense will be, really?"

"The usual, I suppose. Lie, deny, alibi." She laughs and repeats it to herself. I am encouraged to see her soften. "Everything I tell you is old old old, Ashfield," I say. "I'm not clever, you just haven't heard it before."

"I wish you wouldn't do that," she says. Her expression darkens and so does her voice. The smile slides away, just like that. "You always infer—you're constantly inferring—that—that I'm—" Her sentence becomes a confused fractal until she abandons it, saying instead, "Will you please stop?"

"Yes," I say, having no idea what I am agreeing to do.

"Really, though," she asks after a pause, "do you think they'll put on a defense?"

I shake my head and bite at a hangnail. "You're looking at it. A suit and a family, that's the defense."

"You're serious, aren't you?"

"Kid's never been in a suit in his life." At last she turns to

Pool, and I examine her face as she does. Her clear brown eyes appraise him without interest. "Piss me off," I say. "These guys—thugs in suits—"

"What do you call a black kid in a suit?" she asks me. "The defendant. Is that what you mean?"

"Oh, Christ—"

"He's on trial. Why do you mind?"

"Because it's what the jury sees, all right?" I say. "They don't see Haskin Pool out there—out there in his world. They don't see him with his do-rag on, out there under the lamppost. Playing C-low."

"They don't see you in your—in whatever you wear."

"No. No, but the jury doesn't let the guy go home because I'm wearing a suit," I tell her. "They see him and think he's a sorry little spud. *How could he kill someone? He can't even tie his own tie!*"

"They don't."

"They don't? You know how many guilty motherfucks I've seen let off just because they come in here looking fourteen? Because Mommy's in the back row bawling?"

"Listen to you," she tells me.

"Yeah. Listen to me, Ashfield. I know what I'm talking about."

"No. Listen to you. Saying they let defendants go when you did the same thing!"

"I—" I start, but there is nothing I can say.

I do not know how she knows, but the way she looks at me, wholly without shame, tells me that her remark did not fly involuntarily from her pretty mouth. She knows, of course, and while two days ago, alone in my Appeals office, I would not have minded, now I mind. At least I mind that *she* knows. I mind that she is right, and that she so effortlessly put me on the defensive. This morning I woke up believing she has a dirty little secret, but here we are talking about mine, Nicole Carbon, and staring at each other over opposite sides of a bright line Laurel has cut into the varnished linoleum between us, staring at me from the side where I should be standing. While there is nothing I can say, nevertheless I start to say, "I did what I did because—"

"Because you felt sorry for her?" she says, and she relishes this moment more than she should. She gladly throws Nicole Carbon in my face. "How did that make her less guilty? How is that different from what you say they do, the jury?"

I fix her with a stare, trying to make it angry, although I suppose I look like I feel: betrayed. She stares right back, joyfully vindictive out of all proportion to this argument. She is fighting as though the outcome actually matters.

"So it's okay when you do it? Because you're smarter than they are?" she asks, pushing the blade of her fingernail file even deeper into my gut. Then she takes a reasonable tone. "The jury humanizes the law. It's— Giobberti, it's what they're *supposed* to do."

"Humanizes the law—fuck that. The jury sucks the guts out of the law. Fucking *ignores* the law."

"You have no idea," she says, smiling at last, but the smile registers no victory nor humor. She is shaking her head. "What it's like. To grow up in these places. You have no idea—"

"No idea what? What it means to be black? Is that what you're saying?"

"You think you know?" she asks, and the last vestiges of her empty smile drop away. Her eyes flicker. She anticipates my answer and is ready for it.

"No, Laurel," I tell her in a careful tone, "but I have some idea. I was born here, remember?"

At last she turns grave. I knew it was only a matter of time. She says, "I'm happy for you. But don't you ever, *ever* think you know what it is like to be black. Because you will never know, Giobberti. You never will."

Now Gewirtz is here. He slipped in unnoticed. By the time I look from her to him and back, she is already at work on her legal pad. With the air conditioners turned off, I hear her pen scratching over the paper and wonder how much of a mistake I just made.

"I don't see much of a difference, anyway," I say, retreating gingerly. "Not in Brooklyn, anyway. Only difference is our wheels. And our sneakers." I wait. Nothing. "And black women talk in movies. And spit on the sidewalk."

She turns again to me and seems to contemplate being offended. Slapping my face, maybe, but she merely sighs inaudibly and takes it for what it is. I suppose she wants away from the topic as much as I do.

From the forty-seven Brooklyn civilians led into Gewirtz's courtroom at ten-thirty that morning, six have doctor's appointments, three hate cops, two think the system is a joke, five do not speak English, three believe Arabs deserve what they get, one has a plane ticket for Jackson Hole, and eight are manifest idiots. So an hour later, Gewirtz puts the balance in the jury box, and everyone else walks out the door. They are let go with the thanks of the court. They are sent to the elevator bank, where they wait for the single working elevator to return them to the Central Jury Room. There they are formed into another jury panel, along with others let go from another trial, and all of them are sent to another courtroom where they are determined to have doctors' appointments, to hate cops, to believe the system is a joke, et cetera, and excused with the thanks of the court and returned to Central Jury, where they are reassembled into another jury panel, et cetera.

Upstairs, I talk to the remaining nineteen while Gewirtz picks up the telephone. Throughout my voir dire, the buzz of Gewirtz's pillow talk is in my ear, although I cannot make out a word. Cully watches me like a wicked presentiment. Luther is standing in the back, and I notice him only because he sneezes; then he turns and walks out. Yost is reading a *People* magazine someone left behind yesterday; he sets it on his lap so no one will see it, but I can. A court officer is doing a crossword puzzle and does not care if anyone notices. Pool's family sits in the back row with their coats on, as if expecting to be asked to leave, sent to Central Jury, perhaps, along with everyone else they watched walk out.

After Yost has his turn with the nineteen of them, after he apologizes because it is almost lunchtime and apologizes because they had to wait so long and apologizes because the elevators do not work, we pick our last four and finish the jury.

The courtroom is nearly empty when Gewirtz calls us up to the bench and says, "Listen. Where are we, here? You ready to start this thing this afternoon?"

"I can open," I can tell him.

"You have witnesses?"

"You know how it is, Judge."

"The thing is," Gewirtz says, and by his tone I understand that he had hoped I would said no, "I have a doctor's appointment this afternoon."

"I hope it's nothing," Yost says immediately.

"No, Yost," Gerwirtz says, annoyed. "It's not serious. Just a boil. *On my ass.* What I'm going to do is call the jury in and tell them we can't start the trial today. But I want you both ready to open tomorrow. And I want witnesses. No excuses." He stands and unzips his robe. As he does, in a lighter tone, he asks, "Any chance of a disposition of this case, Mr. Yost? Your client looking for anything?"

"There's never been an offer," Yost says, picking up the judge's nameplate from the bench. JONAS A. GEWIRTZ. JUSTICE SUPREME COURT. He spins it on one end. "I mean, if you want me to ask—"

"Ask," says the judge, rolling his eyes. "And—just stop handling that. You see? Look. That's how the thing gets all scratched. Look at that."

Yost sets the nameplate down with exaggerated care and walks over to the defense table. He sits and talks to Pool. After twenty seconds Pool is shaking his head. Yost stands and says, "He'll take straight probation right now." He says it as if he is serious.

"I think the People are looking for jail time," Gewirtz says in a dry voice. "Aren't you, Mr. Giobberti?"

"Generally in murders, Judge."

"Will he take any jail time?" Gewirtz asks Yost wearily.

"Will you take any jail time?" Yost asks Pool in the same voice. Pool shakes his head and says something I cannot hear. Pool then pulls on Yost's arm, and when Yost bends over, Pool whispers in his ear. Yost does not bother to keep his voice down. I hear Yost say, "I'm not saying that. I'm not telling him. No." I cannot hear what Pool says, but he is scowling now, his face an image of his mother's. Then Yost walks over to us and shrugs.

"Well?" Gewirtz asks.

"Says he's innocent, Judge," Yost answers. "What can I say?"

"In that case," Gewirtz says, "he shouldn't even take probation."

In the hallway, waiting for an elevator, neither Laurel nor I are saying much, because Pool's family is here. After several minutes one of them sidles over and tells me she is going to put a chicken on my doorstep.

She is one of the women with Pool's mother. Already she has turned her back to me. Laurel heard but does not know what it means, so she does nothing. I do nothing myself except feel my face getting hot. The woman who said it is standing back again with the others, and none of them faces me except the boy.

"*What?*" Laurel whispers to me, trying to speak without seeming obvious.

"What did you say?" I say to the woman who said it. In the empty tenth-floor hallway, the sound of my voice resonates, and they all turn and the boy keeps staring with his watery eyes. "What did you say to me?" I repeat, and I barely recognize my own voice, so choked does it sound with spit and anger. I step closer to them, and the boy walks between the women and me. He pushes right up against me with his pigeon chest, and I could knock him down, he feels so light. I walk through him to the woman who said it, and the kid is grabbing at my arm.

"You hear me right," the woman says. She has, I notice, a single gray hair on her chin, an inch and a half long. It moves when she speaks. Behind her the elevator chime rings like a round bell, and the women hurry inside. The boy follows anxiously, but I put my foot in the way of the closing door.

"You want to kill me?" I say to her. "Is that what you want? That's what you want?"

"Yo, mister," the boy says now. "Step on outa my mom's face."

"You know where he is? Haskin?" I ask the woman and the others, too.

"Bomba clot," the boy is saying under his breath, but I ignore him. "Bomba ras clot."

"You know where he's sleeping tonight?"

"Why you is lying?" Pool's mother asks in thick West Indian. "Why you lie? *Answer me dat!*"

"Jail," I say, spitting the word as if it were something I wanted out of my mouth.

"The lagga head," she says. "Why ain't you put *him* in jail. Tell me!"

"You know how many badasses I got on Rikers would love to do me a favor? One phone call, lady."

"The lagga head! Arrest *him*!"

"One phone call," I say before letting the door rattle shut. "That's all it takes. One fucking phone call and a pair of Air Jordans."

Laurel takes my arm, pulling me gently but insistently from the door. When they are gone, we wait for the elevator to begin its slow return to us.

CHAPTER 14

In Wendy's on Fulton Street, standing in line in the greasy humidity, as abrupt as a slap, after the clean cold outside, I have the only white face. Everyone is lining up. Everyone is checking me out, throwing queer stares my way because I look like Five-O, because I look pissed, because I am white and Wendy's on Fulton is black. Not that anyone gives a shit. Not really. This is Brooklyn, after all, and we all swim in each other's pool. But we notice. On the train and on the street we see one another, and we notice. Here they notice me and they notice Laurel beside me and wonder, *What's up with that?*

In a moment I stop thinking about that chicken business and let it go. I smile a little to myself and wonder why Laurel is here. This is not her scene. She would never allow any of this. Not a

Bacon Double anything or a *Biggie* anything or anything involving one of those forlorn baked potatoes that repose under a heat lamp, ready to be stuffed with something. *You have no idea what it means to be black,* she told me, but what she meant is *You have no idea what it means to be Laurel Ashfield.* Look at her. Why she is here I have no idea. Followed me from court, I suppose, wondering if I was looking for a pay phone to *call someone* on Rikers. Here, she is more an oddity than I am. She would not know how to order. She would not know what's on the menu. She stands with her head fixed, moving only her eyes at the twelve-year-old girls next to us, pushing each other, falling down, squealing in voices like a subway train entering the bend at Union Square.

You're not from around here, are you? I remember Gewirtz's question and her reaction to it. *Tell me, what is black?* I should have asked her. Would that be born-here black? Would you mean the hard boys of the vertical squalor of the east Brooklyn projects? Or maybe their Carolina cousins, softer in every way—so trying that much harder to be hard, chilling under the lamppost with them but not knowing even how to walk like them. Or perhaps their sisters who are nothing like them, except in their faces, and sometimes not even then. Or black from the islands, maybe—gaunt and poor Jamaicans, dark enough to suck daylight. Or from Puerto Rico, even—*and don't say you ain't black, bro, your hair nappier than mine!*

And what the hell is white, for that matter? The investment bankers in their apartments along Prospect Park West and in Second Empire town houses on Pierrepont Street? Or would that be the Satmars on New Utrecht? The superannuated Park Slope hippies? The Irish and Italians who circled their wagons in Windsor Terrace and Gravesend and Dyker Heights?

Arabs inhabit Atlantic Avenue under the long afternoon shadow of lower Manhattan.

Koreans. In every Thai restaurant, every Japanese restaurant. Eighth Avenue at Sixty-eighth Street looks like Chinatown.

So, Laurel, tell me, what is black? Tell me what is white. And while you're at it, tell me all about Brooklyn. And don't pretend you know.

I've lived here forever, and I don't know.

There is no black and white. I know enough about Brooklyn to know that. Black and white: an oversimplified dichotomy, a handy way to explain differences evident only at the extremes. There is on the one end Dellroy Dunn, and Pool, and his mother and sisters and cousins and aunts. And on the other, there is . . . not me, surely. On the other end there is: Laurel. In between we are the crayons melted in a kindergarten project, melted down in a coffee can to make a single candle colored a muddy gray. In the crucible, everything blurs.

And yet—and yet—I know that I will give my order to the girl and she will write it on a paper slip and the paper slip will go into the back and a bag will appear a minute later and in the bag will be a hamburger and on the hamburger will be ketchup. Which I fucking hate. Which I will have told the girl I do not want, and which I will have known even as I told her that it was a pointless exercise because I always tell the girl. I always say *No ketchup,* and it never makes a difference.

"And no ketchup," I tell the girl when she asks me. "All right? No ketchup. Please." She makes a check on the paper slip: *no ketchup.* "No," I say, and look at her. She is a fawnlike girl I have never seen before, pretty, too shy, almost, even to speak. She is wearing a little polyester outfit that will stink of grease when she gets home. "Can you check it again?"

She does. A bigger check with her pen. She laughs, for some reason. She thinks I am funny. The white guy in black shades is funny. He hates ketchup. She checks it again with her pen, which has a pink plume attached to it, and she laughs without making a sound.

"What was all that upstairs?" Laurel asks as we wait.

I take off my sunglasses. I am over it and starting to feel foolish. I put them in my breast pocket. Her complexion is wan and weak under this light: dilute, bleached. I take the bag another kid gives me and do not answer Laurel's question. I am over it, but I do not want to talk about it, not here. I do want to look in the bag, but I lack the heart. I want to trust, to believe. A flaw in my character, which I should have gotten over by now.

We walk outside, and the early-afternoon sky has no defined origin of light, no sun, no shadows. The buildings seem oily and brown, and we walk under a construction scaffolding of corrugated metal and tubular gray supports. In an unused doorway two sixteen-year-olds, white, kiss and reach in to each other, and you can see their breath. The boy's hand is on her back, and he does not know what else to do with his hand, so he moves it in concentric circles. Laurel and I pretend not to see them. Unable to resist, I take my hamburger from the bag and heft it; it feels warm and pliant inside the paper wrapping, like a freshly killed pigeon. Opening it while walking, I am not surprised to see—ketchup! I am surprised only to see that, if anything, I have been treated to a double helping. Ketchup is smeared on the top and on the bottom, and the whole sodden mass bleeds through my fingers and onto the sidewalk below. A blood-spatter pattern on the pavement, reminding me of a scene inside a bodega. A scene Pool may or may not have made.

Laurel says something, but I do not hear because of a helicopter beating overhead. She looks up, forgetting we are beneath a temporary portico of corrugated metal. As the rotors resonate off building after building, she waits, whatever she said disturbed by another suicide on the Manhattan Bridge.

"That woman. What was she saying? Ladder head?"

"*Lagga head*," I say, rewrapping my hamburger. "Jamaican slang. Means *dope*."

"Dope—like drugs? Like an addict, you mean?"

"No. A dope, you know? A dumb-ass."

We walk. Near the Municipal Building is the bum from yesterday. His hungry puppy is asleep, or dead, starved to death because I did not let Laurel give the man a quarter. The man sits on a small kilim carpet he found in some Brooklyn Heights garbage can and spread over his subway grate. He sits pulling a plastic fork through his beard. "Another great day," he tells me. I nod. "Like the tie, fella," he says as I pass, and involuntarily I stop walking and look at Amanda's tie, now stained with a single teardrop of ketchup. In disgust I nearly tear it off, give it to the man. Instead I hand him the Wendy's bag. "Has ketchup on it," I tell him, and it sounds like an apology. He reaches out to take it, leaving the fork jutting from his beard.

And so, when Laurel takes me to her lunch spot, I think, *Why not!* Here the wooden floors are scattered with sawdust for no good reason. The aisles are stacked with small bottles of pills and capsules of roots, and everything is aromatic, exuding the sort of sickly sallow health of a marathoner, the rotten core of an organic apple. In the back they are serving up vegetable hamburgers and tofu heros and chicken-free chicken salad. I wait for her, imagining people are watching me, wondering about me.

We leave with her lunch, and in her gloved hand there is a carrot juice, which she drinks through a straw as we walk. I have my hands in my pockets because of the cold. I bought nothing. I am thinking I need to talk to her soon, or now, as we walk slowly together through the open plaza across from the Municipal Building. The residue of yesterday's carnival spills from the wire trash cans, and all that remains of the earlier snowfall are small redoubts of black-tinged snow that dot the path all around us and dissolve into gray pools.

"So," she says in a cool voice. "What's that mean—*chicken on your doorstep?*"

"Voodoo," I tell her, jarred from my thoughts about her, and her light tone does not match what I am thinking, but of course she does not know what I am thinking. "Santeria—I don't know. Some wild-ass island shit."

"Like a dead fish in a newspaper," she says, smiling. "Isn't that what your people do?"

"My people?"

"You know, *mobsters.*"

"That's right," I say. "Italians are all mobsters."

"You seem to think we're all alike."

"Laurel—" I stop and turn, but instantly I see from her expression that it is not like that at all. She smiles with the straw in her mouth, depressing her lower lip so that pink shows like flesh of an exotic fruit.

Again we are walking along together, and still I do not know how to begin. Behind us, on Court Street, cars idle in a jam, and their exhaust makes a theatrical ground fog. The horns start soon, and a Chinese guy in a panel truck is working his horn and a man walks over to his window and they start up for a while. The guy in the truck keeps repeating, "I fuck you up!" in a way that suggests he does not really know what he is saying. "You fuck me up?" says the other man in mocking disbelief, and so forth, and the cars are still not moving. More horns start in—the New York Symphony—and I lose interest.

"Tell me," Laurel says. "Do you like this job?"

I repeat the question, and then I answer, "Sure. Has its moments." I suspect she is not making cocktail conversation, but she says nothing more. We walk, so I ask her, "You? I mean, why aren't you at Shearman & Sterling or someplace? Make some real scratch instead."

"No, thanks." She laughs a little at that, and I understand it is not the first time she has been asked the question. "I like doing this."

"Why?"

"Because I feel like I'm doing something—this is hard to explain—something real."

"Can I ask you a question?" I say, and she gives her permission with a nod. "What's it like? Doing this job when . . . you know, what we were talking about before."

"I have no idea what you're talking about."

"You know," I say, sorry I started on this topic. "You know, being black and working this job? I'm just—because most of our defendants are black. Do you ever feel like—"

"Like a traitor to my race?" she says, making me feel ridiculous with her tolerant smile.

"No," I say. "Just like—I don't know. *Damn, not another brother in jail.*"

"No. I think, *Damn, not another wasted life.*" After we walk fifty feet she tells me, "What I do—what you *have* to do—is remember that justice is an individual right. You can't give justice to groups. Sometimes you can't even define the group."

"You think that's what we do? Give justice?"

"Yes. Yes, of course," she says earnestly, believing it entirely. "Don't you agree?"

"No. I think we try. I mean, what we do here on earth? It's never going to be perfect. The most we can do is . . ."

"What?" she asks when I do not finish.

"The most we can do is—what we do."

"What do we do, Giobberti?"

"Enforce the law."

She thinks about that, and I wait for her reaction. It becomes more important to me as I wait for it. She seems to understand that I am waiting for her, and she turns her eyes to me as we walk and says, "That's true."

"I feel funny agreeing with you," I say. "Let's fight about something."

She frowns neutrally and says, "You don't really know people—on Rikers—that would—" I shrug in answer, embarrassed that she had to see that display. "Well," she tells me, "I don't think you do."

Suddenly I stop walking. I say, "Dellroy's in the wind." She stops also and sits on a low metal fence and cocks her head at me, saying nothing. "He left, Laurel. In the middle of the prep, he left. I've had people out all night. He's nowhere."

Her expression does not noticeably alter. She seems to shrug. "Why, I wonder," she says to herself. Then to me: "Did you say something? He's not that bright, you know. Maybe you said something that—" She sees the way I am looking at her, and her face clouds. "What?"

"Tell me."

"Tell you what?" She smiles a little, drinks a little from her straw.

"The truth. Just say it," I tell her, bluffing it out. "Just say it, Laurel. I already know." She laughs because I must seem very grave. I say, "It's a put-up job, isn't it? Heatly is pinning this job on Pool."

She stares past me, the smile still fixed.

"He's using Dellroy. Isn't he, Laurel?"

At once all life drains from her face. She says, "You don't know." Not a question. She is explaining the way it is to herself. I do not have to answer. I stare back at her as she reacts. "My God," she keeps saying. "Oh my God."

"Laurel—"

"Oh my God."

"Laurel," I say. "Just tell me." But she stands, and I follow her as she starts to walk in widening orbits around a point, and she drops her Styrofoam cup. Carrot juice spreads over the cement. This puts her over at last—the simple loss of a cup—and she finds the cast-iron fence again and sits. She sits slumped forward.

"How is it possible you don't know?" she says, looking up at me, her eyes unblinking and large.

"Tell me," I say, ignoring the way she makes me feel. "Heatly pinned—"

"No. *No!*"

"Who, then?" I say, shouting the words. "Who? Tell me. Luther? Was it Luther?"

"No," she is saying, shaking her head from side to side.

"Goddammit," I say, and I step to her and hold her shoulders between my hands to make her face me. "Tell me who did this."

She stands and frees herself from my hold. I do not follow. I watch her walk away, her long black coat sweeping behind her as she walks, then runs.

CHAPTER 15

The station is in motion. I am looking into the tunnel, through the progression of geometric girders, and everything is off-kilter. I turn my head, but that does not help at all, so I sit. The station is empty and too bright, like a sordid Lower East Side apartment at three in the morning when the lights go on and the party is over, and the few survivors left in corners and bedrooms come blinking into the open. I sit that way now on a bench, feeling exposed and pale. An old man appears in a frayed three-piece suit, no overcoat, porkpie hat. He hawks phlegm, and the sound of it resonates through the still tunnel. I wait an interminable while for him to spit, paralyzed from any further thought or motion until he does. He does at last, then he wipes himself with the cup of a hand. You can hear his hand running over the stiff bristles of his chin.

A train comes. From the distant end of the tunnel, a half mile away, I see the point of light. When I look again, the train is in the station. I am on my feet. I board. The doors close and I stand by the door and see myself reflected in the glass on the other side. A watery reflection.

I am drunk, I decide, and I enjoy it. The novelty of it. The nostalgia of it. Standing drunk in a moving train. I am a hearty sea captain! Knock me down!

I see my reflection in the window glass and wonder, *Am I drunk?*

I sit. Everyone is tired. Everyone is white. A downtown train to south Brooklyn, so what do you expect! I look at people and look them in the eye, as if I were from Rochester. No one looks back for very long. Everyone feels sorry for me. Everyone is ashamed for me, because they know.

Across from me sits a Hasid with side locks and the whole regalia, skin yellowed from five thousand years of history. He is squint-eyed with thick eyeglasses, looking at life through two aquariums. Next to him a man is having some sort of low-caliber seizure, ticking regularly in tiny tremors not associated with the movement of the train. Two sixteen-year-old boys sit nearby with their legs spread into wide vees. One is saying, "I listen to everything you do. Except Metallica." Another kid—a waxy rat of a boy—starts calling his sister names suffixed with *head*. Then a wise guy walks by with a clown nose on, red. No one notices, except me and the kid, who grabs his mother's sleeve and points. His sister, *farthead,* looks, too. Then the boy and his sister start laughing their asses off. A Chinese guy walks by selling batteries. Batteries and yo-yos and gum. He sets an electric monkey on the floor, and it lights up red and yellow; it turns over, then back again, while making a tinny mechanical whir. I cannot tear my eyes from it. I watch, transfixed, interrupted by a clown nose rolling across the floor and under my seat. I bend down to get it and feel a rush of vertigo, and when I sit back up, I cannot focus right away. I toss the thing to the clown guy, and he puts it in his pocket.

Fifteenth Street station. I walk up the concrete stairs alone. Outside, the streets are oddly dark. Some streetlights are not working, and the snow is over, and the wind, so everything seems still and very late. I turn toward home, but I do not want to go home. I walk around for a while. I wish I were sober. Or drunk. As it is, I am neither. Or both. So I walk around some more until I start to feel cold and am not thinking at all. On a side street a homeless woman crouches between two cars, holding up her layers of coats with two hands. Her ass is chapped red. On the avenue there are some lights, some people walking. Steam rises from a manhole cover, blooming and dissipating, and Christmas trees lie dry and stricken on the curb. A garbage truck with a plow attached drives by. A dog tied to a parking meter smiles hopefully at me. The video store is empty except for a kid with a bone in his nose and a local alcoholic asking for Jean-Claude Van Damme movies—the same guy I see sitting on a milk crate shaking coins in front of the corner Korean market and in the pharmacy buying isopropyl like fifths of cheap vodka. *Not my future,* I think, *yet here I am. Here we are.*

I walk home and with plodding feet climb the stairs to my door. Ann is not here. The lights are off, and it feels like it used to feel after Amanda left. I cannot stay, not with the place dead and empty like this, unlived in. Nor with me like this, the way I was in this place, when it was this way.

Without taking off my overcoat, I walk to the kitchen telephone. I dial the office desk and they connect me to Laurel's home number. The line rings and rings, and if she does not answer, I do not know what I will do next. When she does, I tell her I am coming over. She does not say anything for several seconds, then she gives me the address and repeats it while I write it in the dark with a broken pencil on the back of a birthday card. *So she lives in Brooklyn,* I am thinking.

Outside, I walk and keep walking. I come alongside Prospect Park, and the buildings recede, revealing a velvety black dome and no moon. I see, high against the night sky, an airplane's foreshortened contrail hang like a falling star. I make a wish upon it with misplaced hope and superstition.

Laurel is standing at her apartment door, which features a Santa still taped to it, a Santa complete with eight tiny reindeer. I barely notice. I am off balance, not drunk. The walk in the clean night air cleared my head. I am instead put off balance by everything about this place, beginning with the doorman. I stood outside the building, checking the address against what I wrote in the darkness of my empty kitchen, and there was no mistake. Her building is a pile of carved limestone, entered through a tunnel of green awning. I stood against a brass pole supporting the awning. The doorman, liveried like the czar's footman, eyed me from his lodge window, then asked questions I answered with alcoholic breath. He pressed a number on the phone, and after an interlude of rumbled whispers into the receiver, he let me up, closing the elevator door behind me. I could see his face, stern in the porthole window, as the car rose. I wondered if I should have tipped him.

Laurel waits in her doorway, leading onto the carpeted seventh-floor hallway where I stand, tie undone, probably looking like all hell. She, on the other hand, is wearing a T-shirt, blue on white, Yale. And with her hair undone like that, she has a startling offhand beauty that I notice right away without comment. I step inside, hands in pockets, and I look self-consciously at my shoes and behind me, where three liquid gray footprints lead from the doorway to where I am standing on the black-and-white tiles of her foyer. I step out of my shoes, and she comes over. She smiles, and that helps.

I walk in her living room across an elaborate hardwood parquet, and with my socked foot, I step on something small and blunt. A red LEGO, which I pick up and set on an end table amid photographs in oval frames, little boxes, and whatnot. She sits cross-legged on the flowery couch, toenails painted maroon, soles pink. I move to the window, uncertain how to start. The window is a prewar rectangle that does not take real advantage of the view, rendering it almost as a framed painting. Still, the car alarms and sirens below seem muted and blend in with the night and the carpeting of Brooklyn lights—yellow, white, and red—laid down between here and lower Manhattan, where the distant skyline winks, white under black.

I face her again. In the quiet—now without the distraction of activity, of motion—the booze catches up with me. I have to concentrate to keep my eyes on her. With my right hand I take hold of a chair near me, but I do not sit down. I must keep standing, knowing I do not have long.

She says, at last, "I was born in Brooklyn." I do not know how to answer, so I do not. "I suppose you wouldn't know that. Anyway." She makes a small shrug.

"I don't know—a lot about you."

"I was," she says as a matter of fact. "Here. Park Slope. Methodist Hospital on Sixth Street. We lived here until I was four. I don't remember it. Not well. All I remember were these really tall wooden stairs in our house that we used to slide down. On our behinds. It was fun." I smile at the idea, but she does not. "We moved to the city later," she tells me. "Hamilton Heights. Do you know where that is?"

"Sure. West One-fifties, right? Nice neighborhood."

"Nice black neighborhood, you mean," she says. "This was—God—in the mid-seventies. I remember my dad always talking about *gall-damn junkies*. I never knew what junkies were." A moment passes. "He wasn't a very articulate curser, my dad. *Gall-damn junkies!* I just thought they were, you know, like Sanford and Son—junk dealers in old red pickups. I kept looking for them. I didn't know. I didn't know why they made him so angry. Redd Foxx is harmless enough, right?" She pauses. She looks at me, really looks at me, but quickly adds, "I'm telling you this for a reason, you know."

"Go ahead."

"We'll talk about everything else in a minute."

"All right," I tell her. "Right now tell me some more about when you were a kid."

She shifts on the couch, putting her legs down and bringing herself more into the light. Her arms are still crossed, and one hand pulls distractedly on the hem of her T-shirt sleeve. I am still standing, holding the chair. If I sit, everything will stop. I want to hear her, so I will know what I have to do tomorrow.

"We weren't very popular there," she says. "Because my dad agitated some people. But because of my mother, too. I guess. There were other reasons—I don't remember. It was a weird time. There were always these . . . discussions with the bedroom door shut. I didn't understand it. When you're a kid, you don't understand things; you feel them. I just remember always feeling afraid. Incidents. Words."

"Like what?"

"I just— I don't know. Stupid things I don't remember now," she says in an even, conversational tone—intentionally even and conversational, I think. We are each trying to subjugate our own bodies, to hold ourselves level long enough to do this thing. "I just remember my dad telling us to keep walking. *Keep walking. Look straight ahead. Just let it alone,* he'd say. That sort of thing. And I was always asking, you know, *What? What?* And he wouldn't say." She pauses and concentrates. "My brother would tell me later, and I still didn't understand."

To me it seems she is talking to herself. She is not looking at me at all anymore. She is looking here and there. Out the window. "Once, though," she says. "Once we went to this little diner on Columbus? I loved it, because when I was a kid? You could get breakfast there, even for dinner. I thought that was the greatest thing, and I was always, *always* asking to go there. Driving my parents crazy. Once we went there for . . . something. After a recital, maybe. As a treat, you know?"

I nod.

"And we go there," she says, frowning with concentration. "All of us. My father and my brother and my mother who— I didn't tell you," she says and starts to laugh at the recollection, finding it funny all of a sudden, and talking to me while she laughs, remembering it. "She isn't just white, okay? She's *so* white. And she has red hair and freckles and skin like—okay?"

"Okay."

"You get the picture?" she asks, no longer laughing. "We're sitting there and we're this happy little family. I'm six or seven, so what else am I supposed to think? And next to us? At the table next to us? There were these two—gorillas. I didn't hear what they said, but my brother told me later that one of them passed a remark about my father. *Uncle Tom,* or something clever like that. Even when he told me, I still had no idea," she says, putting her hands together. "*Uncle who?* And my brother had no idea, either. He was just like, *It's bad, it's bad,* but he didn't know."

"So what happened?"

"All I saw was my dad," she says. "He very carefully put his napkin down. Then he said, *Excuse me, son.* He was speaking to the one who said it. He said, *Excuse me, son. Was there something you wanted to tell me?* And that's how my father speaks. Very— I mean, you *know it* when he's talking to you. And the guy looked at his friend and then said something else. Just a smart-ass, I guess. I didn't hear that, either, but my dad just—right across his face. Like this. And you could hear it. And the whole place, the whole restaurant, went . . . dead. Nobody was moving. Nobody said any-thing. And my father, he was standing over the guy, waiting for the guy to do something. But he didn't. He just sat there looking at his plate like he'd been—whupped."

Remembering after a moment, she says, "My dad is pretty big, you know? But that isn't why the guy did nothing."

"Why not?" I ask her.

"Because my dad would have killed him," she says simply. "I remember, though, when my dad sat down, he reached over to get the salt or something, and his hand was shaking. Like this. That was all."

I keep looking at her, knowing that she is telling me something because she needs to, not because she wants to. She is telling me something important so I will understand. But I do not under-stand.

She says, "You want to know something else? It never— I mean *never*—dawned on me that it was because of my mother. Because I was always so proud of her, that she was my mother. She's very refined, very beautiful. So what I thought—everything— I thought it was all because we were from Brooklyn." She turns to me and smiles very sweetly, innocent. "Isn't that funny? I thought people were always angry at us because we weren't from—" After another moment, she says, "And that's what Heatly said to me."

"I don't understand."

"I suppose you think I just went along, don't you?" She looks right at me. "For a long time I kept telling myself that I had no choice, that if I went public, they would say just what you're thinking right now. That I went along from the beginning."

"Did you?"

"I knew, and I didn't do anything about it. Whatever my reasons—"

"It was Heatly, then."

"And it wasn't what he said," she is saying, but she is not answering me. "It was more just the way he *looked* at me. Like I was . . . pretending. That bastard." Here she begins to laugh lightly. "I'm following him around the squad room like this—this stupid annoying little girl. I'm telling him I know. I'm telling him. And he just looks at me. He just looks at me like I'm—like I'm something he doesn't even have a word for. Like I'm this little . . . counterfeit."

"Laurel," I say. I sit next to her on the couch.

"I went along. Isn't that what you want to know? I went along, Giobberti. So just go, do what you have to do. I don't care any-more."

"Tell me, Laurel," I say, feeling the exhaustion begin to pull at me. Deliberately I ask her, "Did Luther know?"

"I was all alone. Don't you understand? I was frightened! I didn't think this happened. I'm following Heatly around the squad room like—like an idiot! I'm asking him why. I'm telling him that I know. That's when he said it. That's when I just— stopped trying. I let him. That's what you're asking me, right? Well, I let him. He just looked at me that way. *You're not from around here, are you?*"

"Laurel," I say.

"God, I hated him!" she says, concentrating on a point right ahead of her. "Do you want to know something, though? Why I didn't say anything? Do you really want to know?"

"Why?"

"Because I wanted it. In that moment I wanted it like he wanted it. I let him," she says, "because I thought he was showing me something. Something that I didn't know—something that happens out there—in the world. I thought, *So this is how it is.* Sometimes this is how it is, and I didn't know. He made me ashamed I didn't know." Abruptly she is angry. "He made me ashamed of who I am. Goddamn him!"

"This isn't what happens," I tell her. "This is fucked up."

"Don't tell me that! Don't you tell me that!" she says, turning her anger on me. Once again I am the handy proxy, and wearily I take it. "You have no right to—patronize me—or act like—"

"Wait."

"I mean, that's why they picked you, right?"

"What are you talking about?" I ask. "Who?"

"Luther. The D.A. I don't know," she says. "Of course that's why. You have no problem with *moral ambiguity*—isn't that what you said?"

"Don't make me defend what I did," I tell her, too tired to fight. "I can't. But you're talking about pinning a murder on some mope—"

"Pinning a—"

"—so Fister can get a headline."

"Giobberti," she says after a full minute in which the silence of her living room settles over us. The sounds of the city below are the only sounds. She says my name, not understanding, and then at once she understands. When she finally speaks, she speaks very quietly. "Giobberti, Pool killed him."

"He—" I say, and then I, through the haze of my alcoholic stupidity, understand, too.

"This was Pool," she tells me, and written in her eyes is the minor reprieve I have just given her, the relief of knowing that whatever she has done, it is not nearly so bad as what I had ac-

cused her of when I walked inside her home. Yet I still need to know.

"And Dellroy?"

"Yes," she says, nodding. "Pool and Dellroy."

"I don't—"

"And Lashawn Sims. And Heatly. And Luther. And me—all of us, Giobberti. Do you understand now? All of us—this was all of us."

"Dellroy?" I ask, my head all aswim.

"He went along, Giobberti. Just like me."

She says it with a desolate sadness. I would do something for her, anything, but I do not know what. She seems to register my helplessness, but she has told me all she wanted to say. Now she nods and purses her lips with a certain satisfaction. She stands and walks away. I hear a door gently close.

I wait for her, but she does not come back.

CHAPTER 16

Open my eyes. A different light from a strange window, slanting at an unaccustomed angle, and nearby the sound of mornings echoing from the past—plastic toys dropped on a wooden floor— crayons rolling under the bed—the small voice of an imaginary friend, or a doll, or a bear. The sounds of a child playing.

Heart pounding the veins of my neck, and *Is it a dream?* and *Why here?*

Why now?

Where am I?

Beneath everything else I feel festers a malignant germ of hope—hope that it is not a dream, that it is she, although I know it is not. The cruelest sort of hope you let yourself have, knowing that it is not hope at all.

Violently awake now, and my daughter is not here. Nor is Laurel. I am in her empty living room on a workday morning, a Thursday morning, and it comes back to me, although my mind is wet tissue paper. Talking—talking with her, and then—nothing. Yet all that is distant from me. I am listening to the sounds of a child playing, and the light from the window is very bright. I am wedged into the couch, still dressed. I stand and walk to the window and recognize Prospect Park from seven stories, with the sun already well up over the spread of oaks, bare and brown. The war monument at Grand Army Plaza, with its ironic dedication in Roman capitals across the entablature for all Brooklyn to see— DEFENDERS OF THE UNION—is a confused tangle of verdigrised infantry and cavalry, never intended to be seen from above, erected when it was as tall as things ever got. Everything has a skewed, uncertain perspective, and still the sound of the child is in my head.

My tie and shoes are off. She must have done that. Or maybe I did. I stand and give myself a once-over in a gilt mirror hanging over a sideboard. What I see is accurate enough, I suppose.

In my socks I walk into the kitchen, where Laurel is sitting with her back to me. Her unplaited hair from behind is beautifully wild. Diffuse copper corkscrews. Hearing me, she turns and smiles. A weak smile but genuine.

"I heard someone," I tell her. "A little kid."

"Sit down," she tells me, but I walk to the sink, which smells like hot water and soap, unlike mine, and with that I think of Ann sleeping alone after coming home and waiting for me. Another mess to clean up today, although I am in no shape to deal with that, either. With one hand holding the black granite counter for support, I slap cold water on my face and neck. When I straighten, Laurel is behind me holding a dish towel. I take it and run it over my face, and she is standing close to me, unmade up, teenage skin delightfully unperfected. I notice for the first time the pale freckles that play lightly across her nose and cheeks.

She turns and walks away, to the kitchen table, where she sits. She is wearing flannel pajamas patterned with green snowflakes. I follow and sit near her, where a *New York Times* is laid open near a bowl of milky cereal. We look at each other with embarrassment and recognition, and a little girl pads into the room. She is wearing flannel pajamas in her mother's pattern. She is a mother, Laurel, and so natural are that moment and the realization of her motherhood that I do not even wonder: as though I have known it all along, as though it is far less remarkable that a little girl should appear in the kitchen than I should be here in the first place.

"Um, Mommy," the girl says, taking no more than a brief, uninterested notice of me. Like her mother's, her eyes are as light as her skin—stained cream.

"Come up here, Faye," Laurel says, and the girl sits on her mother's lap frowning, concerned about something very, very important.

"Faye," I repeat. "How old is she?"

"Five," Faye says for herself, while pulling on Laurel's arm to get her attention.

"Almost," her mother says. "Faye, say hello to Mr. Giobberti."

"Who are you?"

"Faye!" Laurel says, and we both laugh like grown-ups always do when a child asks the right question at the wrong moment. "Mr. Giobberti is my friend. Now, go get dressed," Laurel tells her, lowering her voice, sliding the girl from her knee, and smacking her lightly on the behind as Faye turns away. Faye takes an apple from a bowl and walks off, her bare feet playing soundlessly over the hallway floorboards, her gait altering only for the moment it takes to adjust her underpants beneath her pajamas. I have never told Laurel about Opal. I wonder to myself whether she knows.

"So," I say. "You weren't running home to watch *Wheel of Fortune,* then." She laughs. Or rather it starts as a smile, ends as a laugh. "Faye. She's—" I start to tell her, but Laurel seems already to understand. She nods in anticipated agreement. There is something she wants to say as well, and I give her a moment, believing that she is going to tell me about Faye. She lets it go, whatever she wanted to say, and the moment passes. Now is not the time for this conversation. She asks me what we are going to do.

"I don't know." Her question catches me off guard. What I am thinking is now that I know everything, I still know nothing at all. "I need to see Luther."

"Luther," she says, not bothering to conceal her shock.

I shake my head to let her know it is not like that. "But you need to tell me, Laurel. You need to tell me."

"All right," she says, cautiously relieved. "But later—I have to get Faye—"

"No. Now, Laurel. You have to tell me now."

"Giobberti!"

"Now," I tell her, meaning it. "From the beginning." I remain seated, but she cannot. She stands and turns away. My hands are clasped on her table in an imitation of patient calm. "You went to the Seven-Five that night. Start there. You went with Luther."

"Yes," she says, turning to me again. "No, Luther was there already."

"You came down alone?" I ask.

"Yes."

"Why, did he call you down?"

"I was in Investigations then, I—"

"He asked for you?" I ask.

"No. No, he didn't even know me. I was up. It was my night. He— They were done with Dellroy when I arrived," she says. "All Luther needed was for me to write it up. Just draft the complaint and get it filed. We didn't talk about—Dellroy. Not that night."

"How did you—" I start, and I cannot help but sound skeptical. She hears it, too, I am certain, because she is very serious all of a sudden, standing there in her snowflake pajamas. "You said you confronted Heatly. That night."

She blinks and momentarily falters. "I talked to—someone else."

I wait. When she tells me no more, I ask, "Who?"

"He—Dellroy was down there. With a friend. Someone who came down. With him."

"Who?" I ask again.

"Just—a friend, Giobberti. It's not important."

"What the fuck, Laurel? Who?"

"Her name is Santra. Santra Flowers," she tells me, understanding that she has no choice. "But you have to promise me you'll leave her out of this. She's not—"

"What's she got to do with it?"

"Nothing!" she says. "Nothing at all."

"So why would I bother her?"

"Just—*please.*"

"She knows about this?" I ask.

"Dellroy told her. As I said, she brought him down," she says in a flat voice, telling me that I can believe her or not, she does not care. "He came down to tell Heatly."

"Bullshit he did." She shrugs. I say, "She's going to bring her boyfriend down—Dellroy's going to come down to Heatly, why? To hang himself on a hook?"

"There was no other way. He was scared," she says. "Santra

was scared for him. You don't know how they are together. She's not his girlfriend. She's like—his mother, almost."

"So Mommy brings him down to confess to a—"

"They didn't see it like that!" she says. "You've met him, Giobberti. My God, he's not capable of something like this."

"Why did he partner up with Pool, then?"

"Partner. It—it wasn't like that," she says, the emotion plainly welling up in her throat, making it difficult for her to speak. "They were never partners. He was scared. He was scared of them, but he looked up to them, too."

"Them?"

"Pool and—Lashawn Sims. Sims was—"

"Sims," I say. "The beanpole? From the lineup?"

"—partners with Pool on this. This was theirs. Not Dellroy's. Never Dellroy. God."

"Why Dellroy?" I ask. "Why did they bring him in?"

"They used him," she tells me. "Like everyone else, they used Dellroy."

"Why?"

"Because of how he is," she says. Her voice implores me to believe.

"Used him for what?"

"There's a surveillance camera in the store, right over the counter," she says reluctantly, sounding almost ashamed to know this, to be telling me the details, the facts I do not know, as if she herself were confessing them all to me. "Didn't work. It wasn't connected to anything, but Pool didn't know that. They sent Dellroy in with the gun. Pool and Sims stayed in the doorway. Out of sight."

"Holy Mother," I say, seeing where this all is leading. "And Gomez went for his gun."

"Yes," she says, facing me before saying, "Yes, and Dellroy shot him." The news is meaningless at first. "Dellroy," she repeats.

"Fucking hell," I say, standing suddenly, knocking my chair over. It clatters on the tile floor and neither of us rights it. "Fucking hell, Laurel."

"He didn't kill him, Giobberti! He—" she starts to say, then she just tells me. "Pool ran inside after Hamadi went for his gun. Pool's telling him to shoot and—"

"And he did," I say, calmer now.

"Yes!"

"That was the shoulder wound."

"Yes," she says. "I'm getting this from Dellroy, so it's kind of . . . you understand. But I can't believe he would have shot Hamadi on purpose. My God, the man used to feed him. Dellroy had nobody in the world—his grandmother, Santra. This man, he— The only thing I can figure is Dellroy panicked. Hamadi goes for his gun, Pool comes running in, Hamadi stands up, and Dellroy must have just—" She shakes her head at the idea, at the ugly horror of the scene she has described for my benefit.

"And afterwards Pool finished him."

"Yes," she says.

"Where's Sims in all this?"

"He left," she says. "He ran down Sutter. When the shooting started."

"Beautiful. *Beautiful!* Jesus, you couldn't pay me to make this shit up." I am still trying to sort the pieces out in my head. They mostly fit; Laurel has hammered them into place with the heels of her shiny black shoes. They fit except for two. I ask her, "Help me understand. Why's Dellroy going along with this? The man means so much to him—he's gonna go and rob him up?"

"Giobberti, you know how he is."

"No. No, I don't know how he is, Laurel. I don't care who stuck an ice pick in his head, he knew this sucked. Don't tell me he didn't."

"Who told you that?" she asks, sitting.

"Moss." I pull the chair upright and join her at the table. "Squad lieutenant, why?"

"No. Nothing. I just didn't know how you would know about that," she says, and her mistrustful expression falls away. "Look, I can't explain why he went along, but he went along. No one put a gun to his head, if that's what you're asking me. He— You have to understand that he looked up to them. *Convict* and *Slim*—they were the big kids, you know? The ones who hung out under the lamppost. And when they came to him— You have to understand that they came to him."

"That's not an excuse."

"No," she says, deadpan. "It's part of Dellroy's psychological whatever."

I smile but do not laugh. She does not even smile. I put my head into my palms and rub my eyes and ask her my second question: "So why's he going to give himself up for this? He walks in the door two weeks later?"

"He was scared. I told you."

"Scared of what?" I ask. "Heatly didn't have shit on him."

"Pool. He was scared of Pool."

"Pool?" I ask. "Why Pool?"

"He believed Pool was going to kill him."

"Why would he think that?"

"Because Pool killed Sims."

I just laugh. After hesitating, after turning to her, I laugh. She looks at me and does not, because it is not funny. I am not altogether sure why I am laughing myself. When she tells me to stop, I do. "All right," I tell her. "Let me have it. Let me have it all."

"Pool thought Sims gave him up."

"He never," I say, then realize the answer. "The lineup."

She nods. "I mean, he is a beanpole. I'm sure that's why Heatly ran a lineup with Sims. Two weeks with nothing, he was just playing hunches."

"A good hunch," I say. "She never made him, though. The woman who saw him running. Henkis."

"Too bad for him she didn't," Laurel says. "Pool killed him that night."

"Pool figured Sims snitched him or—"

"—he wouldn't have been released," she says. "Right. Anyway, Dellroy supposed he was next. That's why he went in. Wait here." She stands and walks down the hallway. I wonder if, as with last night, she will not return, but she is gone only a moment. When she returns, she is holding a legal pad. She offers it, barely raising her hand to do so, as if her arm is weighed down by it. "Here," she tells me, after I do not take it. I do not want it. I am bruised from all her information, and I cannot imagine what this is now. Undaunted, she sets it on her kitchen table in front of me. I see the first page; it is not her handwriting. The handwriting is so poor that I think it may be a child's, Faye's perhaps. I turn one page, then another, and without reading it realize that no child would write this—the words are all wrong. I face her with an implicit question.

"Dellroy," she answers.

" 'I'm gonna tell you about murders and shit,' " I read aloud, turning back to the first dog-eared page and reading the beginning. "What is this?"

"Dellroy," she says again. "I asked him to write it down." She offers nothing more. I look at the pages, six legal-sized pages written in the same tortured hand, worse than mine, with no evident punctuation. I have seen these precinct confessions and witness statements, barely literate, scrawled on legal pads or whatever else was handy, often about three in the morning in a windowless interview room. One I have seen on a take-out menu, written in the interstices between entrées and appetizers and beverages. I have seen thousands. I could paper my apartment with them if I had them all. But I do not have them, any of them. I do not have them because they never come home. They are written and sworn and signed and slipped into plastic evidence bags and sealed until trial, when they are cut open and revealed with some small drama. And they are never secreted down the hallway in your apartment, near your child's bedroom.

"Giobberti, I have to get her to school," she says. "Please go now. Just read it, and then we'll talk."

At last the violent nausea washes over me. I am sick, and I am sick for her—sick for what she has done and sick for what has been done to her. Sick. Sick for what I must do. I walk away from her, into the living room, where I tie my shoes on, as if blindfolded, sitting on the couch where I slept. On the other side of the wall I can hear Faye playing, and I pause to listen. After that I let myself out and sit on a bench in the chill morning air.

CHAPTER 17

"Read this, you shitbird."

I throw Dellroy Dunn's handwritten statement at Mark Luther, and the legal pad fans out noisily on the air of his twelfth-floor office. We watch as the legal pad glances harmlessly off the edge of his desk onto the dun-colored carpeting. There is a newspaper in his hand and there are three other newspapers on his desk. He is wearing eyeglasses—the little wire eyeglasses you see on Italian men in ads inside the Sunday *Times* magazine—and he would have taken them off when I knocked, had I knocked and not just walked in.

"What's this?" he asks, cocking his head at the legal pad. I am watching him. None of my subtle psychology now. I am fascinated by his self-control. He knows, the fuck. He knows, *but look at him!*

After a moment his mouth turns up at one edge, and he takes the statement from the floor, holding it between thumb and forefinger. He sets it on his desk and runs his eyes quickly over the front page without reading it. He takes off his glasses now and turns his cool gaze on me. He says, "All right. Who wrote this?"

"Dellroy Dunn."

"Ahh, of course," he says, trying for rich sarcasm. His eyes roll merrily to suit the act, but they are flat. "Dellroy Dunn, of course. Now, tell me, who the fuck is Dellroy Dunn?"

I walk closer, until only the desk is between us. He recoils, pushing back instinctively in his swivel chair and crossing his thin legs as he does, to make it seem intentional. When I do not answer him right away, he knits his fingers and lays them across his chest and waits.

"That really is the question, isn't it, Luther?" I say. Behind him is a bookshelf and to the side is a wall of memento photographs and framed certificates for doing God knows what. "He's either a witness or a perp. Depends who you ask."

"I'm asking you, Giobberti."

"He's a perp," I tell him. "Before you got to him, anyway. You and Heatly. Before you cleaned him up." He laughs. There is no other answer he can give me, but I will not take that from him. I would slap his face before I let him laugh at this. Knowing that, he knocks it off. "You cleaned him up, didn't you?" I say. "He confessed to Heatly. You knew it." I can hear every sound now—the secretaries nattering outside his door, the car horns on Court Street below, the vapor rising through the steam pipes in the wall. "Tell me."

"You're out of your mind," he says at last, reorganizing himself in his chair.

"Tell me, goddammit." I do not move.

"I knew you weren't ready for this," he tells me, shaking his head, not watching me anymore. "Two days back and you're— Listen to yourself! My God, I— Look at you! You look like hell.

Did you even shave? You look like you slept in that suit. How the hell are you going to open to a jury this morning when—"

"Open?" I ask, making a short laugh at the idea of finding an opening statement for a jury somewhere in the twisted metal of this wreckage. "The case is over, Luther. There is no case."

He considers that. "You're sick," he says. "That's what you are." He picks up his telephone and starts to dial. I nearly laugh again, because it is like something from a movie. I imagine two expressionless men appearing to escort me out. "You need help," he is saying, stabbing at the buttons with the index finger of his left hand. Improbably, I am thinking, *Is he married?* And *Is he left-handed?* Then I find I have thrown the telephone to the floor and have kicked it. He is right. I am sick. I'm stark raving. But kicking the phone, his phone, anyway, feels good. Heavy, with buttons that light up, the phone makes a mournful foreshortened ring when I kick it again. "You tell me now," I say when I am done.

"Giobberti."

"You tell me now, so help me God, Luther, or—"

Still he hesitates, his mind always working. "If this kid confessed to Heatly—like you say—then why the fuck didn't Heatly arrest him?" He lets the question hang in the air along with his aftershave. "Did he arrest him, Giobberti? No, he didn't. No, he did not."

I do not know why Heatly gave Dellroy a walk. I wondered the same thing as I sat on a park bench across from Laurel's apartment building after reading Dellroy's statement in her elevator and under her building's green awning. I thought about it walking over the bluestone pavement along Prospect Park West, walking not home but to the train. I read the statement several times, trying to understand.

I'am a tell you about murders and shit But I wasnt with all that. What happen is Convic come over to the play ground with Slim + they both is like *come on* because they have some thing for me to do. I say what? + they dont say. They is just like come on U do this + U can be with us. So wear they is taking me is the Arab spot on the corner + when we is all most there Convic pull out this gun he have. I seen it + was like oh snap! That is when I know what they is planning. Convic then say U take this + we all be cool. And we get there + I was like why aint you come in? but they say no cause Gomez know me or what ever. After may be 10 minutes I go up to Gomez and say yo Gomez U kno what this is. And Gomez just be shaking his head at me But he kno some one is in the door + was keeping looking at it all the time. All he do is say No + dont do this Dell or what ever. And I am confused For like 1 minute he do nothing He did not take no money out + is only looking at me + is sad because he kno. He was like oh Dell why is U mixed up wit this?? I was just telling him come on Gomez cause it aint me doing it And I hear Convic yelling I shold hurry up. That is when I say *yo Convic it aint happening* + I turn to walk out or what ever When I turn that is when Gomez go down by the counter wear the meat is at. I turn + I aint see him no more Same time Convic bust in and be saying *hit that nigga* and was bugging And then Gomez jump up + he have a gun That is when I shoot one time. I aint kno then but that is when Slim dipped out the doorway. After that Convic take his gun back + in 1 minute I hear a other shot. I think may be he shoot me because he was mad he was like why U aint tell me Gomez have a gun inside? I say I did not kno Any way Convic say I must have killed him because he is dead and thats a fack. Next thing Convic is throwing every thing down + and aksing wear the tape is. I tell him I do not kno Then we both dipped He go his way + I go mines Next time I seen Convic was when Slim got rested. Convic come over to the play ground + is like *sniches get stiches* and keep my mouth shut or what ever. I aint sniching I am jus doing what I got to do to survive. If U from wear I'am at then U kno what I'am saying

But after I had read it and read it again, I still did not know for certain why Heatly had done it that way. I remembered what Moss said about Heatly's own history with the kid, but that did not explain it, or all of it. So the best reason I could come up with I now tell Luther:

"He wanted Pool. You wanted Pool."

Luther is quiet. He makes a gesture, but he says nothing, and I know I am right.

"It's the co-conspirator rule, Luther. You can't use Dellroy's confession against Pool. Heatly knew that—Christ, you probably know that much," I say, walking to his bookshelf, pulling out his unthumbed copy of the *Criminal Procedure Law*. I drop it on his walnut desk, onto his newspapers, and say—in Laurel's tone of voice, as a joke for her, as if she were here with us—"Section Sixty Twenty-two." He does not move. He sees the *CPL*, not me. I say, "You had nothing to corroborate Dellroy's confession. All you had was one perp pointing a finger at another. That didn't get you Pool, just Dellroy."

"Dellroy was enough," Luther says. "If all I wanted was an arrest—"

"No," I tell him. "Not on this case. Not in an election year, Luther. Not with Cully out there staring at you." He waves his hand at that but says nothing. I say, "This was Pool's caper, and if you were gonna get Pool, you needed a witness, not another perp."

I wait, watching him. "So you made one. Didn't you, Luther? You and Heatly."

When he does not answer I ask him, "That's it, isn't it?"

"What?" he says, and his eyes come up. He was not listening, I realize.

"You didn't want Pool's boy, you wanted Pool," I say. "What would Cully do with that if you put Dellroy under and let Pool skip? *D.A. Collars Patsy, Mastermind Goes Free!* That would have been beautiful, right? A month before the election." I sit across from him. "He knows, doesn't he?" I ask. "Fister knows."

Luther's tongue bulges the side of his cheek. Then, mildly, he says, "Shut the door, Giobberti." His Alaskan-husky eyes are unblinking, unashamed. He sees me like a problem to be solved, that is all. He is wondering what it will take.

For no other reason than that, I sweep the contents of Luther's desktop—his newspapers, his leatherette blotter, his paper Starbucks coffee cup, his NYPD mug full of pens, his paper-clip dispenser, his Barbados souvenir letter opener—onto the carpet, where it makes less racket than I expected. We both contemplate that separately. Then Luther says again, sullen and serious, "Just shut the goddamn door. Please."

I stand and walk to his office door and, holding the doorknob with a backward glance at him, pull it behind me as hard as I possibly can. I walk down the hallway, and rows of secretaries stare at me with startled amazement. I continue to the elevator bank while something, a diploma probably, or a framed photograph of Luther on a beach somewhere in a Speedo, belatedly falls from his wall and shatters.

Laurel's eyes come up when I step inside her cubicle, and right away I see she is not this morning's Laurel of the snowflake pajamas and wild hair. She is inviolate again, wearing black, with wide white pinstripes and shoulders like razor blades. Her hair is tied back and brought to heel. Freckles erased. Lipstick. Yet the expression on her face is different than yesterday's, softer, and it makes me pause in her doorway. "I talked to Luther," I tell her without sitting. She waits for the rest of it.

"Something stinks," I say finally, and she shakes her head because she does not understand. "Not metaphorically, like Denmark," I tell her, glancing around. She points a pencil at the corner of her cubicle, at a garbage bag with an orange sticker affixed. BIO-HAZARD. There is a police Property Room document taped to the bag.

"They brought it this morning," she says, and I understand she does not know what is inside the bag. She does not know that particular smell, the stink of decay, of death vitiated by layers of plastic.

"Gomez's clothes," I tell her, and she turns to it again, frowning. "You ordered the evidence from the Property Room?" I ask. "The evidence you didn't keep yourself, I mean?" I say it as a joke, but it is not funny, and she does not laugh. I take the bag to an unused corner of the floor and return two minutes later with a rusting aerosol can I found along the way. "Stand back," I tell her, spraying the can everywhere until a gray miasma forms around her desk and she is coughing and waving her legal pad in front of her face. I say, "Better?"

"It's worse," she says.

"Right," I say. "Smells like someone died in a pine forest."

She comes over, joining me in the doorway. She says, "If someone dies in a pine forest, and no one smells it . . ."

"He's still dead. Sort of explains the job, don't you think?" I ask her. "If someone dies in Brooklyn, and no one cares, is it still murder?"

"Sure it's murder," she says, smiling a little. "But we plead the case down to manslaughter."

"You know what, Ashfield?" I say. "I think you're spending too much time with me."

She gives me as much smile as she is able, and I know we both have waited as long as possible this morning. Something passes between us, and I nod. I tell her to follow me. She follows me through the bureau, past cubicles and shelves and conference rooms, until she speaks my name in weak protest at the end of an unused hallway as I push twice on a heavy door painted red. A sign attached to it makes a false promise: ALARM WILL SOUND. On my third try, the door swings open and only creaks. She follows me into the empty stairwell. Inside, the air is used up and stale, like air from a bicycle tire. Everything is painted battleship gray in gloss enamel. Walls, steps, handrails, and floors. There are cigarette butts scattered all over, and one Coney Island whitefish, used. I pull the door shut, and there she is. She stands facing me with hollowed eyes, her hands together, and her shoulders narrowed inside her jacket.

"He knows."

"Of course he knows," she says, relieved nonetheless. Still, she asks, "He told you?"

"He didn't say it, but he knows." My voice is too large in the stairwell, so I lower it to a hoarse whisper, my throat raw from alcohol and useless sleep. "He didn't know about Dellroy's statement, though. He seemed kind of—" I remember that I left it with him. That was a mistake.

"He didn't know about it."

"I showed him."

She bites her lip. The silence thickens around us, and it is her turn to talk. She tells me of that morning when she came to Luther, clipping her sentences as she does when she is emotional that way. My mind is going too fast to allow everything in, but I hear her tell how she came to Luther to give up Heatly but found herself promoted to Homicide. She is saying, "And Luther wanted me to. To just play it out. While he dealt with it on his end. You know? Said it would take time. Which is why he put me in Homicide. I believed him, Giobberti. I wanted to believe, you know? That he would. But—"

"This isn't just Luther," I tell her, interrupting the disjointed narrative, not caring enough about how the jagged iron jaws clanged shut around her, caring only about prising them open without tearing away too much skin or unstopping a vein. "Or Luther and Heatly."

"Or us."

"Right," I say, and it is true. This is mine as much as hers, if not more mine than hers. I am here for a reason; she is here only because her name was at the top of a list six months ago. She was up for the ride that night, that is all she did to get Haskin Pool. Me, Christ. Fister had me on this one before he even heard of Haskin Pool, before Gomez took the first bullet. This job was mine after I sent Nicole Carbon home. "And us."

"And me, I mean."

"*Us,* Laurel," I say with some force, and she appreciates my saying it, although I am giving her nothing but company and an empty promise full of good intentions. "What I'm telling you is Fister knows."

"*Fister?*" From her mouth the word seems impure, if not vaguely obscene. I turn away. "Luther didn't tell you that. Of course he didn't tell you. Giobberti?" She is making me meet her eyes and I do not want to, because it will not help. Seeing her expression will confuse me more. I am thinking that I do not know my next step. I can't even imagine what I will be doing an hour from now. "How do you know?"

"He knows. It's like you told me. Why else am I here? He picked me for this, Laurel. He knew I'd see what it was, and he knew I couldn't squawk when I did."

"You can't be sure of that," she says, although neither of us believes it.

"I know Luther," I tell her.

"How do—"

"Because Luther doesn't wipe his ass without Fister didn't tell him to," I say, irrationally angry at her because she does not know Luther as I know him, and because she could have prevented all this by assuming the worst rather than the other way around. I am angry because she trusted him. "You have to know how people are. That's how Luther is. Ah, Jesus."

She says tentatively, "So we can't—drop it. The case. We can't dismiss. That's what you're telling me?"

She gives me an odd accusatory look. Her face is Ann's face. She looks at me as Ann will look at me when I tell her. *All I wanted was a case,* I am thinking. All I wanted was a case to try. I did not want a good case. I did not want to win. I just wanted a case. I wanted to show Ann something—that there is a reason to stay with me—that I may not be ready for her, but someday I might be. That is all. So how the hell did I end up here? In a gray stairwell, trying to explain the facts of life to a woman I did not know three days ago. The walls feel very close, and I am shaking my head and am abruptly very tired. Then, without answering, I am aware of her waiting for me, relying on me to know more than she does. To do something. I start to leave. I am pulling on the door. It is stuck.

"Giobberti. Wait."

"Goddammit." Ignoring her, I force the door with a brutal pull, and the inertia swings it open roughly into her shoulder. The door gives her a sharp solid hit that spins her back a step. She makes a small, wordless sound, hurt or just surprised, I cannot tell. I do not walk away but stand watching her rub her shoulder. Her eyes peer at me without blinking, blaming me. With that I come back to myself. Whatever that was just now—not panic but near enough, something I have never really felt before and do not want to think about because it is a shameful thing—has passed, and I am here with Laurel again.

"That's what you want?" I ask softly. "To dismiss?"

"*Yes,* that's what I want," she tells me with disbelief and disappointment. I realize now, a moment too late, that she intended this morning to walk to court and dismiss the case against Haskin Pool. Somehow my knowing, when I had not before, changes everything, like magic. Despite knowing better, that is what she thought. She wanted me to do that for her, to make it possible. I wish I could rearrange the world that way, but I cannot.

"We can't dismiss," I say, my voice nearly gone.

She waits. She throws her arms down. "Don't you see, Giobberti? Don't you see that I cannot live with this thing anymore? I cannot."

"It's not as easy as that," I tell her as she starts to walk in a circle, her fists clenched. "This isn't about what you can live with, Laurel. We can't walk away." She is not listening to me. I say, "If Pool gets out, Laurel—Laurel, listen to me!" She stops circling. Her expression is a cocktail of hurt and sorrow and possibly contempt for me—pity, at least, but after all, pity is nothing less than a species of contempt, a milder iteration. "If we dismiss this case? If Pool gets out? Dellroy's dead, he's fucking dead, do you understand that?"

She shakes her head without much conviction. "Maybe Pool will—"

"What? Laugh the whole thing off? Hook up with Dellroy for a cigarette, maybe?" I nearly smile at her, seeing that even now she is not disabused of her instinctive, willing trust, which springs from the part of her that Luther mistook for naïveté. I say, "Pool doesn't know Heatly worked Dellroy, he just thinks Dellroy ratted him." I see from her eyes that she understands. "We've got to get Dellroy. He's got to testify," I tell her. "Running, he cut his own throat."

"No. No, I'm not putting him on the stand to lie."

"We have no choice—"

"No!"

I hesitate as the sound of her voice dies away inside the stairwell. Quietly I tell her, "There isn't a right move anymore, Laurel. There are only wrong moves left."

"I don't believe that," she says, a breathless whisper. I say nothing, so she asks me, "Giobberti, what do we do?"

"Find Dellroy, goddammit. I don't know."

"How can you not know? You're supposed to know." She does not believe me entirely, wanting me to reveal the answer that I am withholding. She pulls back and says, "What do we do—*now*, anyway? I mean, we need to be in court—God, ten minutes ago."

"We go to court, then," I say. "We make an opening statement. Play for time."

"Pretend nothing happened?" She laughs at the idea, then stops laughing. "That's your plan?"

Angry, ashamed, I say, "Then give me another plan, goddammit!"

"I don't have one!" she shouts right back.

"That's all I got, sister!"

We hang fire, looking into each other's eyes in the dimly lit stairwell. Improbably she starts to laugh again, lightly and infectiously, and I smile against my will, wondering what the hell now.

"What?" I say.

"I was just thinking," she says. "Maybe you shouldn't have gotten that haircut."

CHAPTER 18

Standing before the prosecution table, facing the jury, Laurel tells them a story. In her story a man dies and another man is responsible for it. She tells them a crime story, all of it true. She tells them how a man conceived of a robbery. She tells them about a bodega in East New York and the man who died. I sit up in my seat and listen as if it is the first time I am hearing this story, fascinated by it and by her, by her unwillingness to utter a single false word.

It is not enough for her, I know, that she speaks only the truth, for she withholds more than she tells. Yet somehow she seems to relish this. She needs this. She asked for this on our otherwise wordless walk to Schermerhorn Street. She asked me to let her open, and I knew why she asked, so I agreed. She asked so that I would not have to lie. She wanted to open—for me but mostly for herself. Her opening statement is a braided whip and I watch as she flagellates herself with it, ripping open great bloody tears of flesh along her back. She is Dimmesdale in his closet. I watch her and feel weak.

She tells them that the man responsible for the crime is right over there. She points, in general, with a wide sweep of her arm that encompasses Pool but also Heatly, and Fister, and Luther. The jury believes her; without knowing more than what she tells them, they believe her because the truth is in her and because Pool looks like a thug. She tells them that the evidence will prove Pool guilty, and here she turns and again points. She points at Pool now and at no one else. I see in her accusation, in the vehemence of it, the one thing that allows her to do this, the one aspect of this horror show that allowed her at least a fitful sleep these last six months: Pool is guilty. No matter what else, no matter who else, Pool is guilty. That is not enough, but it is a lot. As she points at Pool with her painted fingertip, and as her arm falls and the court-room goes dead in the vacuum following her accusation, she pauses. Here, her eyes meet mine for the first time since she stood before us all. She turns from Pool to me and seems for a heartbeat to falter, knowing that the diaphanous veil she has woven over the stinking turd in the corner of her story has been pulled momen-tarily away, because I know. I watch her expression soften, then build again in resolve. For an instant I think she may say to hell with it, that she may tear the veil fully away and show them. I imagine her pinning her gold shield on the foreman's lapel and walking out the back door, her heels clipping lightly, purposefully, over the varnished linoleum to the staircase, not even waiting for the elevator. But her eyes drop from mine and she resumes her statement, unwilling to let herself off that easily, unable to afford the extravagance of washing her hands. I feel a certain twinge of disappointment. In some way I feel responsible for it, her new appreciation of moral ambiguity.

I smile privately, though, when she does not call Pool *the defendant*. He is *Mr. Pool*. And we are still *the Government*.

Distracted, listening to her, thinking of her, thinking of my next move, I am startled when, after ten minutes, she sits. Next to me, she breathes with the subdued excitement of having done it. Gewirtz stirs. In the quiet that drops, everyone faces the bench, where the judge has slid out of view. The only indication that he is still with us is an elongated coil of beige telephone cord stretched taut across his desk. Presently I see the high leather bolster of his chair move, and then Gewirtz pulls himself straight and blinks at Laurel and says something inaudible. He looks at the jury and tells Yost, "Go ahead, ah, Mr. Yost," as if it were his fault.

Yost brings himself to his feet and walks to the jury box. Paging through yellow leaves overwritten in blue pen, he comes to a place in his legal pad marked with a sticky. One hand holds the pad, the other searches instinctively, unconsciously, along the frayed warp of his tie. "You know?" he starts, his gaze fixed upward. "You know? You know, I think I fell down that rabbit hole." A pause. The jury waits. "You know the hole I'm talkin about is that hole that the girl there—what's her name?—Alice. The hole Alice falls down, and everything inside it there is all upside down and topsy-turvy and all mixed up and what have you. Because I'm sittin there with my client, with Mr. Haskin there, and we're listenin to, ah, Miss Ashfield, and, ah—"

He keeps talking and I have heard it all before. A canned defense opening. Number sixteen. He is saying even less about what happened inside the bodega that morning than did Laurel, if possible. Yost's opening statement is all *reasonable doubt is a very high standard* and *the burden never shifts from the prosecution* and *keep an open mind, ladies and gentlemen.* While that goes on, Laurel listens attentively, or pretends well, but I slip her a corner torn from her legal pad, on which I have written a note. While Yost goes on and on, she pretends not to notice. Then, with an elliptical fingernail, she slides the note over the walnut Formica, but she does not read it yet.

"And you're gonna learn that a woman by the name of, ah"—Yost opens his legal pad—"Marjorie Henkis saw someone— someone she described as a 'beanpole,' ladies and gentlemen. A beanpole! She seen him leavin the scene! Runnin down the street! Around the corner from the grocery store! A beanpole! Look at my client. Please. Hello. Does he look like a beanpole?" Here Yost returns to the defense table and tells Pool to stand up.

"Object," I tell Laurel in a whisper without turning my head, but either she does not hear me or is ignoring me. "Objection," I say, standing. I cannot see Gewirtz, only the phone cord leading to the turned back of his chair. Yost and Pool face me. Pool remains seated, without expression. I repeat my objection, adding a *Your Honor* this time to get his attention. The judge's head peers around the chair. He sustains the objection, and I sit.

"What I'm sayin is there's room for reasonable doubt," Yost says. "And we already know that this Dellroy character—Miss Ashfield didn't bring him up, but I'm gonna bring him up. You bet I am. He's their main witness, and what do we know about him? Well, for starters, we know he's a liar—"

I face Laurel. Yost, in fact, faces Laurel. He drew the objection intentionally, calling Dellroy a liar for rhetorical effect; he wants the objection so he can throw up his hands and shrug at the jury when Gewirtz sustains it. She remains stock-still, however, not even moving her eyes.

" 'Jection," I lazily say, not even bothering to stand. Gewirtz sustains it, and Yost moves on with no theatrics.

188 • *Robert Reuland*

"Well," he says. "You're gonna learn that the very day of this incident, the police ask him, 'Did you see anything?' And guess what he says? 'No,' he says," and Yost goes on and on, working it, and Gewirtz has submerged again, leaving only a periscope of hair visible above the edge of the bench. My note to Laurel, my little joke, is still in her fingers. She reads it at last, inclining her head imperceptibly. *We're fucked.* I suppose she does not remember the other note, still tucked beneath the peeling Formica. Perhaps she remembers but simply does not think my note is very funny. When she does nothing other than pinch the paper slip between her fingers and let it drop unobtrusively to the floor, I decide that it is not funny at all.

Gewirtz calls a recess, and I watch the jury walk in an obedient line toward the back door and see Cully sitting there but not Pool's family. Cully rises with surprising agility and walks toward me as I step into the gallery.

"Hell was that?" he asks me, sounding angry and making a gesture of disbelief. He is speaking loud enough for Laurel to hear, so I take hold of his arm—thin, like an old man's arm. I walk him several steps away. He is saying, "She didn't say squat, am I right? Just a lot of blather."

"Just—"

"I mean, you listen to her and you think all Pool did was put the evil eye on the guy. And Yost is right. Why in fuck didn't she tell them she had a witness to all this? What's his name, Dellroy? I mean, Jesus! She's not going to open with her witness?"

"Her first homicide, Cully. All right? Cut her a break."

"First homicide. More going on than that," he says with a queer stare. "I think the both a youse are in the shitter. For what it's worth."

Gewirtz's clerk has walked over to us. He stands there holding a piece of paper in his two hands. "You stand up on a plea?" he wants to know. "Judge is bringing him up now, and the ADA on the plea ain't here."

"Can't get an elevator," Cully says to the clerk, "probably," and I ask Cully how he got here. "Judge's elevator," Cully tells me, and I hear him jingle his key ring to prove it as I return to the well with the clerk. "You better give me something when you feel more chatty, boy-o," Cully says.

"Let's go, People. Let's go," Gewirtz is saying before I have even gotten to my table, where Laurel still sits. She does not appear to see me when I come over. She is moving her pen over the tabletop, pushing it around in a circle with her index finger. Gewirtz says, "Step up, Mr. Hyman. Let's go," and the lawyer on the plea is standing at the defense table, crowding Yost. Mr. Hyman evidently does not have a comb. Or a liver. He is rooting through his lit bag with two hands. Things fall out of it onto the floor. The clerk calls the case in. "This your case, Mr. Giobberti?" Gewirtz asks.

"No, Judge. This is a negotiated plea," I say by rote. "The People rely upon the prior negotiations."

"Mr. Hyman," Gewirtz says, "do you or your client wish to say anything before I impose sentence?"

"Hey!" someone says, and I turn in the direction of the voice, to the defense table, where Valentino Burton is standing in handcuffs between Mr. Hyman and the court officer who just brought him out. "ADA Goberry," Burton says. "Whassup, cuz?"

"Hey, bro," I say. "Guess they ain't drop it."

He shrugs. "Three months on Rikers. I do that shit in my *sleep*. Ha ha ha!"

Then Gewirtz puts him in. "Take charge," Gewirtz says when

it is over, and Burton is led out again, still chained to himself. Halfway to the door behind the bench, however, he stops walking and is too strong for the court officer on his arm to do anything about it. He turns to me and says, "I call you, Goberry. I seen some shit since I get out—nah sayin?"

I nod and turn to Laurel, wanting to smile at her over what just happened, only to see her walking away without a word. She walks to the back door, and I follow. I walk past Cully, who stands, thinking I am returning to talk to him. I walk through the swinging back door into an oddly partitioned space of impromptu Sheetrock hallways and drywall offices in a once spacious foyer where a beaux-arts chandelier still blossoms from a coffered ceiling, burning fluorescent bulbs. There I walk over the echoing terrazzo floor past windows screwdriven shut to keep despairing prisoners from breaking from their escort and leaping to their deaths down airshafts that the sunlight never touches. Turning a corner, I see Laurel on a bench, alone. The hallway is empty but for a civil lawyer schlepping a boxy lit bag on an airport wheelie and talking on a cell phone in pure fluent low-rent legal. I sit next to her.

Laurel says nothing for a moment, and then she says, "I feel like—shit."

From her tongue the word is vivid and new. We do not talk. When I feel I can, I say her name, and she tries to change the subject, telling me, "I called the Seven-Five."

"Laurel."

"I talked to Lieutenant Moss," she says. "But even if—"

"Laurel."

"Even if they get him," she says, ignoring me but turning to me. Her expression is dead, but her eyes glisten like polished stones under cold water. "Even if. What then? Are we going to put him on the stand? And have him say—what, exactly?" She is not on the verge of tears, I see, nor any great emotional display, but not because she is one of those women who cannot cry or refuse to. Perhaps, like Ann, she cries during airline commercials and other small, unwarranted moments, simultaneously laughing at herself because she knows she is oh so predictable that way. This, however, I imagine Laurel Ashfield has cried out long ago. The tears have hardened her, calcified into a salty pillar in some dark place within her. Yet seeing her expression, the utter desolation written there, jars me. I do not answer her question, knowing it would be pointless.

She stands. "You asked me yesterday why I wanted to work here," she says. "I remembered thinking that I could—I don't know—do good. I thought I would always know what to do, and I'd just have to do it." She sits again and leans forward with her elbows on her knees. "And what I don't understand is now—*now,* by doing the right thing, by dismissing, we end up doing something so . . ."

I nod. "And the other way around," I tell her. "Don't forget. If Haskin goes upstate, that's a good day's work."

"I don't know, Giobberti. He deserves it. God, he deserves it, but that's not really the point, is it? If that was what this is about, we should just send Valentino Burton that pair of Air Jordans." She gestures with her hand in the direction of the courtroom and then glances at me before turning away. In her short glance I see something that chills me—she had not seriously considered it, of course, but she considered it. For an insignificant moment, she considered it: a moment so brief as not to be a moment at all, and yet it was a moment longer than she would have spent conspiring to murder, a few short days ago, before meeting me.

"The job is shoveling shit, Laurel," I say carefully. "You're gonna get some on your hands."

192 • *Robert Reuland*

She says to me, "The worst thing about—*this*. Almost the worst thing, anyway, is I don't trust myself anymore to do the right thing. I don't know what's right anymore." She goes on, "I'm just going to leave it to you. You'll have to do what you think. Whatever you do, I'll be okay with."

We hold each other's eyes. "So you trust me?"

"I don't trust myself." Without fanfare, she tells me, "I know where he is. Dellroy. That is, I have a pretty good idea." I nod and wait for her, and she seems to have a second thought. She tells me anyway. "With Santra Flowers."

I recall the name. "The friend? Who brought him down?" She nods and says nothing more. I do not ask her how she knows, but having told me, she wants to tell me something else. I can see that, but I know that if I reach too fast, she will give ground beyond me; like trying to catch a cat.

After a time she says, "Pool killed her brother. She saw it."

I remember Pool's conviction when he was eighteen, the one that earned him his street name—*Convict*. I ask her if that is what she means, but she says no. "Who's her brother, then?" I ask her.

"Lashawn Sims." Her voice is factual; her eyes, in contrast, watch me expectantly.

"Sims—*Slim?*" I ask immediately. "Her brother is Slim?" She nods. "Santra saw this?" I ask her, my mind working again after a morning given over entirely to self-pity and lethargy. Now I have something. "You said she saw it." She does not answer me right away and seems not to like how my voice has changed.

"No, Giobberti," she says, but it is not an answer to my question. "No, I didn't tell you so you could—"

"Laurel, goddammit—enough!"

"No," she says, shaking her head slowly and saying, "No. She won't testify."

"It's her brother, for chrissake!"

"She *knew*," Laurel says. "She knew what Heatly was up to. Don't you understand? She was there all night with me. And I promised her— God! I must have sounded just like Luther!"

"Heatly let Dellroy off!" I say, absurdly revitalized all of a sudden. I have to stand. "What's her bitch with that?"

"You don't understand. Santra, she never wanted Dellroy *off*." She says the word with a slight contemptuous inflection, batting it right back to me, accusing me of something. In a milder tone she says, "It's the way she is. She brought him down there to tell the truth." She shakes her head and says to herself, "She must think I'm—"

"Does Heatly know about her?"

"No," she says, her fight nearly gone. "I mean, I don't know. We never talked about her. We never talked much at all."

I walk to a window opening onto the airshaft. I stand there and try to add it all up, trying once more to arrange the pieces in this vertiginous chess match, to snatch them from midair and hold them in place a moment, at least. I feel Laurel behind me, waiting. Without turning, I ask her, "Santra can ID Pool?"

"Leave her alone," she tells me. I turn and ask her again in a voice that she must answer. She nods. "He doesn't know about her, does he?" I realize, saying it aloud. "Pool doesn't know she was there."

"No," she says.

"Tell me."

"Oh, Giobberti, does it really—"

"Tell me."

Her shoulders fall farther, and without emotion, as if reading from an uninteresting menu, she tells me, "Santra saw it from her bedroom window. Pool killed him outside. On the stoop. She came in with Dellroy. That night." She fixes me with her eyes because she knows what I am thinking. "He would kill her, too. You know that."

"You brought her in?"

"I tried. It's no good."

"You tried," I repeat, angry because no matter how impossible it was, Santra did not come in. "How'd you try? You subpoena her to the grand jury or—"

"No!" she says, shouting. "She won't testify."

"Why the hell not?"

"Can you blame her? I don't trust us, either."

"Jesus Christ." I kick a steam radiator, but it does not help.

CHAPTER 19

In the tenth-floor men's room three unindicted murderers loiter in the corner and do not care if I care. I don't. They are part of the topography of my world, and I would not give them a second thought even if this were any other Thursday morning. I enter the stall and a toilet flushes nearby. I read the familiar graffiti and watch a caramel-colored cockroach gamely swim in a circle, looking for purchase on the enamel bowl. I finish my business and walk to the sink, where a little man wearing a beret is washing his hands. He turns to me in surprise, and a gray, inky vortex swirls down the drain. "I didn't think they'd have soap!" he says. I smile in answer, and the man is very satisfied and helps himself to some more soap. I put water on my face, and of course there are no paper towels. Soap but no paper towels. The man in the beret leaves, shaking dry his hands and pushing against the door with his shoulder. The water is dripping down my neck, under my collar, and I stand hunched and immobilized by indecision.

I ask my reflection, "Hell you gonna do, asshole?"

I say it as a sort of joke to myself, the spare locker-room atmosphere of the men's room prompting me to give myself a pep talk, but the way it sounds against the baritone murmur of the wise guys in the corner makes me realize I have no answer.

We're fucked.

The three boys walk out and I turn, dripping, to follow when Yost walks in. He gives me a brief self-conscious nod, as men do in men's rooms. He leaves the stall door open, and in the mirror I can see the left side of him as he stands there with legs spread. I am nearly to the door when, from the stall, Yost calls out, "You got that kid Dellroy, huh?"

I could say something different, or nothing, but what I say is "Talked to him couple days ago." Something in Yost's tone tells me that is the right thing to say.

"Kinda surprised my guy," Yost says. He reappears, zippering his fly and not flushing, not washing his hands. I am leaning, with crossed arms, against one of the sinks in a long row. Yost faces me with his hands in his pockets, rocking on his beat wing tips. Turning to inspect his tie in the cracked mirror, he says, "A real surprise, anyway. 'Specially if he sits in the box. When's that gonna be, anyway? Today?"

"That would spoil the surprise, Yost. If I told you."

"You wanna bet he don't?" He is inspecting his chin in the mirror. "Five dollars, say?"

"Never bet on a trial—bad karma."

"Like haircuts. So they say." He turns from the mirror and steps closer to me. "Listen, Gio. This kid a mine? He can throw out some bad karma himself. Not that I wanna know about any of it, like I say."

"Marty," I say, shaking my head and deciding to bluff it out. "Guess what happens if Dellroy goes missing? What happens if I prove Pool's been calling Dellroy from Rikers, and not just to catch up on old times?"

"Mm?" Yost narrows his eyes.

"I'll move for a Sirois hearing." I put an index finger on him and say, "I don't need Dellroy to testify, Marty. Fuck, I don't *want* him to testify. Jury hears your boy scared him away? You lose, Yost." He looks me up and down. "So tell *Mr. Haskin* next time he picks up the phone I'm gonna be pissing on him from the other end. Right?"

I open the door to leave and Yost snatches at my arm. I do not like it, and he lets go. "Gio. Giobberti, wait," he says, his voice having lost its brazen edge, having returned nearly to its usual wheedling pitch. "Here. Shut the door. Shut the door, will ya? I don't wanna talk to you out there. Kid sees me talkin to you all the time. The mother and them, too. Don't like me bein too friendly. Nothin personal." I nod. "Just listen, Gio," he says. "Here's the situation. I'm not sayin that the kid will bite, but let's just say for the sake of argument you get your Dellroy Dunn. Say you can get him in the box. Just hypothetically, say."

"A plea?" I ask, shaking my head more from surprise, but Yost takes it as a rejection out of hand.

"Listen," he says, moving his fingers in front of him as if adjusting the knobs in a shower. "Before you say no—"

"What's he want?" I ask. I ask it as if no possible answer could please me.

"Let me talk to my guy," Yost says. "But you gotta, you know—you gotta give me somethin I can *work* with. Give me an offer I can take to the kid."

"Man Two. Fifteen straight."

"Manslaughter," he says, rubbing his chin. "Can't do better than fifteen years? Say ten. I coulda got fifteen from the judge without your okay."

"Fifteen to life, you coulda got. I'm offering a straight fifteen."

"Come on, Gio. I'm not even sayin the kid will take it—just give me somethin. So I look good. To the kid. What do you say? Give me the ten fuckin years."

I do not answer, and someone walks into the bathroom. Yost and I both shut up. We walk out together, but in the hallway Yost is not so voluble anymore, and he twists his head anxiously from side to side to see if anyone can see us together. Pool's family, for instance. They are not here. Nor are the two cops I notified to be here—filler witnesses, to give the jury something to do while I think about what to do. Later they will show up with a coffee for me. The foyer outside Gewirtz's courtroom is lifeless. Under his breath, Yost tells me to think about it.

"I'll think about it," I say, and realize that whatever else this means, it may solve one of my smaller problems. "But listen, Marty. I gotta—you know—go to my boss on this."

"No problem."

"So I gotta have a day."

"I'll agree to an adjournment."

"No, you're gonna take the adjournment. Tell Gewirtz you got a doctor's appointment or something. Tell him you got a boil on your ass, too."

"He'll shit a brick," Yost says. We are standing together outside the doorway of Gewirtz's courtroom. We are late, and through the crack between the door and the jamb I can see that already the jury has been brought in. Gewirtz is walking around behind the bench, clearly wondering where the hell Yost and I are.

I shrug. "What can I say, Yost? You want me to look into this offer for you or what?"

Yost sighs with the usual resignation. "All right, all right. So I got a boil on my ass. But you get me that ten, Giobberti."

My lunch is on white butcher paper, on my desk, my desk in my office in Appeals. A better lunch today than my last lunch in this office, three noontimes ago.

Lunch today is something on whole-wheat bread that Laurel picked up. Whole wheat with a whitish paste that is not mayonnaise and something firm that is not meat. The alfalfa sprouts I have already scooped out with two fingers and a thumb. They lie in my wastebasket in a hairy ball; there is only so far I can go. I am wiping my fingers on a recycled paper napkin when I see Mark Luther standing in the doorway with the same hang-dog expression Bloch wore when last I sat here, before I would eat this sort of thing, before I would not lose any sleep if I learned that a seventeen-year-old boy had been found dead in some alleyway in East New York, a single bullet making a bindi on his forehead. Now I would. Now I want to see Dellroy Dunn make it to twenty-one. After that he is on his own, but today I've got his back.

"What do you want, Luther?" I say, without any real bite. I will get around to him later. For the moment he is just a nuisance.

"This . . . statement," he says, holding Laurel's legal pad, a neutral expression on his face. "Interesting."

"Let's go. I'm on trial."

"Good. Good. That was my second question. Make sure you're not thinking about anything . . . rash." He smiles his smile, and I wait. He comes closer. He sets the pad on my desktop and raps it once with a finger. The smile goes slack presently, and he says, "Look, I can guess what you're thinking, but listen. We never knew about it, you know."

"*We?*" I ask.

"I never knew," he says. "I never seen it—that's what I'm here telling you, whatever you think."

"*I?* First-person singular. You said *we*. First-person plural, Luther. Who the fuck is *we?*" He watches me, amazed, because he knows where this leads and because the arrangement of his world does not let him believe I would go there. I am speaking heresy into his pre-Copernican ears. *Yes, Luther, the world is round, and I will take this where it must go, but right now let me finish my—sandwich*. "Just say it, Luther. Just goddamn say it. Fister never knew about the statement."

"No. He didn't."

"But he knew about everything else, didn't he," I say, waiting for him to deny it. He does not. "Jesus. Whitey knew."

"It's political," Luther says. "You don't understand."

"*It's political*," I say, and I say it seriously, very seriously, as Luther tried and failed to do just now: to make it all sound like the work of deep and dangerous men. Men who bend the rules because *it had to be done—in the interest of—blah, blah, blah*.

"There's more going on here than you know," he says in the same tone.

"Give me a fucking break."

"Giobberti, you—"

"You schmuck. This isn't—a John Grisham novel. This is just Fister and you. That's all this is."

"Don't be so damn—" Luther gives me his cold stare that tells me he is not going to take much more of this. "We arrested a killer. Don't forget that."

"So everyone's happy. The *News* lays off Fister. Fister gets to swing his balls a little. Is that it, Luther?" I stand and put my fists on the desk, leaning in to Luther. "Meanwhile, you got someone down there—a woman who would bleed for this job. And you let her twist in the wind on this."

"No one made her do nothing."

"The hell would you know?" I ask.

"She went along," Luther says, smugly indifferent.

"Bullshit she went along."

"*Bullshit?*" he says. "Fucking ask her."

"I did."

"And what did she say?" he asks. "That I made her? I threatened her? If she said I did, she's a liar."

"She trusted you."

"She saw what it was and she let it ride. Why can't you?"

"And what is it?" I ask, knowing better.

"It's the job. It's putting people like this little criminal in jail."

I shake my head involuntarily. "Not this way, Luther. Not like this."

"Would you—! Would you listen to yourself?" Luther says, smiling with disbelief. "You got a lotta ass, talking like that after what you pulled."

"Here we go. Yeah."

"Listen to you. Going on about your morals. Standing there looking at me like I'm—" His face contorts as he says it, accusing himself of something. He opens a window on himself, but I do not care enough to look. He does not interest me, and the moment passes soon enough. "Well, screw you, too, buddy," he tells me, meaning it. "I don't give a crap what you think of me. You're entitled to your opinion, but you owe him. You owe Fister."

I sit, suddenly tired of this conversation. Mildly, I say, "That's what this is? Payback?"

"You want to make this thing big, then yeah." I do not answer, and it seems that Luther feels the tide of this argument turn to him. In truth, there is not a lot I can say. He steps closer to my desk, after having retreated a step earlier. In fact, he lowers his voice. "You let her go," Luther tells me. "That mother what pooped her own kid. Fister let you pretend you didn't know, but you knew. You knew, didn't you? How's that any different than this?"

"You can't turn this around—"

"Hell I can't," Luther tells me. "We had no case against this murdering Pool fuck. And Heatly made it. He made the case. This woulda been the second body this kid skated on. This is how we do it. This is how we put this kid inside for the rest of his life."

I listen and wait for him to leave, but he does not leave. He says, "What you did with that mother? You read the law and said, *Fuck that, I know better.* How's this different? Tell me." I shake my head. Luther gains momentum. "And something else for you to think about: if I'm crossing the line, okay? If I'm crossing the line, it's to put a killer—*a fucking murderer*—in jail." Luther pauses. I hear him breathe. "That's what we do here, Giobberti. We put the people who kill people in jail. We don't let them go home to their families. Because we feel sorry for them. You read me?"

I stand again and walk to the window to get away from him. He does not let me. Now he is behind me.

"Heatly made a case, Giobberti," he says. "He threw Dellroy a break—so what! I mean, you talk to this kid? He's a fucking retard!"

I turn to him and say, "When did you see him?"

"Who?" he asks, and a vertical line appears on his forehead. I see the line on his forehead and the triangle of smooth skin on his scalp that shows where his hair once was. "What are you saying?"

"Dellroy," I say. "You talked to him at the precinct, didn't you? The night he came in."

After a moment, he says, "Does that really matter?"

"No, not really," I say. "But you're wrong about one thing."

"What's that?"

"We have no case. All your hard work, Luther, and we still have no case," I say. Luther does not understand but he concedes nothing. "He skipped," I tell him. "I haven't had him for two days."

He reacts, giving a skeptical wave.

"I got no case, Luther. And even if by some fucking *miracle* Dellroy Dunn shows up in my office tomorrow morning, I'm not using him. I'm not putting him on the stand to lie."

"You're not—is that what you just told me, counselor?" Luther says, not believing me yet, or not entirely. I am not certain I believe it, either.

"I'm not," I say. He puts his hands into his pockets. "Go now," I tell him.

"All right, Giobberti. I'll leave." He thrusts his chin upward before he turns and starts to walk out. By my desk he pauses to pick up Dellroy's written statement, and at the door he stops. Without turning entirely around, he says, "They used to call it hindering prosecution, what your girlfriend did." He lingers there so I can get his drift. He could shut up there and walk out, but Luther feels the need to be more blunt, to tell me more specifically what he is going to do with the weapon I handed him this morning. "Maybe it's obstructing justice. The penal law was never my strong suit. You can figure that out, smart guy. Something else for you to think about. Before you go and do something stupid."

I am upon him in two steps. He holds his ground, but I drive an index finger into his breast. Beneath his suit and vest and carnation he is all packed muscle. "Get your meathooks off me," he says.

"Hear me now, Luther—I will lay you out. I will lay you out and Fister with you."

He seems to consider a response in kind, yet all he says is "You're done here." There is no inflection in his voice when he says it, no rancor, no emotion, and all at once I have no energy to say anything more.

CHAPTER 20

"Something else I was** thinking—" Laurel starts to say to me before I interrupt her. We are sitting on the gray velour backseat of a
Crown Victoria in the midafternoon, and she is speaking as she
has spoken during the five miles of this drive out to East New
York: in her delicate whisper that the office detective at the wheel
cannot hear, that I myself can barely hear over the radio he has di-
aled to *All Sinatra, All the Time.*

"Listen, Laurel," I say, cutting her off at last, tired of ideas
and thinking about them. Mostly tired of not having any, or any
good ones, anyway, or answers; just questions without answers—
just one answer: that there is no answer. "We got another problem.
Not a problem, really, but—anyway. Remember that hypothetical
question? If your only witness dies on the eve of trial, would . . ."

"Gio?" She turns. Her voice is full of horror. Her hands reach to her face, which has abruptly drained.

"Oh—no," I say. "He's not—not that I know, anyway." Her arms fall heavily back onto her lap. "I'm sorry," I tell her, but she turns away.

At a stoplight a yellow pickup pulls up beside us, its suspension lowered; it looks like a short-legged terrier. Overtaxed speakers distort Spanish music into a fringe-edged thump audible through my closed window, over Sinatra.

"You started to say something," she tells me, her voice curt, after we drive another five blocks. She faces her window, although there is nothing to see. This block of Atlantic Avenue is low-rent commercial, with gas stations and car-parts stores and storefronts a hundred years old retailing car alarms and cell phones and beepers. Some are boarded up. Livery cabs dart around us, changing lanes without signaling. Now we get jammed up between a panel truck and a flatbed. Traffic stops, but there are no horns. The detective chirps the siren, but no one can do anything about it, so we wait. We are caught beside a sequence of R.I.P. paintings on roll-up window gates. Tombstones, and five-foot-tall heads wearing earrings, and crucifixes. LI'L JULIO, one reads in bubble letters sprayed in white and neon green, DEAD BUT NOT FORGOT. Then the siren chirps again, overloud in the cold quiet, and a heavy shoe on the accelerator sends the Crown Vic forward again, pushing Laurel and me against the velour.

This is Brooklyn, too, I am thinking. *There is her Brooklyn, there is mine, and then there is this*—we are passing through Brownsville, over the hill into the periphery of East New York. Pool's Brooklyn. So she is from Brooklyn after all, but what does that signify? Irrelevant as the hue of our flesh. She is from Brooklyn, but all that means is she is not from anywhere else. She is not from Chillicothe, Ohio.

"I talked to Yost this morning," I tell her. "And I was remembering that hypothetical we were talking about. If your defendant says he wants to plead guilty before trial and your witness is dead—"

"I remember," she says, sitting up very straight. She understands. "Haskin wants a plea?"

"Yes. Maybe."

"To what?" she says, her voice no longer a whisper.

"Man Two," I say.

"Time?"

"I said fifteen," I tell her. "Yost is looking for ten, but if that's where we are, then we got a deal. He goes up and I go down and we're done."

"Why didn't you tell me until now?" She is very excited.

"I figured you'd say no," I tell her, remembering her answer to Fister's interview question, and remembering my answer to her answer—that she needed to see something of the world. I suppose that now, two days later, she has seen something of it. I know that even when she told me her answer Tuesday morning, she had already seen more of the world than I gave her credit for. Still, I am thinking that today she may answer the question differently, and I am sorry for that. I blame myself, in a way.

"God," she says in uncertain anticipation. "Gio—"

"I don't know if Pool wants anything, anyway. This was just Yost's idea."

"Do you think Yost knows? Do you think Pool told him about Dellroy?"

"I doubt it," I say. "And if he did, Yost wouldn't believe him." Laurel nods. "Even if Yost believed it," I say, "where's that get Pool? Pool can't point the finger at Dellroy without pointing it at himself." She nods at that, too. Pool is flypapered to the truth—as we are to the lie.

"He won't take fifteen," she says after a pause, trying to sound skeptical to avoid sounding hopeful. I agree with a nod, and she thinks about it, her eyes bright but fixed. Then she abruptly asks me what we should do about it.

"It's a damn fine plea," I tell her. "Case like this—hell."

"That's not what I'm asking, though," she says, and I know she is not thinking about the plea but about what it would mean for us to offer it to Pool. I am talking about the plea to avoid talking about the other thing, but she makes me talk about it, saying, "You know what I'm asking, don't you?"

"Yes," I tell her. Then, "So what's your answer?"

"Are we talking about the hypothetical or . . . ?"

"The hypothetical."

"I already gave you my answer," she tells me. "I wouldn't take it. It's based on a lie." Her prim, reedy voice again, which I have not heard in a day. She is too emphatically certain, however, for me to believe she means it wholeheartedly. "I'd tell the defendant my witness was dead."

"What if the defendant is who bumped your witness?" I ask.

She nearly bites a nail. Instead she presses it into her cheek, creating a hollow but drawing no blood. She says, "I guess he'd already know, then. Wouldn't he?"

In this overcast block of East New York, shadowy even in the mid-afternoon, Laurel seems unwilling to walk away from the car. All is thickly quiet. When we shut our doors, pigeons fly from telephone wires, and the sudden winged flutter of the birds makes Laurel start. Behind windows of the three-story houses—all of them attached to one another, all of them fronted by little stoops with metal handrails—curtains are pulled back and spectral faces appear.

The detective asks me a second time if I want him to come inside. I tell him no. The girl is not going to like this scene much, as it is. She will like it even less if we come unannounced into her home with a detective smelling of cologne and gunpowder. He nods and tells me he will be back in thirty minutes, and the unmarked car leaves me standing alone with Laurel on the sidewalk. The cold makes the exhaust plume from the tailpipe as the detective floors it down Blake Avenue, the way cops always drive.

"Here we are. Hansel and Gretel," I say, but her mood is somber all of a sudden. "Where is it?" I ask, and she starts to walk. I follow her to a narrow house like all the others. Santra Flowers's house is redbrick with a single bay window to the left of the stoop, and three windows each on the two floors above. Three doorbells. Three apartments off a common stairway. Laurel reaches around me, pressing the bottom bell. Nothing happens, and after a full minute I press the bell again. Then I back down the stoop to the cement walkway leading to the house. I see nothing in the windows. In the one closest to the stoop, a bay window, the pink cloth blinds are drawn tight, and there is too much daylight to tell whether there are any lights behind them. Laurel, her hands pressed together, stands on the stoop, which I now remember is a crime scene. The bay window is Santra's, then. The pink curtains are Santra's.

From inside comes the sound of a deadbolt sliding open. I rejoin Laurel. Through a porthole in the door, finger-smeared glass reinforced with chicken wire, I see a woman peering out. I take out my wallet and tin her, and all she says is *What*. I say I am with the D.A.

"Jus' a minute."

The woman's face disappears from the porthole and nothing happens. Across the street four boys have arrived on three bicycles. One sits on the handlebars. They ride the bicycles in tight concentric circles until one of them drops his; the others squeal and point. Already their voices are cruel. Hearing them, Laurel turns but says nothing. Then the woman reappears. She opens the front door, which leads into a small foyer paved with encaustic tiles from another century, shaped into a geometric pattern and mostly broken up. A single lightbulb hangs from the ceiling on a wire. Another door separates the foyer from the common hallway, and that door is kept open with a wooden block. There is that boardinghouse smell of cats and dank carpets and the slightly nauseating hint of other people's dinner.

I tell her, "I'm looking for Santra Flowers."

"What you want her for?" She stands pulling a shapeless robe around her shoulders, which are very thick and round.

"She's not in trouble, ma'am."

She snorts a laugh without altering her dull expression. "Santra couldn't be in trouble if she tried," she says, pointedly withholding anything more. She squints at Laurel in the weak light. "Ain't you that same D.A. that was here?" she asks her.

"Yes, Miss Flowers," Laurel answers. "It's Laurel Ashfield."

"Oh, I din't recognize you." The woman's face brightens. "Wait here and I bring her out." She turns and heavily walks away, her shape filling the narrow hallway. She disappears into the black at the hallway's far end, and I hear a door close, and whispered voices. Someone down there is waiting by the door. I turn and see, through the glass porthole, as if in a fog, the kids on bicycles. All of the bicycles are too small, and the kids' knees come up when they ride. Dellroy must have watched their older brothers, longing to belong.

"Santra," Laurel says at that moment, and I turn around. A girl appears, or rather the form of a thin girl whose face I cannot see. She is watching us behind large glasses that reflect the bulb overhead. She says nothing, but she comes toward us and into the light. Laurel tells her who I am and the girl nods; she knew already. She is a slight girl with fine, delicate features obscured by her eyeglasses: great rimless ovals that glint in rainbow refractions as she turns from Laurel to me and back. The three of us stand there, none of us ready to speak. The air seems close around us, as if it could carry the vibration of our voices for miles, as the ocean carries whales' songs from one continent to another. All of us know what this is about, but none of us wants to say it.

"Santra, I—" I start to say before she interrupts me, and my voice, slow and easy, is a voice you use for someone standing on a ledge, the voice I use for young boys who see their fathers killed by strangers, their mothers killed by their fathers. There is about Santra's manner, her slim, flat-chested form, that same vulnerable quality, although I put her age at eighteen or even twenty.

She nods when I speak, as a child would nod, quickly, but she cuts me short and with a voice I do not expect tells me, "You're here for Dellroy."

"Yes."

"He's not going to testify," she says, and I was wrong about her. Her voice is not a child's voice, and she is no child. She is not in awe of me. She is telling me politely to go to hell. More—she is telling me that whatever I have seen out there, she has seen it, too, so I will not get over on her with the usual, with my psychological whatever.

I face Laurel, but her expression is ambivalent. "He's here?" I ask Santra.

"Does that matter?" she says. Something in her voice, in her eyes—which are lit intelligently behind the glass—suggests to me an instant familiarity, and I am wondering if we have met, or if she testified for me in a forgotten trial. If she recognizes me, however, she says nothing about that. "He's not testifying," she says again, no longer defiant. She states it as a fact, as if stipulating the color of his eyes for a form I am filling out.

"Santra—" Laurel starts.

"You people," Santra says to me, not to Laurel, and she sounds almost amused. "You want him to tell the truth now? You told him that, didn't you? Now you want him to tell the truth?" I do not answer. "The truth," she says, saying the word with an open irony. "As if you people care about that."

"Santra, please," Laurel says.

"It's too late for that!" she says to Laurel, now angry. "He told you the truth!"

I am quiet, thinking it best to let Santra get it out. Laurel waits, too, cowed by the ropy girl standing in front of her. With her long coat still on, Laurel seems twice her height—like an American in a *National Geographic,* standing before a native in a far-off land. "You come around with your lies and promises," Santra tells her, her voice breaking. "Why should we trust you people anymore?"

Her anger is for Laurel. While Santra generalizes to me and nameless others, she means everything for Laurel alone. "Santra," I say at last, and both women turn to me, almost with relief, but before I can say anything more, the door opens down the hallway, and standing there, backlit by a wan yellow light, is Dellroy Dunn. He walks over, hands in the pockets of the crotch-hanging blue jeans that give him a saddle-sore cowboy stride.

"I know you." He says this to Laurel.

Laurel does not know how to answer. Her eyes go to Santra, as if seeking her permission, and says only, "Hello, Dellroy."

"Hello," he answers in a gentle voice. He fixes Laurel with his good eye and his mouth makes a shy, self-aware smile. Again we are standing under the bare bulb not knowing what happens next, although now there are four of us. Dellroy still sees just Laurel; if he recognizes me, he gives no indication. Santra crosses her arms, and I see that a patch of pigment on her right wrist is missing, as if oxidized by spilled bleach. She wears her watch on that arm, the band partially hiding it.

"I need to speak to him," I say to her.

"Well, you can't," Santra tells me, inserting her narrow body between Dellroy and me. "I want you to go now. You have to leave if I tell you. That's the law. Isn't it the law?" Behind her lenses I see the black and white of her eyes in the dim light. She is right— we have to leave. Nor is there any point in keeping at her, I can see that. I turn away, but Laurel does not. I take hold of her arm, yet she stands fixed in place.

"Santra—" Laurel starts, but Santra turns on her, as if she has been waiting for an excuse.

"No!" Santra says, telling her what Laurel wanted to say to me Monday. "No. I'm through with you. With all of you. You change the rules. You . . . play with people. With our lives! Get out."

"Santra, that's not—" Laurel tries to say, but again she has to yield and stand listening.

"You say you care, but you don't. You say you want to help, but what do you do? You lie. And you want Dellroy to lie for you."

"Stop it, Santra," Laurel says, resorting to her mother's voice, trying to reestablish some moral authority over the girl but failing. She ends by saying weakly, "You know that's not fair."

"Then why is he here?" Santra says, not loudly. She makes a quick gesture at Dellroy, who stands with a guilty floorward stare, wrongly believing this is about him. If this business between the women started over Dellroy, it is now about something else. Santra watches Laurel in a way that puts me miles distant. Like Dellroy, I am a voyeur here, watching a private dialogue come at last to a sordid denouement beneath a hanging bulb. Santra's expression (her flickering eyelids give the lie to her slightly haughty upturned chin) exposes a shared history of many hours with Laurel before this afternoon. There was the night spent together in the Seven-Five, waiting for Dellroy, as there must have been other nights, other days—Lashawn Sims's funeral, I realize, and other hours spent in this very house while they talked about that, and about other things I will never know about. I see them together in the room with the pink curtains overlooking the cement stoop. No, they are hardly strangers. A stranger cannot betray you, and that is what Santra believes happened. "He trusted you," she says. "I trusted you—and look! Who's going to help him now? Where's he going to go?"

"Santra," Laurel says. "You know this was not my—"

"You—" Santra gives Laurel a sharp, merciless stare. "Everything you told me. I believed everything you told me."

"Santra, please."

"You come out here. With your ideas. About everything. But you don't see anything. You never seen your brother shot, have you? You come out here with your promises, but you don't know how it is."

I take Laurel's arm again, and this time she yields gratefully to me; she becomes pliant at once in my grip. I pull her around to me, and she feels very light, nearly hollow. We turn through the doorway, and in the daylight Laurel's pallor is frightening.

Santra calls from the doorway as we step onto the cement walk, "So just—go back. Just go back where you're from. Stay out of here, because you don't know where you're at!"

Behind us the door closes and we wait together. There is nothing to say. Across the street the boys have left. We wait in the still afternoon until the gray car pulls up, and then we drive away. In the backseat I sit and stare stupidly out the window and listen to Sinatra crooning "Night and Day," and after we pass it, I realize we have driven by the bodega on Sutter. I turn and see it in the rear window. The metal window gates are drawn and padlocked and overwritten with graffiti. One reads GOMEZ PEACE! Laurel is silent until Crown Heights, and then she asks the detective in a businesslike voice to take her home. She gives the address. When she steps out, I follow.

CHAPTER 21

Across from me, on the other side of her kitchen table, Laurel sits and watches her daughter without expression. There is a book in my hand. *The Tale of Jemima Puddle-Duck*. Faye, pajamaed, brought it to me, offering it with eyes huge and earnest. She had been sent to bed a half hour earlier, and in that time Laurel and I have gotten nowhere. Now Faye waits until Laurel says her name. Laurel says it in two syllables in the same vacant voice she used with me before Faye got out of bed. Faye says nothing but looks at the book, then at me. I feel guiltily complicit, because I want to read to her as much as she wants me to read to her. Laurel secretly welcomes the interruption of her daughter, I think. We are each sick of the other by now, sick of the other's face and answers, sick of talking, just sick; we are talking only to avoid thinking, coasting uphill on momentum, nearly spent, waiting for the long slow slide back into the inevitable dirty conclusion of this dirty business.

Ignoring her mother, Faye climbs onto my legs. I nearly leap to my feet. Yet I stay still, and my lap instantly recalls the sensation— the warm fidgety feel of a little girl, small muscles, small bones. I await whatever reaction my mind or body will see fit to summon up in answer. "Read this," Faye tells me, settling in. So I do. I read to her about Jemima, a resolute puddle-duck, a single parent who decides to hatch her own eggs and raise them. Laurel looks on, still without a meaningful expression, her eyes focusing intently on nothing.

"But *what happened* to the foxy gentleman?" Faye asks me when I shut the book. I wait for Laurel. Faye is paging backward, wrinkling the pages, dissatisfied. "What happened?"

"Well, Kep took him into the woodshed," I tell her when Laurel does not move. "Didn't he?"

"Kep left him there?" Faye says, turning on my lap to look me in the eye. Her little forehead furrows, as her mother's does sometimes. "In the woodshed?"

"I suppose."

"What—" says Faye. "But what did Kep *do* to the fox in the woodshed?"

"Well, Faye." I turn to Laurel for help, but she is someplace else. "I guess Kep took him in there and, you know—threw him a beating."

"Is he dead? The fox?"

"Yes," I say, thinking about it really for the first time since I read the story to my own child so long ago. "Yes, I suppose he is, Faye."

"My father is dead," she tells me. Now she understands. The fox is dead. She slides lightly off my knee and onto the floor. I feel vacant and strangely light. I stand, unable to sit, and at that moment Laurel does, too. She is back again. She comes around and takes Faye's hand after no more than a backward glance at me. *I should leave,* I am thinking. *I should not be here.* I should run out the door and keep running until I hit Windsor Terrace. There I should lock my doors and pull shut the curtains.

"Maybe I'll pick up some Chinese," I say, waiting by the doorway. "Or something."

"All right," Laurel calls out as she shepherds Faye down the hall with a palm on her back. Before they turn in to Faye's room, the little girl breaks free from her mother and runs to me on bare feet. She runs down the hallway to me, and automatically I fall to my knees on the black-and-white tiles. Faye kisses me lightly, wetly, on the cheek. And then she is gone.

Outside, I walk along Seventh Avenue, where decorations still hang from lampposts. Mostly giant candy canes and outsize wind-blown bows. I have left my coat behind; I walked to the elevator thinking about something else. I am not cold except for my hands. I pocket them and walk past lit storefronts until I remember why I am here. I am thinking of Dellroy, of course. And Pool. But there is also Laurel and Santra. And Ann. And Faye and Opal. *And there is me,* I think. Me, and all of these. I walk along and try to think a straight thought about one of them. I stand in the Chinese restaurant, waiting for my takeout, and the front window is fogged gray inside. Only a moment earlier, as I walked from her building, the wind made a cold circle on my cheek where Faye kissed me.

I take the elevator to Laurel's floor and see myself in its polished copper door. I am jaundiced in the reflection, sorry, with my plastic bag of Chinese food smelling up the place with that greasy steam-table smell. When I press her bell, my hand is red. From inside, she tells me the door is open. I come in and cannot shake the feeling that I should have just left when I left, that I should be someplace else. I wipe my feet on a sisal mat.

Laurel at the kitchen table, alone in a circle of light, is all I see except for city lights in the living room window. "Shrimp fried rice, cream sodas," I tell her. "Couple Butterfingers." We eat and do not talk about the case. She uses chopsticks and I do not. I tell her I am very impressed, and we talk about nothing at all. Then I say, "Faye is . . . perfect. A perfect you."

That is when she tells me of her husband. Lymphatic cancer. And I tell her about Opal and the car crash. We do not talk about them after that, and we do not pretend to know how it is for each other. The parts missing from our lives misshape us like puzzle pieces, but that does not mean we fit each other. We do not say any more about them except this: Tom Ashfield was thirty-one. Opal was five.

"Five," Laurel says, and I know what she is thinking.

"No, it's okay," I tell her, and it is true. It is true. I held a little girl on my lap and waited to feel either a dead girl or nothing at all; instead I felt only Faye. Faye is Laurel's. Opal is mine, and I will never see her again—not in another girl the age she was, nor in any other child Ann wants me to give her.

And if that is true, wouldn't I be a different father for a different child?

I am thinking about that to myself, and the epiphanic certainty of it is so sudden and natural that I wonder why I had not realized it before—*was I stupid?* I am so distracted by the thought that at first I do not understand Laurel when she says something to me.

"What?" I say.

I hear her tell me, again, "Let's take the plea."

I see her over a miniature city of white take-out boxes and

Styrofoam clamshells. Her eyes are tired and flat. I suppose I look the same. We are sitting here in the kitchen half-light, beaten, dead, but for me the final kick is hearing her say that, because I know what it means. I stand and begin gathering the aftermath of our dinner into a plastic bag. I will not look at her.

"Did you hear me?" she asks, her voice cautious and low.

"No."

A pause. "No, you didn't hear, or—"

"No," I say. Not an answer but a reaction. A reaction against what she said—or against what I have done to her. *I brought it into her home,* I am thinking. I tracked it over her black-and-white tiles with my dirty shoes.

"Gio, we have to."

"It's over, Laurel." I want her to stop talking.

"Dellroy—"

"He's dead already." I say it very loudly, but I still do not face her. "He's been living on borrowed time since he was nine."

I feel her eyes on me. She whispers, "You don't believe that."

I walk away with my plastic bag. I am searching for the garbage can, but I cannot find it, so now I am walking in her kitchen with a plastic bag, and I do not know what to do. She comes to me. She is trying to make me look at her, and I cannot. She is saying my name, once, twice, and at last I drop the bag on the floor and face her. She seems unable to withstand how I am looking at her, and her hand comes up as if in defense.

Her mouth opens, but she says nothing. Then, "There are no right choices anymore." I can barely hear it. "You told me that."

I breathe and wait. I am looking at her face. It is no good. "No," I tell her again.

"Gio!"

"No!"

In a different voice I ask her, "You want to know something? A few days ago? I thought you were—" I shake my head, unable to find the right word.

"*What?*" she asks.

"You," I say, feeling myself involuntarily smile at the memory of Monday's Laurel, Tuesday's Laurel. "You, with your ideas about truth and justice. You looked down at me, didn't you?" She turns her head away, but I take hold of her shoulder and her face comes around. "You thought you were better than me," I say. "Didn't you?" Still she says nothing. I feel my eyes begin to burn with an unforeseen emotion. I cannot recognize my voice. "And you shamed me, Laurel. You shamed me because you are."

I release her and she goes slack. We stand that way until I walk to the door. Turning before I leave, I say, "So to hell with you for telling me different now."

CHAPTER 22

Jackhammered awake in my own bed into a leaden January eight o'clock. Awake after lying awake for hours next to Ann, who slept and did not ask why I was wearing the same suit or had not shaved or had not come home at all, and she happily believed the lie I made up for her. The case, I told her. Which was not entirely a lie, although it hurt like a lie to say. She believed me. She said *oh* sympathetically and touched my cheek, and I suppose that if she were going to walk away, it would not be over something as parenthetical as a fuck. I could not tell her—it would not have been just a story, not last night. As it was, she smelled disaster on me and took pity on me and fed me and told me to take a shower. I went to the bedroom exhausted and wide awake, and I watched shadows play along the wall long after she fell into an innocent, openmouthed slumber. Then I went to the kitchen, six hours from morning, where I found a bottle of booze under the sink with the Drano. I did not sleep because I could not sleep, but I did not drink because I needed it; I drank for something to do while I waited for sleep to do for me what I could not do myself.

I slept, but it did not take, and now I am late for court and my tie is uneven. The small end peeks beneath the big end like a tongue. The best I could manage this morning. Tried five times, cursing at my pale self in the bathroom mirror, snapping it angrily off, starting over, all the while thinking, *A man who cannot tie his own tie, he is surely a sorry man.*

To the train, walking along the sidewalk to the station against the stream of Catholic schoolgirls heading to school in the other direction, their legs pink and bare beneath plaid skirts, fat boys running behind them in duffel coats. I heard them laughing as I walked down the stairs underground.

I could not find my overcoat. I heard the landlady's *Today* show on the landing, each step down an effort thrown into high relief against the backdrop of Al Roker. More cold, more snow. Late now, and I do not care. Who could care? Not Haskin Pool. Pool's in no hurry—fucker's copping a plea this very day, so he will wait and be glad to wait. Waiting is all he will have to do for the next ten years. He will wait for me another hour before he goes upstate to wait some more. All the same to him, one day after another for ten years, with time off for good behavior, earning four cents an hour in some upstate cement stall, his every need attended to by the local redneck population of Green Haven, New York. He will wait for me.

Must have fallen asleep the very instant Con Ed started with the jackhammer outside my window. A jackhammer against the frozen blacktop entered my dream, a dream featuring a jackhammer. And a river. I awoke and found myself atop the quilt with my legs pulled up, because I was cold. I opened my eyes as if in surprise. Ann was already gone. I gazed with curiosity into the mirror. No hurry. Al Roker on the television. Along the sidewalk to the station. Walking underground. The laughing boys. Waiting on the platform, cold, supposing I left my coat at Laurel's. Have to explain that to Ann, too, because she will ask eventually. Laurel will give it back, though. She will not want a memento.

I stand by the train door in case I need to jump to a station platform and be sick in a garbage can. Cannot shake the bourbon smell. I am one of those stiff-standing alcoholics you smell on the subway when you do not know who it is exactly. You smell him and look around the car and know only by looking into his eyes, and I look like that this morning, with my eyes listless from too much thought and too little sleep. In the bathroom mirror, haggard, with a shadow already formed under last night's shave. Now I stare vacantly, rocking with the movement of the train, still thinking, thinking. I look and smell like a drunk, like hell. Around me are people, and I am standing at the door. Shrimp fried rice. They do not clean the shrimp. They, the Koreans in the Chinese restaurants, they don't pull out the thready black intestine. I've seen it. That's why I am sick. Drano bourbon and shrimp shit.

Just give him his plea, Giobberti. In the thin light of the morning on the cold mattress, in the mildewy shower, on the sopping bath mat, in the lurching train—nothing else comes to me. But I do not try too hard. I am done with trying. Too goddamn tired, and sick, and sick of trying. I know nothing anymore except that I woke up this day the same man who woke up in the same bed Monday morning, as if I had been visited by a generous angel who gave me a wish and that was what I wished for. *There's no place like home!* Home! Home to the Monday morning before I heard of Laurel Ashfield, before I knew about Dellroy Dunn. Home was a Kansas where I could sit behind my door and not worry about the black letter of the penal law touching ground in East New York and shattering into disjointed paragraphs and parentheses, spitting periods and semicolons like shrapnel that wound and kill.

Give Pool his plea.

End this thing. Fucking end it. Save yourself some other day. This sand shifts too suddenly to draw a line in. He is pleading guilty because he is guilty, and doesn't that count for something? *Hell yes, it counts for something,* I tell myself. *So I'm crossing a line—but if I'm crossing the line, it's to put a killer in jail. That's what we do, right? We put people who kill people in jail.*

And, walking from the station, on Schermerhorn Street at last, under a cement sky I think, *He is guilty, the fuck. So if I'm crossing the line—*

If I'm—

Oh, Christ.

I stop walking. I stop and stand in front of the courthouse, near a line of men waiting ahead of me, and I think, *Oh, Christ,* and maybe I even say it aloud, realizing those words are not mine. *Oh, Christ.* The men do not notice me. None of them even looks, although I feel conspicuous in front of them, open to them, as I see myself exposed and know that it was Luther who said those words.

Oh, Christ, it was Luther.

Yost walks over when I come in. I had forgotten about Yost. He never really entered the picture when I considered what had to happen today. But he is part of it, after all. And Gewirtz. And Pool. The clerk runs to roust the judge from chambers the moment I swing open the back door. Here are Pool's sisters and cousins and aunts, but not the boy; they scowl and point as Yost walks to me, but they, like Laurel and Cully, who picks at a scabrous arm and does not notice me, are spectators. They all might as well have stayed in bed today. The stenographer smiles brightly and winks mascara at me, as if this were another day altogether.

"Well?" Yost asks, and behind him Cully looks on. "You were gonna—you know. Talk to your boss. 'Bout the offer."

"I talked to him," I say, unintentionally vague. Yost follows me through the gallery, but I do not enter the well. There Laurel sits, turned around in her chair at the prosecution table, looking like I feel. "The thing is, with Luther—" I say to Yost. I need to sit. I sit in the front pew, then I turn and lie down on it. Yost is over me, looking down. Strange to see him from this angle. He missed a triangular patch, shaving.

"Not for nothin," he tells me, "but you ain't look so hot."

I fold my hands across my chest and face the ceiling. "Shrimp shit!" I say.

"You get me that ten years or what?"

I feel a sudden slight vertigo, and there is a chance I may drift suddenly upward, up to the ceiling, maybe, where I would disturb some of the cracked plaster and it would fall over everyone like a light white snowfall. Yost keeps talking, saying, "A good plea, Giobberti. Tell me it ain't good. Come on."

"It's no good."

His face changes from one of hopeful expectancy to one of blank disbelief. "You fuckin me?" he says, his voice still wheedling. "Come on, you tell me Luther turned down that plea?"

"You know," I say, "I think I forgot to mention it to him."

"What are you, funny?"

"No."

"What did he say?" he asks. "I'm standin here askin youse what Luther said. About the plea."

"It's—political, he said."

"Politics," Yost says. Now he understands. "All them articles is why." He repeats it, louder this time, and casts a look toward the back of the courtroom for Cully's benefit. "We wouldn't be here if it wasn't for all them articles. In the papers."

Then I have to leave. I spin upright to my feet, and the vertigo nearly sends me back down in the other direction. When I can stand, I start walking to the back door. Then I walk faster. "Fifteen," Yost is calling after me, "all right? Fifteen. *Fifteen!* Fuck—"

Through the swinging back door and into the foyer, I run to the men's room, where I kick open the stall door and spill last night's shrimp fried rice into the rust-stained enamel bowl. When all of it is out, some more comes. And when all of that is out, some more after that. Shrimp fried rice comes from my stomach, and when that is empty, from my intestines, and then from my veins and muscles and bones. I toss it all, and when I am at last done, I am sitting at a right angle on the floor, sitting on the tiny black-and-white hexagonal tiles that are cracked and stained from cigarette butts, dirty shoes, and snot, and dried whatsit from masturbatory daydreams dreamed by court officers on slow afternoons. I am trying to get up and getting up and trying to get up and not getting up, and I am wedged into a corner of the stall while someone keeps saying, "Hey, buddy?" I open my eyes and see Jesus' face in the rust stains in the bowl, and I stop trying to get up. I stay wedged in my corner and still hear the guy talking. "Hey, buddy?"

"I'm okay."

"Hey, buddy. You okay in there?"

"I'm okay," I lie. The guy is waiting, I can tell, because he does not believe me. Finally he walks out. Afterwards I walk to the sink. I want to wash my hands and face, but there is no soap today. Today there are paper towels but no soap. My eyes are all bloodshot from the violence I did to myself in there. I slick my hair with water. I slap my pockets and find a linty half-stick of Doublemint that I eat. Then I shake my head and laugh at myself for being such an asshole. I feel better now—cured!—but it is only the eye of the hangover hurricane, and I know I do not have long. Gewirtz is on the bench when I return. He shoots me a dirty look.

When I hear Laurel put in her appearance, it is all I have heard her say since last night. I say nothing to her, uncertain what I would say. I feel swept downstream, adrift on a watery current in a rain-swollen river, very far from the banks. The dream I was having when the jackhammer started: I remember now. In my periphery Yost is on his feet. "Your Honor?" he keeps saying.

"We about ready for the jury, People?" Gewirtz asks me, oblivious to Yost.

"Your Honor," Yost is saying.

"Judge?" I say.

"We approach, Judge?" Yost asks.

"What is it, Mr. Yost?"

"The defendant has an application?" Yost says. He says it tentatively, turning to me, then to the judge. "Maybe we have a disposition, maybe?" Pool is looking straight ahead, his head down and his hands clasped atop the table. He puts his head onto his hands. I know what he is thinking. He is thinking that this is it.

"Is that correct, Mr. Giobberti?" Gewirtz asks me. I am still watching Haskin Pool. "Do we have a plea, People?" Gewirtz says, pitching his voice higher, believing I do not hear him. I turn to the judge and see him standing with his hands on his hips, his robe hanging to one side in flat black folds.

"Yes," I hear Laurel say. "Yes, Your Honor," she says again with more confidence.

Only at that moment do I know I could not have said it. *Could not have said it,* I think. *Could not say yes. Could not say yes and cannot say yes and will not say yes.*

The stenographer smiles at me. I smile at her. She does not know, of course. Even when she types it all down in a moment, she will not know. Her fingers are on her machine, ready for me. I envy her life of buttons to push and fingernail polish and word jumbles, and in the distance I hear again the siren call of Appeals—a second thought! There's no place like home! Home to Appeals, to Kansas, to a warm kitchen of canned tomatoes and navy beans. *Come back, Giobberti!*

No. Fuck that. I am ready, but give me a minute. God make me good, but not just yet.

"Now, Mr. Yost, do you have an application?" Gewirtz says, pausing while he sighs and runs a hand over his head. He opens a three-ring binder that contains what he is supposed to say.

"Yes, Your Honor," Yost says. "After speakin with my client, Mr. Haskin has authorized me to enter a plea of, ah, guilty to the charge of manslaughter in the second degree in, ah, full satisfaction of the indictment."

"All righty. Is that what you want to do, Mr. Pool?" Gewirtz asks. Yost is gesturing for Pool to stand. Now Pool and I are both standing, both facing the bench. "You want to plead guilty? Is that what you want to do?"

"Yeah," we say.

Gewirtz: *Swear him in.*

Clerk: *Raise your hand. Do you swear or affirm that the answers you are about to give will be the whole truth and nothing but the truth?*

Pool: *Yeah.*

Gewirtz: *All righty.*

Yost: *Judge?*

Gewirtz: *What?*

Yost: *Can we— No, forget it.*

Gewirtz: *Is there a problem?*

Yost: *No, I was just lookin at the wrong thing.*

Gewirtz: *You have it?*

Yost: *I have it now.*

Clerk: *He's got a prior felony.*

Gewirtz: *Who?*

Clerk: *The defendant. He—*

Yost: *That was a Y.O.—check it.*

Gewirtz: *People? He's got a prior Y.O.? Wait, I see it—it was a Y.O. For, ah—*

Yost: *Possession of a weapon.*

Gewirtz: *He was eighteen. He got a Y.O. for that? If that's what— Oh, I know what I was going to ask. What's the plea to? Murder Two?*

Yost: *Man Two.*

Gewirtz: *Manslaughter? Why manslaughter?*

Yost: *It's the plea.*

Gewirtz: *Okay, ah. Are we ready? Mr. Giobberti, you with us? Here we go. Everybody ready? Oh, what's the promise?*

Yost: *Ten? Ten, I— Fifteen.*

Gewirtz: *Fifteen?*

Yost: *Yes.*

Gewirtz: *That's straight. On the manslaughter, right? All right, let's go on the record. Are we on the record? Thank you. Mr., ah, Pool. I'm going to ask you some questions, and you just—answer. Let me ask you first if anyone is forcing you to take this plea?*

Pool: *Nope.*

Gewirtz: *Are you taking this plea of your own free will?*

Pool: *Yeah.*

Gewirtz: *Did you use any alcohol today or any medications that would affect your judgment?*

Pool: *No.*

Gewirtz: *And are you pleading guilty because you are guilty?*
Pool: *I guess.*
Yost: *You have to say yes. Speak up.*
Gewirtz: *I need a yes or a no, sir.*
Pool: *Yes.*

Gewirtz is wearing glasses. He is reading everything from his three-ring binder. I realize I am still standing. Next to me Laurel manipulates a pencil in furtive nervous movements until it slips and shoots from her hand and onto the floor, where it rolls out of sight. She then knits her nervous fingers in front of her and arranges herself in her chair. I say nothing to her. We are strangers again. It is Monday for us, that same Monday evening when she came back for her keys and found me. We were thrown together, briefly coupled like oil and water in the instant you finish shaking, two irreconcilable opposites conjoined by movement and momentum into a dirty momentary swirl before they separate. After this we will have nothing. We will give slightly embarrassed nods to each other in hallways and on Joralemon Street.

No, I realize, we will not even have that.

I stand, missing her in a way, already sorry. We are no good together, and yet she gave me something. Or gave me back something I had lost. We are no good together, I know—but she was good for me.

"Your Honor, at this time the Government moves to dismiss the indictment against Mr. Pool."

That is all I say. A simple sentence. Subject. Predicate. The stenographer is smiling and winking. Yost does not turn, nor Pool. Gewirtz is paging through his three-ring binder. Beside me Laurel sits motionless. Evidently no one hears me. Or pays attention. Or understands. So I repeat myself, louder this time. This time they do.

CHAPTER 23

Upstairs in Appeals, I am filling a cardboard box. Nothing remains on the white walls except yellowed tape where I pulled things
off, here and there taking one of several layers of paint. Nothing
on my desk except the box. Computer screen blank. Wastebasket
full of crap I do not want, desiccated erasers and so forth. The
cardboard box contains law books, a stapler, some coffee-stained
papers, a snow globe, photographs, drawings, and a pencil holder
made from a soup can and construction paper. Phil Bloch has seen
this same box before in his two A.M. imagination, prefiguring my
return to Homicide. Now Bloch stands in my doorway and sees
the box on my desk and knows it means something different. Yet,
as if nothing happened this morning, as if he did not already hear

about it, he asks me, "Going somewhere?" I do not give him an answer, since he does not need one.

I look at Bloch and he grins, and I have to smile sheepishly back and shake my head. *No you don't, you bastard! Don't make me smile!* But hearing Bloch's voice and then seeing him in my doorway, knowing that he labored up here for the second time in a week, his shirttails hanging out, an isosceles triangle of exposed gut, I have to let it go. This was never Bloch's show, anyway. Even if he knew anything, and even if he had told me what he knew, it would not have changed a thing. Like Laurel and me, Bloch was someone else's creature in this. This was Heatly—Heatly and Luther—Luther and Fister—Fister and Cully.

Cully. There are two pink telephone message slips from him in my wastebasket. The first came ten minutes after I arrived back from court without Laurel. Where she is now I have no idea. I had a notion she might be packing a cardboard box of her own, so I went to her cubicle. I was shocked to find it empty. Then I saw her hand sanitizer, her change dish, her pen set—which I nearly took. She has my overcoat, after all. We could meet on some neutral ground and exchange them.

Laurel bolted the instant Gewirtz stood. I suppose she did not even wait for the elevator, since she was not in the foyer when I swung open the back door. I had remained only a moment longer than she; I waited and watched as Pool stood and was handcuffed. Some small consolation to learn that he had a parole hold, that he would have to wait the weekend on Rikers until it could be cleared, until he could go home Monday morning to the women who even then still scowled and pointed, not understanding.

Cully caught the irony.

"Two days in the clink!" he said as I hurried past him, trying not to meet his haunted gaze, needing instead to catch Laurel.

"Less than he got for his first blood, Giobberti. But I suppose if you add in his time served—"

I stopped short, my hand resting on the door.

"You want to tell me what the hell just happened, Giobberti?" he called out. "I mean, the guy's going home."

"He'll be back" was all I said.

Cully laughed a short laugh and coughed a little. "Yeah, that's what they always say," he said. "But someone has to die. Before that happens. Someone has to die before you get him back!"

"Someone already did."

"Yeah, Phil," I say when Bloch asks me if I am going somewhere. "You know, thought I needed some air."

Bloch stands there nodding, no longer smiling. "Fister wanted to see you," he says. He says it like he does not care one way or the other. He uses the past tense, knowing it is all largely irrelevant now. "He wasn't gonna chew your ass, if that's why you're leaving."

"No. That's not why."

"What I'm saying is, you have him by the balls and he knows it," Bloch tells me. "He and Luther—they want to know if you talked to anyone about this."

"That why you're here?"

"No," he says, sounding a little hurt. "No, it's not."

"Talked to anyone," I say. "Cully, for instance? No, they should know that. I can't cover her if this comes out into the open. Fister and me, we're both pointing guns at each other's head."

"Not *your* head." Bloch walks to the window. The snow threatened by this morning's sky has been falling silently for the past hour. He says nothing about it, or about anything else. His hands are in his pockets.

"Anyway," I tell him, "I suppose we're even-steven for that

other thing. For Nicole Carbon. Tell Fister that, if he wants to know what I said."

Bloch nods, his back still to me. I fold over the top of the box, shutting it. I pick it up, then walk to the door. Shut off the lights. Bloch, backlit in the window, turns. "So that's it?" he asks. "Just like that? How about a drink—something."

"Next week," I promise him, oddly touched by his sincerity, something I never expected. Now would be a fine moment for a nostalgic thought. I hesitate in the doorway, waiting for something like that, but nothing comes. In life, moments and their significance never match up, or rarely. Later, I suppose. Later I will think about my years here and what comes next. Right now I have something else I need to do. "Now I gotta take a run out to East New York."

"East— What the hell?" he says, laughing at me, because it is a place you go only for the job. "What, you got friends out there, maybe?"

"No."

"Well—what?"

CHAPTER 24

Outside, alone with my cardboard box, I move tentatively over the slick sidewalk along Joralemon Street. The snow gathers momentum, making a cab impossible. Snow catches on my eyelashes and melts. My shoes are full of it. I pause. A block away on Court Street, barely visible, a blur of yellow behind faint headlights. I put a hand in the air, although no one else is around at all. Off duty, I see, as the cab nears. I wave at it anyway, figuring what the hell, but it slowly passes, as expected, its tires throwing great arcs behind them as they spin on the roadway. *Do I even have cab fare to East New York?* I have been there only in office Crown Vics and marked cars.

In the temporary shelter of a construction scaffolding, I balance my box on a tubular cross-member rimed with frost. I reach

into my suit jacket, my shoulders heavily powdered after five minutes outside. I withdraw my wallet with numb fingers, and it slips.
Credit cards scatter on the sidewalk, colorful against the even cover
of snow. I retrieve them one by one, and a new twenty-dollar bill
that looks counterfeit. Enough for a one-way trip, I suppose, and
a train back afterwards. A happy couple passes me wearing stocking caps; each is holding up the other and laughing about it. Their
voices seem flat in the snow-thick air, but that is all I can hear except a distant car alarm. And a dog. A few more people. Some of
them walk under the scaffolding, and one of them is Heatly.

He wants to shake hands, so we do. Seeing him, I realize I did
not have a clear picture of him before this moment, it has been so
long. He is acting very friendly, trying to remember the last business we had together. He throws out names of killers, and I am
saying no to all of them. He is very well dressed under a black felt
Borsalino hat, and I remember that about him: his hat. I also remember that he is one of five first-graders in Brooklyn North.
And I remember that he has killed three people—all clean line-of-
duty kills. That changes how you look at a man; it changes how I
look at Heatly, anyway. I wait for him to get to the point, because
there must be a point.

"Just came down to get a take-out order signed by the judge,"
he tells me. "Thought I'd stop by. Say hello."

I cannot tell if he knows I do not buy his act, for Heatly's cop
face gives nothing away. He says, "Bloch said I might catch you."

"I'm heading out your way. How about a lift?"

"Sorry," he says, shaking his big head. "Gotta run out to Rikers." He taps his breast pocket to indicate the folded take-out
order, I suppose. "Walk with me. Let me buy you a drink."

I hesitate. *Not with you* is my first thought. *I don't hate you,
but I won't drink with you, either.* He puts a hand on my shoulder,
however, seeming to understand that. "Let's talk," he says in a dif-

ferent voice. I tell him he can buy me a coffee, which seems less like consorting.

Inside the corner coffee spot, Heatly hunches his body onto a stool made for someone smaller. We sit at the window, facing outside. He does not say anything for a while. Just blows the surface of his coffee. He is a large, neckless man with a head bulging into the bows of his eyeglasses, which leave visible marks on his temples when he takes them off. He does not know how to tell me what he came to say, so he asks me what I have in the box.

"Artifacts," I say. I have kept nothing from the job. Except for the stapler, all I am taking home is already mine. I have my shield, though, still pinned inside my wallet. I take it out and the leather is still slick from the snow. I unpin the shield and hold it in my hand. The gold has worn away in places down to the silvery base metal, like cheap jewelry. I heft it in my hand, then turn to Heatly, who watches with interest. I slip from my stool and walk to a tall canister: RECYCLABLES ONLY! The pointy piece of tin makes no sound at all when I drop it in.

"Let's do it this way," I say to Heatly when I return to him. "I'll start by telling you what I know."

"All right," he says, laughing. "Let's get it on."

"First thing first," I say. "You don't like Haskin Pool. You've had a hard-on for him for a long time."

"Very true."

"Ever since he bumped that kid over there in Brownsville," I say. "When the murder count didn't stick and he got the misdemeanor on that one. That made you mad. You didn't want him to skate on another dead body."

Heatly shakes his head. "No. No. Wasn't my case. I heard about it after I came up. I wanted him for capers he was pulling in my neighborhood."

"All right, Bill, just tell me your end on this. It's why you came down here, right? To tell me?"

"No, I had some other news."

"Save it," I say. "I want to know about this."

"Why can't we say it's water under—"

"Because I got played for a dope," I tell him, allowing myself open anger at last. "That gives me the right to know, so tell me." Heatly gives me a hard stare. "Bill," I say, shifting on my stool, softening my voice, "Moss said you had something with Dellroy before. With the mother."

Heatly turns away and blows on his coffee, which is cool enough already. He remains still. Then he shrugs his wide shoulders and says, "I put her in jail, the kid's mother."

I nod. "That have anything to do with Pool?"

"No. Not really," he says. "Dellroy I knew from way back—back when I worked a foot post. New Lots down to Flatlands. One of these kids that had a thing for uniforms—this was maybe ten years ago, remember." He takes a long drink and wipes his stiff mustache with the back of his hand. "One of these kids that always come up to you. Asking you all sorts of questions—where I got the uniform, where I got the gun—you get me? Got to be a regular feature." His large, dark face softens, the corner of his mouth curves. "Used to buy him candy bars."

"Butterfingers."

"Butterfingers," he says. "His brand. After a while I was calling him the Butterfinger Kid." He laughs to himself. "I'd see him coming and say, *Here comes the Butterfinger Kid,* you know? One of these street kids. Didn't even know he had a father until I met him couple years later. After I got kicked upstairs to the squad."

"What, you collared him? The father?"

"Took a call one evening," he says. "Shots fired, man down—

this is back in the early nineties. Used to get four or five of those a tour."

"I remember."

Heatly says, "I get there and it's the usual—body spread out in the kitchen. So that's when I met the father. Didn't know it when I got there, though. Just the guy in the kitchen and the woman sitting at the table. Ask her what happened. Right? The kid's not on the scene when I get there—I don't even know it's his place."

"What happened?"

"What happened is I get there and see all this. And I, you know, ask her where is it. I'm there asking her, and she just points."

"At what?" I ask him.

"The sugar box," Heatly says, shrugging. "Where else you gonna put a gun, Giobberti? I look in the sugar box, and there she's got herself a gun. Nice little Sig—don't know where she got a nice little gun like that. So I police up the gun and ask her was there anyone else in the place."

"Dellroy."

Heatly nods. He takes out a cigarette box and knocks one loose. Lights it. It moves in his lips as he speaks. "Kid's back in the bedroom. In the closet. Playing in the closet. And I says to him, 'Hey, Butterfinger, what you doing in the closet?' And he says, 'Playing.' And I ask him why he's playing in the closet, and you know what? Says that's where he goes when the old man comes home."

"The closet?"

"I ask him did his father put him in there, and he says no. Guess that's just where he would go. To keep a low profile, I'm guessing. Then I see it—the blood on the back of the collar. Just a line. And he's got—little kid's got—I don't know what it was. He's got some kinda . . . tool, stuck in the back of his—" Heatly cannot finish. "Long story short," he says, straightening himself. "The father's in the ground. The mother's out there in Rose M. Singer. She cops to—Man One, I think they were offering. Fifteen-year bid. Child Services ships Butterfinger out to Grandma. Over the river and through the woods, you know? But he wasn't the same. Never the same."

"And you?"

"I . . . remained in touch," he tells me, the cigarette on his lips going up and down. "Kids. You try, but—" The thought drifts away with the smoke. When it is gone, he asks me, "You got kids?"

"Me?" I say, startled by the question. "No. No, I'm not—"

"I got four. Je-sus Christ, you believe that? Don't know how *that* happened," he says, laughing about it to himself. I laugh, too, politely. "Four! I'll keep them all, though. I'll keep 'em all," he says, as if to himself. Then, to me, "You'll see, Giobberti. You'll get you some kids. You're a young guy yet."

I sit still, not disagreeing.

After a pause Heatly stands, pushing out his cigarette on a plastic coffee lid. "Gotta run. Doing God's work today." He shakes my hand, and I am still sitting on the stool. Heatly fixes his hat onto his head. "By the way, that collar I gotta go make?" he says, unable to suppress a sly smile that spreads all over his face, a black face that matches exactly the deep black of his hat. "Friend a yours."

"Okay."

"Haskin Pool."

I feel my heart flutter in the back of my throat and my stomach goes all tight. I am trying to make sense of it, but I cannot think and just want to be told.

"Gonna pin another body on that criminal."

"Lashawn Sims," I tell him automatically. I say the name so quietly that I would not think Heatly heard except I see his eyes change. His cop eyes turn black and lose all their light. He is a different man now, and I would never want to be on the other side of the table from this man. "Your witness," I nonetheless tell him. "You have a witness—Santra. Santra Flowers."

At last he says, "You're a dark horse, Andrew Giobberti."

"Am I right?"

"I don't—"

"Am I right, Detective?"

"Yes," he says, and momentarily I stop listening. I feel—wonderful.

"Could have made this collar months ago—*months* ago," he is saying when again I am listening. "Had her nailed as a witness from Jump Street. Her brother, you know that? Half brother or something. Anyway, you think she'd want to step up, you know? But no. I mean, I don't need to tell you about these kids out there—got no respect for the law no more—want to do things their own way, you know what I'm saying?"

I smile at that, but he does not get it. I shake my head and he moves on.

"Anyway," he says, "zipped her lip and there wasn't a thing I could do about. All my charms. Nothing." To illustrate, he zips his lip. Throws away the key.

"You went to her," I say. "Today you went to her?" My voice quavers but I do not care if he notices.

"No, brother," Heatly says, seemingly relieved that I do not know everything, however I came to know everything else. For that reason, he happily admits he did nothing to bring in Santra Flowers. "I figured she was a dead end. Real nervous personality, you know? Seemed to hate, I mean *hate,* my guts." He shakes his head in disbelief. "Guess she don't like cops. So what else is new, huh?"

"So?" I say, but as I ask him, the only possible answer comes instantly to mind. Still, I ask, wanting to hear him say her name. *"Who?"*

"It was— What's her name?" Heatly is snapping his callused fingers to remember, making a succession of dull thuds. "The princess they had working this— Ashfield."

"Laurel Ashfield."

Heatly nods. *Laurel*. Of course it was Laurel. "Went out herself. This afternoon," he tells me. "Walked into the squad an hour ago. The two of them. Holding hands like sisters." He shakes his head. "I'll be damned, right?"

"I'll be damned," I say and would like to say more. For instance, I would like to tell him I foresaw this—that letting Pool go was the only way to bring Santra in. I would like to tell him I had hoped to accomplish that this very day.

But that is ridiculous. All that happened today was I offered my king in a game already played out long before I arrived. Santra Flowers is my queen in another match entirely. The simple irony of letting Pool out to ensure he stayed in was not a solution but a present—unsought, unearned, undeserved. And at best it gave me a dicey move. Even if Santra let me over her threshold this afternoon, carrying my cardboard box, news of Pool's release just as easily could have driven her deeper into her pink-curtained bedroom, convincing her of the truth of the words written in spray paint on Dumpsters and hallways and brick alley walls in her neighborhood: THE SYSTEM IS A JOKE.

Laurel somehow persuaded her it is not. But Santra, I think, already believed that. Or wanted to believe it, despite everything. *Like sisters,* Heatly said, and that is about right. I realize now who it is Santra Flowers reminds me of.

"I tell you," Heatly says, "when I first met that Ashfield? Didn't like her. Did not like her. At all. Figured, you know what I'm saying—right, brother? Figured she—"

"Wasn't from around here?"

"Right! Didn't know the score!" Heatly says, pleased with my answer. "Kind of surprised me, I'm saying. Her bringing the girl in like that."

"Surprised you?" I ask him. "Don't be surprised, Detective."

"No?"

"No. She's a Brooklyn girl."

ABOUT THE AUTHOR

ROBERT CHARLES REULAND is the author of *Hollowpoint*. A gradu-
ate of Cambridge University and Vanderbilt Law School, he practiced law for many years on Wall Street before joining the district
attorney in Brooklyn, where he was assigned to the Homicide Bureau. Mr. Reuland spent his youth in Iowa and now lives with his
wife and two young children in New York City. He is engaged in
private practice, specializing in criminal defense.

ABOUT THE TYPE

Designed by the combined efforts of Edward Johnston, J. H. Mason, and Gerard Meynell, this versatile face shows an affinity with eighteenth-century Old Faces. Cut in 1912 specifically for mechanical composition, it takes its name from the magazine it was designed for, *The Imprint*. published by The Monotype Corporation. The large x-height and open counters lend to its classic quality. It is suitable for printing on a variety of paper stocks.